"The meeting of two personalities is like the contact
of two chemical substances: if there is any reaction,
both are transformed."
—Carl Jung

ENTHRALL
ECSTASY

ENTRALL SESSIONS
BOOK NINE

USA TODAY BESTSELLING AUTHOR
VANESSA FEWINGS

Enthrall Ecstasy

Cover Design: Hang Le
Formatted by: Champagne Book Design
Editor: Debbie Kuhn

For Terri DuQuesnay

ENTHRALL ECSTASY

ENTRALL SESSIONS
BOOK NINE

CHAPTER ONE

Shay

T HIS WAS A PLACE YOU CAME TO ESCAPE A SCANDAL.

I passed the company logo for "Quinn Public Relations and Consulting."

Being summoned to a meeting with an influential figure wasn't unusual. Very often this was how the elite asked to enter Enthrall.

But I'd been around long enough to know this was about something else.

"Your reputation precedes you." Carrie Quinn welcomed me into her swanky office. A business degree hung on the back wall. "You're quite the charismatic figure, Mr. Gardner."

I hated this meeting already.

Quinn's PR approach was apparently ruthless.

"Goodness, you're tall," she said.

I offered a polite smile.

I was rough around the edges, maybe, but I looked good in Armani—the suit I'd worn today. I took pleasure in challenging expectations.

She looked me up and down.

Her stare lingered on my beard. Recent weeks had leaned toward chaotic, my lack of shaving the only indication life had worn me down.

She wouldn't know that, though. To her, I'd merely look ruggedly handsome and aloof.

November rain lashed against the window. I'd barely noticed the downpour.

In a turquoise blouse and tight-fitting pencil skirt, wearing knee-high boots, she'd pass for a Dominatrix in other circles. I clocked her age at forty. She carried a confidence that told me she thrived under stress.

For some reason, I was on her radar.

She strolled by me to get to the door. "We've never met."

"I don't believe so."

A waft of sultry perfume lingered in the air.

She wielded that scent to subdue clients. Get them right where she wanted them—obedient to her demands.

After closing the door, she headed back to her desk and sat on the edge. "There will be no record of this. No one need know you and I crossed paths, Mr. Gardner."

My curiosity spiked. "I can live with that."

She gave a nod. "Thank you for your service. Navy SEALs, right?"

My response was only a polite smile, not wanting to trigger a conversation about Afghanistan. I'd left that experience in my rearview.

Not my friends, though. War leaves scars no one sees. But in each other, we recognized cuts that went deep.

I was good at slaying chaos.

Much like Carrie.

Once someone like me reaches their thirties, little tends to surprise you anymore.

"You served alongside Henry Cole."

The comment piqued my interest.

Carrie might even know that's how I'd met Cameron—through his brother Henry.

"Such bravery."

I met her compassionate gaze. "Why am I here?"

"A situation…one that requires discretion. Being ex-special forces, you're perfect for this."

"I'm not for hire."

"I hear you're a member of Enthrall?"

My expression remained unchanged.

Carrie reached into her jacket pocket and removed her phone. A few swipes of the screen and then she turned it so I could see the photo of a striking, curvaceous redhead. Twentyish, with flowing red hair and a breathtaking smile, her pretty face was covered in freckles. Her blue eyes were the kind that reflected pain. She'd tried to hide it by feigning happiness.

Pretty but complicated was the type I avoided.

"Rue Asher." She looked at the photo herself. "She's stunning, isn't she?"

I didn't react.

I'd done my research, too, and drilled down hard on this CEO. Yet I'd found nothing, which revealed this woman was good at hiding her private life.

"She's a friend," she said. "In a way…"

That wasn't vague at all.

"What do you need from me?" I asked.

Carrie hesitated as though wanting to keep something back. "I'm concerned for her safety."

"Sorry to hear that."

She smiled. "I can see why Dr. Cole hired you."

My relationship with Cameron went deep. We were close, like brothers, really. Cole had hired me as his head of security back when I'd left the SEALs.

That man could read a soul with one glance. He was a god-damned genius—a man who deserved protecting at all costs.

Parlaying the conversation away from him was crucial.

"This is about Rue?" I said.

"I don't need to know the details." Carrie looked uncomfortable. "Just get her out. Extract her. Tonight."

My interest piqued at her desperation. "Out of…?"

"Are you going to pretend you don't move in those circles? I have it on good authority you do. You're the man who keeps everyone safe. You're the tech expert."

Rue wasn't at Enthrall or Chrysalis, which was what Carrie had insinuated.

"Who referred me?" I asked.

"I'll never divulge who recommended you."

She wanted me to go into this situation blind.

"You should share your concerns with her," I said.

Carrie held up her phone again, this time showing me Rue dressed in her graduation gown. I again noted her freckled button nose and bright red hair, a feature that would make a submissive easily discernible if wearing a mask.

Carrie put her phone down. "She has a bright future. Only you can make sure of it."

"That's a curious statement—"

"Get her out of Pendulum."

A jolt of concern hit me at hearing that name.

If Rue was in the clutches of Pendulum she was in danger. If anyone asked about the place, they were told it didn't exist.

Pendulum was where the richest and most powerful men in the world went to misbehave.

Consent was dubious and the play rough.

"I don't know who else has the skill to access the place," Carrie said softly.

"Is she a client?"

"No."

Carrie pressed a palm to her chest. "Please, Shay."

"This is not what I do."

"Enthrall does good work." She tilted her head. "So I've heard."

"This isn't in my wheelhouse."

"How much?"

"It's not about money, Carrie."

"Go to Pendulum. Bring her home." She pushed off the desk and came closer.

Rue would be so deep down the rabbit hole by now.

"What can I offer?" she said. "Access to a public figure? Someone famous you'd like to fuck?"

"There's nothing I need or want." An elegant way of saying *fuck off* with your bribes.

"You must listen to me."

"I've heard everything you've said, Carrie."

I held her stare. A fierce stand-off.

"I can arrange an unmarked car. It will leave in five minutes."

"Anything else I can help you with?" I said.

She softened as though realizing this tactic wasn't going to work with me.

"I don't know who else to turn to."

"I'm sure you can think of someone."

She clutched her skirt and raised it—high enough for me to see she wasn't wearing any panties and view that circle of silver piercing her labia. The jewelry signaled a Dominant's ownership of her. Her clit peeked out between her adorned sex.

We were both silent for a moment, contemplating a familiarity we were both accustomed to.

"Submissive?" I asked.

"Domina. I still switch for my master."

"Do I know him?"

She shook her head. "He lives abroad."

"You can…" I gestured for her to let her hem fall.

She gave a thankful nod and dropped her skirt, reassured by my calm demeanor.

"Speak," I ordered.

"I'm a Mistress at the House of Majestic," she said. "Rue's one of our submissives. She's only been training with us for a month.

She's at Pendulum to be auctioned off." Carrie looked distraught. "She's not ready, Shay. Not for that place."

Fuck.

"How long do I have to get her out?"

"Two hours."

I glanced at my watch and then looked at Carrie. "I'll drive myself to Pendulum."

CHAPTER TWO

Shay

I'D LEFT CARRIE'S L.A. OFFICE AND DRIVEN STRAIGHT TO THE
Strand of Manhattan Beach.

On the way, I'd stopped off briefly at a costume boutique
and purchased a masquerade plague doctor mask.

It reflected a *leave me the fuck alone* attitude.

The disguise covered my whole damn face.

My three-piece suit rounded out the hedonism.

My position at Enthrall meant I was the front man for facing
potential enemies—the one who went ahead to disarm the met-
aphorical explosives lying in wait.

If I didn't get to her in time, they were going to destroy Rue
Asher.

I wondered if she'd be made aware of their rule on consent,
the fact they didn't have one.

I owed the privilege of entering Pendulum to Richard. He'd
made a call and I'd been met at the door by a masked submissive—no codeword required. She'd not be able to pick me out of
a crowd, which protected both of us.

Getting in had been surprisingly easy. If this were Enthrall, heads would roll at this lack of security.

The modern tune was loud, the music heady and unnaturally synthesized—perfect for the atmosphere.

They'd need a larger room for VIPs to mingle while they made their bids on the subs.

This place was a contemporary interior designer's paradise, with an open plan and luxury furniture. Creative lighting showcased the paintings of naked women that charmed the walls. Cozy elements ensured guests had privacy to experience untold pleasure in a lavish setting.

Pendulum was infamous for its wild nights and risky play. The clientele were rich and beautiful and addicted to pushing their limits.

Pendulum. Where you came to mainline sex.

Couples and threesomes and "othersomes" lined the hallways, all of them fucking. Some threw me a curious glance through their masquerade masks as I walked by them, looking out for that distinctive redhead.

Chrysalis could be hedonistic but here the debauchery rivaled our elite manor.

Submissives were guided around on fine silver chains. Not one was free to run off and explore. Or change partners. Or take a break.

Each submissive was owned.

There was a strict protocol of no phones. I'd left mine locked in the glove compartment of my Rover, parked down the road. I'd have to find a landline if I ran into trouble—which shouldn't happen if I remained vigilant.

Having never stepped foot in this five-story building before, I'd have to fake being a regular. Unable to get hold of the schematics meant I was flying blind as I searched for Rue.

Even if my target was wearing a masquerade mask, she'd be easy to find with her distinctive hair and bright blue eyes—unless she wore a wig and contacts.

Anything was possible.

She'd probably be found in the middle of some compromising situation that would be challenging to extract her from.

She might refuse to leave.

I'd cross that bridge later and then burn it to the ground.

Strolling along the labyrinth of rooms, I adjusted my pants to allow for the thrill of the sights and sounds surrounding me. My cock approved of the erotic visions unfolding like a mesmerizing dream as I went deeper in.

Half-naked submissives caught my eye. One command and I could own any of these beauties. Those were the rules—the Doms called the shots. The subs obeyed their masters. They didn't get to choose who they went with—unlike Enthrall, where submissives had equal power until the play began and consent had been given to hand over control.

Rue's extraordinary beauty meant she'd be sought after. I didn't look forward to getting her away from a possessive Dom. The thought of using any kind of violence made my blood run cold.

Opening the door to a dungeon, I peered in to see a blonde submissive sitting in the center of the room, her master peering down at her, an audience sitting in surrounding chairs.

I closed the door and continued through the dim hallways.

God, I'd craved this, erotic delights unfolding around me.

Passing a room where the sound of spanking emanated from behind its closed door, I eased it ajar to see a brunette bending over her master's knee. Her cheeks were scarlet, her moans a mixture of pain and pleasure.

Not Rue.

What had brought her to Pendulum? A kinky friend? Her own desires? Curiosity for this lifestyle?

Achieving rapport with her was essential. Understanding Rue would help with her extraction.

Not causing a scene was imperative.

Down the hallway, a guy was getting a blowjob from two

submissives kneeling at his feet. Their tongues lapped at his cock, his shaft shiny and taut as it rose out of dark curls.

One leaned low to suckle his balls and the other took his cock all the way into her mouth, head bobbing. Their hums of delight echoed around me.

These were the kinds of scenes that were addictive, the reason we came back for more daring acts that delivered a heavy dose of dopamine.

My own passion for exhibitionism added to the thrill. Erotica was an obsession.

This was a decent place to practice a predilection. Even if Pendulum's reputation was questionable, one thing was sure: the subs were typically consenting adults.

Though being selected as a member was only for the elite. No blue-collar workers here. No ordinary guy off the street looking for a rush. These VIP members were let in because their financial portfolios impressed the selection committee.

I was probably too working class for them.

Enthrall was thorough on its selection process; refining it around a more holistic approach.

A butler invited me to enter through two towering doors.

He opened them for me.

Tall palms in impressive vases lined the entrance, the music changing into a more exotic beat; a modern retelling of Vivaldi's "Four Seasons" added an ethereal edge.

Within the ballroom, well-dressed guests mingled, all of them watching the activity in the center—the main show.

Two dominants were showcasing five submissives, each being ceremoniously stripped of their robes. All of them were seductively dressed in scant bodices, no thong required. They were all naked from the waist down.

My gut twisted when I saw *her*.

A jolt of electricity traveled through my veins like a fucking livewire, the visceral response fascinating.

I'd never felt this kind of awe.

The photo of her had not done enough to reveal those crystal blue irises that shone vibrantly through her silver filigree mask.

It was Rue.

She stood out from the rest of the women as a striking goddess, lighting up the room with her beauty, tall and elegant with womanly curves.

It was her proud posture that drew my attention as well...she emanated natural grace. Her complexion was refreshingly earthy.

Nothing about her seemed fake—nothing tweaked by anything but the hand of God.

And God had outdone himself with Rue.

Her sinful mouth was devastatingly kissable.

How could these men look at this striking gem and not desire her beyond all understanding?

I was certain kingdoms would fall tonight. Men would fight for someone like her—a bloody battle would ensue for the damsel in the center.

She stood facing them, proudly voluptuous, her breaths short and sharp—looking like she was in her element.

A long chain dangled from her collar all the way to the ground, ready for some Dom to reach out and grab it.

The Dom behind her was recognizable despite his masquerade mask—his gold Ulysse Nardin wristwatch giving him away. The man had Kaison Faulkner's height and build, too.

Kaison trained submissives at his private estate in Brentwood. Something told me he'd been the one to steal Rue out of Majestic.

His kind of arrogance would be the reason she was being flaunted to this crowd.

The bad boy of B&D had struck again.

He wore a black tuxedo and a bowtie design that revealed he was a member.

I'd run into him at a club in Dubai a few years ago. His wristwatch had been a gift given to him by some rich Arab grateful for the help in keeping his kink fed.

Getting Rue away from Faulkner was going to be challenging.

I didn't have the time to consider the fallout.

No one could see us leave.

I scanned the room, trying to get a feel on who had their sights on Rue. When I turned back, she was looking at me.

An uncommon shudder ran through me, the atmosphere suddenly lacking air.

Time slowed enough to trick me into believing this was a significant moment.

She was special…Rue Asher.

Time with someone like her was the escape everyone craved.

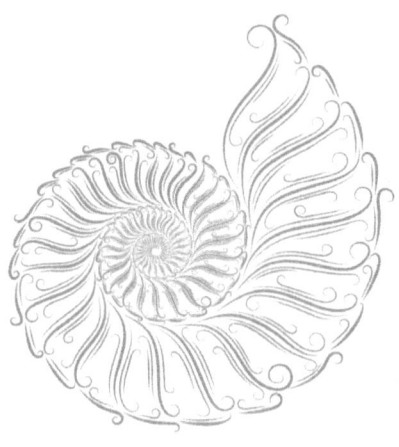

CHAPTER THREE

F INALLY, IT WAS HAPPENING.
I'm here.
In this exclusive ballroom, drenched in a soft blue light that exuded a calming hue, I stood with my heart racing, my skin warm and clammy. I'd wanted nothing more than to gain entry and have all of this attention, but now I was having doubts.

It wasn't like I'd not prepared for this. I'd spent endless hours refining my talent as a submissive at Majestic.

Just breathe.

Faulkner won't let just anyone have me. He'd promised nothing but pleasure when he'd convinced me to sneak out of Majestic for the evening.

Placing my trust in him was all I could do in this moment.

Vivaldi's "Four Seasons" imbued an erotic sophistication to the setting—the mixture of colognes and perfumes bringing a potent richness to the air.

As Master Faulkner lifted off my blue satin robe, his fingers brushed my skin as it fell away, the material gliding to the floor and pooling behind me, exposing my scant bodice and heels.

Panties were forbidden, a dark secret we all knew. We were to remain accessible.

First hearing this had given me a rush. Back when all this had merely been a fantasy.

Reality. So very different.

My tight leather collar felt suffocating. There were too many people. Hundreds of hungry stares from behind masquerade masks, mostly men with a few women present. Female guests dressed scantily to complement the hedonistic mood. At least I wasn't alone in exposing my sexuality.

The exhilaration of finally being here made me tremble.

This, the ultimate debut.

I'm ready.

Even if I have doubts.

I'd been warned at times it might become overwhelming.

Like now.

I'd proven subservient and willing to be a good submissive, attending every session. I had excelled in all that was asked of me and studied the erotic literature given to me.

Back at Majestic, I'd spent hours with Faulkner discussing my limits and pushing through a few of them, seen the pride in him when he'd guided me through riskier play.

I'd excelled to such an extent I'd been brought here after completing just one week of training with him.

Even now, Master Faulkner remained watchful of my every move.

There were five of us, all brought in from different houses. We'd been briefed for tonight's soiree, dressed differently in elegant bodices to reveal our uniqueness: Brunettes and blondes and me, the redhead, who stood out.

Men were often drawn to my titian hair. This masquerade mask hid freckles that made me appear younger than twenty-three.

I'd grown to love them—even though I'd once been bullied for looking different.

I'd developed a sense of my own beauty and uniqueness. That is where my beauty lay. Not in what society demanded of me with its cookie cutter ideals but with how I rose to the challenge of loving myself entirely.

Looking out at the array of gentlemen in classical masquerade masks, all of them seemingly fit beneath their expensive suits, I wondered which one I would be with tonight.

I had always been about the pleasure, the endless arousal that flowed with a session.

In less than five minutes, I could be with any one of them. Given to a master for the night for his pleasure.

And mine.

A stranger who I hoped would be kind and gentle and generous.

I suddenly felt lightheaded with anticipation. The thought of what lay ahead caused the fine hairs on my forearms to prickle. Glancing over at the other subs, I could see they were just as entranced. They, too, seemed to be guessing who would win them.

One of the subs, a blonde, was so aroused her thighs were wet and her breathing rapid. Her breasts rose and fell as Master Faulkner, who stood behind her, tweaked her rosy nipples, seemingly placing her into a delicious trance.

Faulkner left her and came to stand behind me.

If he does the same to me…

In front of all these men.

His body pressed against my back, his hands reaching around to rest on my hips.

Then, his fingers found my labia and eased my folds apart. "Like this," he commanded.

A jolt of panic mixed with exhilarating arousal shot through my body.

He was exposing me completely.

Following his lead, I glanced down and replaced his fingers

with mine, easing apart my folds to reveal my clit, showing myself entirely.

Blinking rapidly, I felt relieved to have my face hidden behind a filigree mask. His fingertips controlled mine, holding my pussy lips wider. The way he'd trained us. It was a pose that would please our audience.

It would arouse these men and woman; our privileged audience observing with a respectful silence.

More of them turned their attention on me, admiring what I willingly revealed—my very essence.

I inhaled sharply in anticipation, my face flushed. This felt raw and vulnerable and deliciously filthy—the sensations building into something so erotic I was afraid I might come from this pose alone.

I felt so turned on that I knew it would start to show; my body revealing its response in minutes.

"They're staring at your cunt," Faulkner said, confirming what I knew.

The thrum down there became more intense, even though there was no direct contact with my clit. My breasts swelled and pushed against the confines of my bodice, the pressure against my beading nipples a distraction.

All of us were ordered to assume the same pose, which made me feel better. I wasn't alone in being slutty.

"Very good," said Faulkner.

Lulled by these overwhelming sensations, my pussy clenched with anticipation.

This, the center of the forbidden.

I raised my chin higher to savor how daring this felt. How high it made me feel—to show everyone that I'd chosen this moment to feel alive.

Eroticism was my drug of choice. I was desperate to chase the multiple orgasms my body craved night after night—an insatiable desire so powerful that as soon as I reached the ultimate pinnacle, I needed it again. My nymphomania was both a curse and a blessing.

Glancing right, I saw that Faulkner was strumming Taylor's clit, the tip of his finger flicking her fast. Her jaw was slack and her moans filled the vast space.

If getting her off was to make the rest of us feel desperate with need, he'd succeeded. A jealousy surged through me like wildfire.

She wailed her orgasm.

I burned to come as hard as she had.

When Faulkner finally seemed content with this exotic display, he gave a signal for the event to begin.

A voice boomed behind us as guests raised their hands and yelled out their generous bids to win one of us. I heard a low rumble of voices as they shared their thoughts with each other about which sub they wanted.

Goosebumps rose on my forearms.

A familiar nervous tremble shook my limbs.

This was my chance to prove I belonged, to make Faulkner proud and let him see that I was ready for this level of play. Let him see he could bring me back time and time again to this secret place.

My heart pounded against my chest.

I scanned the crowd to see if I could guess who might want me, taking in one intimidating Dom after another.

Then I saw him.

He stared back at me with his seductive eyes peering through a plague doctor mask. If the guy was going for scary, he'd succeeded. He looked downright evil in that hooked disguise. Yet his sinister look did something to me, making me heady.

The devil himself wanted me.

He continued to stare with an unmatched intensity.

His impressive height added to his intimidation. He had the muscular physique of someone who was beyond fit. He looked like he could lift me with ease—throw me over his shoulder and carry me off.

He looked like a man who knew how to fuck.

Of all the men here, he stood out.

Thinking he wanted me made my heart skip, touching my soul.

With a subtle nod, I let him know I wanted him to bid on me.

He shook his head *no*. The long beak exaggerated his movement.

Doubt crept in as I watched him fold his arms across his chest, as if I wasn't the one he was after.

My appearance was an acquired taste. I knew that. My hair was an unusual color and my curves made me stand out, waist pulled in tight to emphasize my hips. I was the curvy one, a full-figured woman contrasting with the slender women here.

The tall and hopefully handsome stranger behind that disguise had tucked his hands into his pockets as though he were merely a bystander.

He watched my fate with a cold indifference.

CHAPTER FOUR

Shay

I 'D NEVER BID ON A WOMAN DURING ONE OF THESE EVENTS.
Didn't need to.
Ever.

Fuck to the no if you think I'd waste my hard-earned money on a woman I could make mine with the snap of my fingers. Bidding was something for billionaires to indulge in.

Women came to me willingly.

Always.

Throwing money at a problem like this—a wayward submissive who had waded in over her head—wasn't usually my jam.

After tonight, the girl would be out of my stratosphere.

This wasn't the same crowd you got at Enthrall. This was an entirely different brand of elite. I'd already witnessed a few members snorting cocaine.

Like some of the high assholes bidding on Rue—using Bitcoin, a hundred K's worth. No doubt she would find it flattering.

The bidding continued to rise.

I focused my attention on one Bitcoin guy in particular, an Ivy

League type who was surrounded by his cocaine-loving buddies. They were drinking and cheering him on. He'd have no idea how to handle a submissive of this caliber. Or any woman, I imagined.

My silent question as to whether Faulkner was allowing this was answered when he didn't interrupt the bidding.

I eased through the crowd and worked my way up front, ignoring the glares from the Doms.

I closed in on Rue, towering over her. "We need to talk."

She rose out of subspace. "You?"

"Come with me," I said.

"Why?" Her tone was indignant.

"You're being auctioned off to a stranger."

"That's why I'm here."

In the ultimate tease, her bewitching perfume wafted around me. She was recklessly alluring, and I wasn't so gone I couldn't see she was too innocent for this place—too naive to be let loose amongst these hedonists.

I'd face off with Faulkner another day and dissuade him from ever doing this again—bringing a woman too young to a VIP venue.

I aimed for discretion.

Leaning into Rue, I said quietly, "You don't belong here."

"I do." She met my gaze. "What do you want? Do I know you?"

"You're out of your depth."

She flinched. "Fuck off."

"You're coming with me," I demanded. "Now."

Faulkner interceded, stepping closer. "What's going on?"

I threw out a lie. "I know her."

"Is this true?" he asked her.

Rue's irises twinkled with mischief. "The mask makes it impossible to say."

"I need to talk with her," I told him.

"Not going to happen," he retorted.

Rue smirked. "Bid on me."

Little minx.

Stepping back, I put some distance between us, relieved that Faulkner hadn't recognized me. His disapproving glare caused others to turn my way, drawing unwanted attention that could get me thrown out.

I raised my hands in surrender, gesturing I wouldn't cause trouble.

Rue watched me back away, seductively dragging her teeth over her bottom lip as though trying to entice me back.

She thought I was going to bid on her.

Instead, I slid back into the crowd.

Her expression turned to one of confusion when she heard the cheers accompanied by the announcement that Bitcoin Asshole had won her. He'd thrown enough money into the mix to secure himself a newbie submissive for the night.

Rue was escorted away by the other Dom. She glanced back at me, bewildered. I assumed they were taking her to a room where she'd wait for him. Maybe even prepare her in the kinds of ways I didn't want to put my mind to.

Faulkner grabbed my sleeve. "What was that?"

"What was what?"

"How do you know her?" He was trying to clock who was behind the mask. "Do that again and see what happens."

"Take your hand off me before I break it," I said calmly.

His hand fell away.

"Have we met?" His back stiffened.

When his name was called, Faulkner turned to look in the direction of the other remaining submissives.

He faced me again. "Wait here," he said, and then returned to the center of the ballroom.

The bidding for the other submissives resumed. These were high stake games for the wealthy. The kind you needed a secret society for.

I headed in the direction I'd seen them take off with Rue, discreetly exiting the ballroom and disappearing into the stream of guests strolling down the hallway. Loosening my necktie, I discarded the plague doctor mask and snatched up a new disguise in case they came looking for me—a masquerade mask that someone had set on a table.

Just ahead, Rue was led by the Dom around a corner.

Following them, I noted the long line of rooms, each with a Roman numeral above its door. When I saw Rue and the Dom enter one of them, I held back, waiting in an alcove.

I continued walking when I saw the Dom withdraw from the room, leaving Rue inside.

Before I could reach her door, the guy who'd won her came around a corner with a couple of his friends.

Fuck.

This didn't bode well.

With a nod to Bitcoin Asshole, I said, "Dungeon twenty. We'll bring her in."

He and his two friends ambled off in that direction.

That bought us a few minutes.

With them out of sight, I turned the doorknob and entered the dimly lit chamber.

My breath hitched at the striking vision of Rue in the center of the room, her masquerade mask off.

I should have bid on her. Even one night would be worth it. Then I reminded myself why I was here.

She was secured to the ceiling with a long chain, her arms raised above her head, her wrists captured in handcuffs. Shadows fell over her face and curvaceous body, her sex bare and inviting sin.

I had to keep reminding myself that I wasn't the kind of man who took what he wanted, even as it was offered willingly.

Rue shifted position but her focus remained on the hardwood floor, just as she'd been trained. Her obedience would be treasured.

I wondered how she was feeling, what kind of emotions might be swirling through her mind.

I wondered if she understood the danger she was facing.

She remained still, perfectly poised, giving me time to study her, to admire her long red hair flowing over her shoulders and the way she filled her elegant bodice.

My cock hardened as I drank her in.

Her mouth looked pouty, begging for a kiss. A savage kiss at that. Her long eyelashes fluttered with expectancy or nervousness—or maybe both.

Maybe this was her kink, and I was the disrupter.

I finally dragged my gaze away and scanned our surroundings. The room contained all the hallmarks of a sex club scene, a St. Andrew's Cross and a swing—accoutrements one would expect to be used on a consenting sub. The kind of instruments a Neanderthal might use to harm her.

She'd been handed over for money. Not for love of the lifestyle. I had the urge to go back and punch Faulkner in his pretty boy face.

With Rue's perfect posture she almost looked like she belonged here.

Almost.

She finally looked up at me, recognition flashing across her face.

Not missing a beat, I strode toward her.

"You didn't win me," she whispered, confusion soaking her words.

I checked the handcuffs. "Key?"

They'd literally strapped her up and left her vulnerable.

She tipped her chin at the mantle. I headed over to the fireplace and ran my hand along the marble.

Finding the key, I hurried back and unlocked the cuffs, freeing her hands. Then I unclipped the fine chain from her collar and discarded it.

I shrugged out of my jacket and flung it around her shoulders. "Where are your panties?"

"In the car."

My jacket swamped her. She looked like she was playing dress up.

"You changed your mask?"

"Very observant. Now put yours back on."

She retrieved her mask from a table. "Did the other guy bid on me for you?"

Refusing to answer, I ushered her out, glancing left and right to make sure our way was clear.

She glanced at me. "Are we changing rooms?"

"Not exactly."

"Where are we going?"

"Keep walking."

We passed a couple and I threw them a casual nod so they would think nothing unusual was happening—that I wasn't attempting to extract a submissive from the premises, from Pendulum, no less. If they knew my intention, the powerful clientele here could make my life uncomfortable as a consequence.

Three dominatrices were gathered at the end of the hallway, all of them watching us intently.

I directed Rue to turn left down a different hallway. "This way."

"Who are you?" she asked.

"A friend."

"We aren't friends."

"If I was planning something sinister, you'd still be locked in those handcuffs."

"Take me back to Faulkner."

"He's the reason you're in this mess."

"Mess?"

"Trust me on this."

"I'll scream!"

"You think that would raise an alarm around here?"

"I mean it."

"How old are you?"

"Twenty-three."

I opened a door. Finding the room empty, I ushered Rue inside the private space.

"Kneel," I ordered fiercely.

She sank to her knees, holding a subservient pose. I leaned low and swiped my jacket off her shoulders to expose her.

"You will obey."

A ghost of a smile played on her lips as she shuddered back into subspace.

"Play with your clit," I ordered.

She reached for her sex.

"Wait," I snapped.

Her eyes twinkled with mischief, and it almost destroyed me. But I had a job to do. Get her into a trance. Get her under my command and fast.

I tried to ignore the erection that proved I was enjoying this a little too much. My hands clenched into fists—I needed to pull this off without touching her.

"What do you say?" I asked sternly.

"Yes, sir."

"Better." I gestured. "You may continue."

Reaching low, she began to strum her clit.

"Good little slut," I said huskily.

She let out a gasp. Clearly, she liked me talking dirty.

Again, I reminded myself why I was here.

Stick to the plan.

Seduce her into leaving.

"Slower, my little minx."

She pouted, dangerously close to coming, her soft throaty groans making me harder.

"You like showing yourself to those men?" I asked.

She exhaled in a rush. "Yes, sir."

"You have a pretty cunt," I said softly. "They were all staring."

She let out a sob of pleasure.

"Does that feel nice?"

Her groans grew louder. She was going to give us away.

"Hands behind your back."

The expression in her eyes looked pained as she removed her

fingers from her clit, peering up at me with her carotid pulsing, proving her heart was racing.

"Up," I ordered, placing my jacket back around her shoulders. "Do exactly as I say."

"Yes, sir."

With my hand on her spine, I led her back out into the hallway. "There's more of that if you're a good girl."

We made it to the foyer without causing a scene, which was a fucking miracle. Rue reclaimed her phone and purse from the concierge, and waited for me to grab mine.

"Where's yours?" she asked.

"In my car," I said, not wanting to tell her I didn't trust leaving my phone with a stranger.

The concierge handed Rue her Burberry trench coat. She'd apparently arrived in it wearing only the bodice underneath and nothing else except her strappy sandals and a feisty attitude.

Stepping closer, I freed her hair from beneath her coat collar, the strands tumbling down her back. I stopped myself from running my hand through it again.

She looked over her shoulder at me.

"Let's step outside for some air."

Once out the door, I grabbed her arm and led her away from Pendulum, walking her briskly down the pathway.

"Where are we going?" she said.

"Where do you live?"

"Beverly Hills."

"Then that's where we're going."

"You told me if I was good..."

"The fun's over."

"What do you mean?" Her brows knitted together.

"Just keep walking."

"I know what this is," she snapped.

"Well done, you." I didn't care what she thought.

This annoying submissive was taking up my precious time. I'd gate-crashed the event and done the unthinkable—stolen a submissive, drawn the prize away from the new-money crowd. Who'd no doubt throw a tantrum when they could find no trace of the young woman.

She walked beside me with an annoyed stride, well out of subspace.

"She sent you, didn't she?" Rue asked.

"Want to be specific?"

"You work for her." Rue tried to keep up with me. "Mistress Carrie."

"Not exactly, no. This is a one-off."

"Are you a private detective?"

"No. Where's your car?"

"I came with someone."

"Faulkner?"

"Yes. Am I in trouble?"

I opened the passenger door and reached into my glove compartment, fishing out my phone. "Let's get Carrie on the line."

She rested her hand on mine to stop me. "Don't."

I turned to face her. "She'll reassure you that you're safe with me."

"She doesn't get to do this."

"Get in the car."

"I'm going back inside."

I grabbed her arm. "Not happening."

She tried to get away but then realized I was too strong. I'd seen that look a thousand times. The way a sub reacted to being dominated by a man impossible to escape from. That fiery glint as they processed how much fun they'd have being naughty and then subsequently being punished if they tried to run.

"I'm letting you go." I clenched my teeth. "Don't try anything."

"Sounds like a threat."

"That's why we're getting an adult you know on the line."

"Don't patronize me." She had that exact same glint in her eye she'd had when she'd been playing with herself a few minutes ago.

I raised my mask so she could see my face.

She peered up at me, seemingly impressed with what she saw. Her fiery gaze dissolved into pure want as she bit her bottom lip.

Yet she said, "I'm not going anywhere with you."

"You're not going back in there if that's what you think."

"I'll just stand out here in the cold then."

"Continue to waste my time and see what happens."

"You have no right!"

"Turn your phone on," I said, seething.

She jerked her arm away.

Rue rummaged inside her purse and withdrew her Smartphone, turning it on. It seemed to take a million light years for her to access the screen and read her texts.

She looked up at me. "Shay?"

"What else does Carrie say?"

"You're safe to leave with."

I leaned over to see if Carrie had texted anything else, but the message was brief.

Rue tucked her phone back in her purse. "Shay what?"

"Yeah, you don't get my last name."

"Can I see some ID?"

"Right after you feel my palm on your ass."

Her lips twisted in what could be construed as a smile.

Rue ducked her head as she climbed into the front passenger seat. After closing the car door, I made my way around to the driver's side and got in beside her.

I buckled my seatbelt and started the engine.

"Take off your collar," I commanded.

"Why?"

"Fine, I'll do it."

I felt along her nape for the catch of the collar, her silky locks brushing over my fingers, making them tingle. It was a thrilling sensation—like being kissed by satin. Her hair smelled like flowers.

Rue kept her head bowed, not resisting, instinctively reacting to my control.

Removing her collar, I eased it off her neck.

With the press of a button, I lowered my side window and then threw her collar out onto the curb.

"Hey!" She looked horrified.

I navigated the Rover onto the main road and hit the gas, making sharp maneuvers in case someone from the club decided to come after us, glancing in my rearview until I was satisfied we weren't being followed.

A mile away from Pendulum, I whipped off my mask and threw it onto the back seat. "Take off yours."

She untied the ribbon at the back of her head and slid it off, clinging to the delicate filigree mask as though she'd never get to wear it again.

"How much?" she asked.

"I'm not getting paid for this."

She looked at me inquisitively. "Why are you doing it then?"

"I was the only one who had the resources to rescue your sorry ass."

"I don't need rescuing."

"The guy who won you invited his friends."

She swallowed hard at that, blushing and squirming in her seat.

"Ever tell anyone about this night and I will find you," I said.

"Is that another threat?"

"I'm a man of my word."

"The guy who won me will be pissed off."

"Not my problem." I glanced over at her. "You're a member of Majestic, right?"

Rue stared dead ahead at the road. "Are you taking me there?"

"No, you need some time to prepare for Carrie's wrath."

"I can do what I want, when I want."

"I don't disagree. It's the venue you chose that concerns me."

"You seemed to know your way around." She pointed an accusatory finger at me. "Nothing shocked you there."

"And you know this how?"

"I saw it in your eyes."

I wasn't in the mood to correct her. "Ever heard of discretion?"

"This was none of your business and you know nothing about me."

"I know more than most." I arched a brow at her trench coat and what lay beneath.

That vision of her playing with herself was an exquisite memory, if I allowed myself to replay it, which I wouldn't. That memory belonged to her now.

I'd placed Rue into subspace for one reason alone—to have her compliant. Driving away with her proved how powerful subspace could be when used correctly.

"What's your address?"

"I live at the end of Ellison Drive. It's a cul-de-sac."

"Expensive neighborhood."

"My late father was a defense lawyer." She looked over at me. "Had some big clients."

The property would be worth millions in this neck of the woods.

"I'm sorry," I said. "About your dad."

She gave a shrug as though she was over it. I knew better.

I'd spoiled her fun and nothing I said or did would make a difference.

Rue folded her arms across her chest. "Did you like what you saw?"

I shook my head, amused and sensible enough not to comment.

"I shocked you," she said. "I can tell."

She had no idea the kind of things I'd done. The devilish games I'd played not only in this country but in Europe, too. My kind of kink was off the charts.

Faulkner might be the bad boy of bondage, but I was the devil in Armani.

To keep a place like Chrysalis safe, I'd sold my soul. No regrets. Not when it came to protecting my friends, who were like family.

Rue reached over and rested her hand on my thigh. It was suggestive and dangerously flirtatious.

And evocatively risky because she had no idea what kind of man she was dealing with.

I was not her knight in shining armor.

The sensation of her fingers inches away from my cock made it harden.

Taking Rue's hand, I placed it back on her lap.

A woman this stunning would be fun for a night, but after that she would be a headache. I'd be fighting off the Doms who'd be scheming to claim her, which would cause my protective side to kick in.

After my last relationship, I wasn't in the mood for anything that looked like commitment. It made no sense that I was even glancing in her direction to let my thoughts stray toward that fantasy.

The things I could do to her, though. Give her everything she wanted along with those things she didn't know she needed.

Still, I'd mastered the art of avoiding chaos.

I wanted to get home to catch the Lakers game. Warm up last night's take-out and switch off my mind—even if my phone was always beside me in case of emergencies.

"You're angry."

"I'm not angry," I said quietly.

I wanted to put as much distance as possible between me and this rare creature who was strictly in the no-go zone.

She crinkled her nose. "You called me a slut."

"That was me?"

"Don't gaslight me."

"Rue, it was meant as a tease."

"Tease?"

"I needed you compliant."

"You seduced me."

I gave her a look. "You don't belong there."

She didn't need to know that for a moment back at Pendulum I'd considered claiming her.

Not looking at her in that way made me feel good about myself, even though I was enjoying being this close to such beauty. I'd already seduced her back when I'd sent her hurtling into subspace.

I was the guy who did the right thing.

Faulkner had Rue in that place for his own benefit—financial or maybe even for a business gain. She might like the idea of that level of play but had no concept of what they'd do to her.

Not really.

Within thirty minutes, we'd arrived in the driveway of her Beverly Hills home tucked away in the corner of a cul-de-sac. The lights were out in the entire house, the place seemingly deserted. No other cars were parked outside.

"Thanks for the ride," Rue said in a huff.

Like she'd been dropped off at a shitty location.

"Anyone else here?"

"No, just me."

Leaving her in an empty house with no security was a bad move. I wasn't about to have her vulnerable to Faulkner turning up and taking her back.

I reached for my phone and dialed Carrie's number.

After a few rings she answered. "Quinn."

"Hey, there," I said, switching over to speakerphone.

"Is she safe?"

"Rue's fine. We're outside her house. How long before you get here to pick her up?"

Her sigh was followed by silence.

I glanced at the phone to make sure the call hadn't dropped. "Still there?"

"There's no furniture in that house," she said. "The electricity's been cut."

"Why?"

"Rue's aunt is selling the property."

"I only get an allowance from her," Rue mumbled.

I glanced over at her as I asked Carrie, "I can stay in the house with her until you get here."

"I'm on a plane."

"Headed where?"

"Washington."

What the fuck?

"I've been requested in D.C."

"I'll drop her off at Majestic, then?"

"Faulkner will come looking for her there."

"There's a great hotel close—"

"She'll just go back to the club."

My jaw tightened with annoyance. "Then where am I supposed to take her?"

Rue piped up beside me. "I am sitting right here!"

Reaching over, I cupped my palm over her mouth to silence her. She stilled, either too shocked to move or surprised someone had the balls to shut her up. Her pouty lips felt soft beneath my palm.

I dismissed those thoughts—I was on the phone with her Domina, after all.

I threw Rue a tense smile. "Still there, Carrie?"

"Can I rely upon you to guide her?" she replied.

Rue bit my palm.

I pulled my hand away and glared at Rue as I shot back at Carrie, "I hope you're not suggesting—"

"She has no relatives in L.A., so I'm letting her stay with you," she said flatly. "I'll be back tomorrow."

"This was not part of our agreement."

The phone went dead.

Staring at my screen, I did a mental recap of how I'd failed to get ahead of the conversation.

I called her back and it went to voicemail.

Annoyed, I tucked my phone away and dragged my palms down my face, failing to hide my frustration.

Rue bit her lip seductively. "Looks like you won me after all."

CHAPTER FIVE

Shay

T HE HEAVY IRON GATE SWUNG OPEN, ALLOWING ME TO drive through and up toward Cameron's vast Beverly Hills manor.

He was fifteen minutes away from where Rue had once lived.

This neighborhood was home to celebrities, famed for its lavish homes located not far from Rodeo Drive, an exclusive luxury shopping district that drew locals and tourists alike. A place to get overpriced shit that was in vogue.

Cameron only lived here because it was close to his Beverly Hills clinic, and Cedars-Sinai Hospital was also a five-minute drive.

He no longer needed to live this close, though. Not since he'd turned his focus onto Cole Tea's philanthropy.

I know he missed psychiatry. The call to the family business had been too strong. His dad now had everything he'd planned for; the Cole sons running the empire. Cameron and Henry's sister was on the same trajectory.

A few months ago, the decision had been made that I was to

place all my focus on Enthrall and Chrysalis. Cole Tea's security would protect the family.

For me it meant more time with everyone except Cameron.

Looking toward the house, I realized he may not even be here.

Maybe a staff member had buzzed our car through the gate. Cameron spent most of his time in Venice Beach, preferring his understated oceanside property.

Maybe Mia was home alone with her young son Raif. She'd stolen Cameron's heart and swept him off his feet—just as he had done to her.

And now this big old house was as noisy as hell. Constant laughter and screams of delight ringing throughout the place. The kind of chaotic fun a child brings.

As I drove closer to the mansion it dawned on me how fucking stupid this was.

For God's sake.

Bringing a submissive here, freshly extracted from Pendulum, wasn't one of my better ideas.

No doubt my attraction to her had done the thinking for me. Enticing me to the point of distraction.

Circling the fountain, I headed back down the driveway toward the gate.

I suddenly saw a blur of movement and slammed on my brakes, reacting to the shadows within a line of trees.

A black Labrador puppy pranced around Cameron's feet.

Cameron and I held each other's gaze.

There was a time seeing this man would have an effect on me altogether different than what I felt now. His presence would stir a multitude of emotions. Some expected. Some not. And once he left my sight, his presence would linger not only in my head but in my heart.

Lowering my window, I called over, "You got a dog?"

He glanced down at the pup. "Mia wanted one for Raif. What are you doing in the neighborhood?" He peered past me through my window at Rue in the passenger seat. His quizzical gaze turned back to me. "Is she why you changed your mind?"

"Something else came up."

"Come inside. Let's catch up."

Hanging out with Cameron had been one of the more remarkable experiences of my life. I missed it. But tonight wasn't a good time to fill that void. I had a problem that needed solving.

"You're not leaving without at least saying hi," insisted Cameron.

I put the Rover in park and glanced over at Rue. "Stay here."

I got out and shut the car door. When I reached Cameron, I gave him a warm hug and he patted my back with affection. I guided him away from the car so Rue wouldn't overhear.

"Where's your security detail?" I asked.

Cameron seemed to think on it.

I felt a stab of annoyance. "You sent him home?"

"It's his anniversary." Cameron waved it off. "Anyway, thanks to you it's like Fort Knox in there."

"Yes, but you're out here."

"How's the beach house?"

"Fantastic. Thank you for letting me crash there."

"That's what it's for." Cameron looked over at my car. "You're not going to introduce us?"

"I made a mistake bringing her here."

"Oh?" He peered through the windshield to study her. "Who is she?"

"Rue." I lowered my voice. "She's from Majestic."

"Oh, I like them over there."

"She's not their most well-behaved submissive," I mused.

"Is she wearing anything beneath that trench coat?"

"Yes, actually."

I watched his expression to see if my lie escaped detection.

"Did you come from Chrysalis?" he asked.

The puppy leaped onto my leg.

I patted his head. "Hey, boy."

"Chloe," Cameron corrected me.

"Hey, Chloe." I straightened.

It was good to see him. God, I missed working with this man.

Cameron's mind was constantly processing everything around him.

"Does Carrie know she's a problem sub?" he asked.

Yeah, nothing got by him.

"She asked me to extract Rue from Pendulum."

Cameron cringed.

"Rue and I haven't discussed the details of why she was there."

"Yet."

Which was his way of encouraging me to have that conversation.

"If she needs to talk," he said. "I'm here."

"Not necessary."

"How the hell did she get into Pendulum?"

"She was there with Faulkner."

"That makes things interesting."

"I wore a masquerade mask. No one saw me."

"Carrie reached out to you?"

"Yes, she summoned me to her office downtown."

"She assumed you could get into Pendulum?" He looked annoyed. "Someone told her about you. Find out who it was."

"I intend to."

He shrugged. "Want to come in?"

"We shouldn't."

"What's the plan?"

"I'm trying to figure out where to take Rue tonight."

"You considered us?"

"Before coming to my senses."

"What about Carrie's place?"

"She's on her way to D.C."

"Hotel?"

"Too vulnerable."

Mia appeared in the doorway and made her way toward us. "Shay."

She held out her hands to take mine and leaned in to kiss my cheeks—one at a time, European-style. Her perfume wafted around us like a fresh summer breeze. Her blonde hair was tied back. Even without make-up she was breathtaking.

She looked over at the car.

"Her name's Rue," I explained.

"Introduce me!" said Mia.

"We're leaving. I have to find somewhere for her to stay."

Mia looked surprised. "Did something happen to her?"

"It's complicated."

"But she's okay?" Mia's voice was laced with concern.

"She's fine."

"Come in," she said, gesturing to Rue. "Tell her to come in, too. We can all talk about it."

"I don't think you should formally meet."

Confusion flashed over Mia's face. She looked to Cameron for clarification, and then turned back to me. "You're welcome here anytime," she said. "But you know that."

Cameron handed Mia the puppy's leash. The small dog pranced around her feet.

Mia glanced at Cole, realizing that was her cue to let us talk privately. She gave a nod of understanding as she led the puppy away.

"It was good to see you," she called back.

Mia went inside the house, leaving the door ajar.

Cameron gestured toward the Rover. "Faulkner's making risky moves."

A discomforting thought popped into my head. "You didn't set this entire charade up, did you?"

Cameron looked surprised. "What?"

"Tricking me into getting a new submissive?"

"When have I ever interfered in anyone's life like that?"

"Seriously?"

Like when he sent Scarlet to France to spend time with Danton Belfort because he knew she needed time away in Europe. Knew time with Danton might save her life…and it did.

Or like when he hired Mia to work at Enthrall, manipulating Richard into dating her. Before he finally realized he wanted her for himself. Cut to them living happily ever after in this ridiculously large mansion. With a dog. And a child. And enough domestic drudgery to lose a hard-on.

He did seem happier, though. So there was that.

"No, I have no knowledge of the woman waiting in your car." He narrowed his sharp focus on Rue. "Though if you give me five minutes with her, I'll gain some insight."

"That's not why I'm here," I snapped.

A ghost of a smile touched his lips. "You seem antsy."

"You don't get to do that."

"Do what?"

"Turn this around."

"Turn what around?"

"Make this about me."

"You've been miserable since Carrington."

Just hearing Jake's last name sent a jolt of sadness through me.

Carrington had swept through my life like a fucking tornado, leaving the kind of damage one would expect from a man whose nickname was De Sade—the same De Sade history had proven to be a sick bastard who'd mastered the art of pain a century ago.

It had started off as a joke but, strangely, had turned into reality.

Having retired from the NFL as a star quarterback, Carrington still had this uncanny ability to deal with pain—for himself as well as others.

A trait he was admired for at Chrysalis.

We'd become more.

So much more.

Right up until he'd gone back to his wife. Rylee had initially left him for another man, and then changed her mind—stealing Jake back and making that move permanent.

Over the last month, I'd picked up the pieces of that catastrophe.

I was done inviting in anymore carnage.

"You both agreed Carrington trying again with Rylee was a good idea," Cole said, interrupting my thoughts.

How could I have stood in his way?

I rose out of my melancholy. "If this is your elaborate plan…" I stared off at Rue.

"I'm flattered," he said. "But I introduced you to De Sade and…" He shrugged.

"You never suspected I'd like him that much?" I couldn't keep the surprise from my tone.

After all, he was the great Cameron Cole, renowned psychiatrist known for playing puppet master.

"It's natural to fall in and out of love."

It was the falling out of part that I hated.

He nudged my arm. "She likes you."

"Rue? I've only just met her."

And I was already entranced with her deep blue eyes and flowing hair and those voluptuous curves. She was all woman and full of promise as a submissive, too. I wasn't that much into danger that I'd give her any serious consideration.

"What's her story?" he asked.

I didn't want to get into it. "You better not be plotting."

He scoffed. "That wouldn't be one of my better manipulations."

That made me smile. "It's not like I'm not attracted to her. She's just out of bounds."

"You can handle Faulkner. He has enough ghosts in his closet. So does Carrie, enough to fill Saks Fifth Avenue."

"How do you know that?"

He smirked. "Let me know if you need anything."

Running my hands through my hair, I hesitated to answer.

"It's inevitable." He glanced at me. "You and her."

"It's not a good look. Not when I'm meant to be rescuing her."

"Since when has fucking not been rescuing?"

"Don't."

He lowered his gaze on her. "She's very you."

"What do you even mean by that?"

"She's insatiable."

"You don't know her."

"I know Faulkner. He likes the subs who crave."

"Crave?"

"Pendulum equals exhibitionism."

"Doesn't that make me like him?"

"You are." Cameron patted my back. "That's why I hired you. You're not afraid to go in for the kill. Metaphorically speaking. And your kink is charming."

Right, because I, too, liked to fuck in front of an audience.

"Faulkner's a different species," I mumbled.

"My guess is she's poised to find another place that fulfills her needs," said Cameron. "Somewhere equal to Pendulum. Either you take her on as her new master or you give her back to Faulkner."

"Not Majestic?"

"They can be a little restrictive there." He headed toward the front door, and then paused, turning back to me. "You're insatiable. I imagine she is, too. See how that works."

"I have to drop her off somewhere. Any ideas?"

"No one offers protection like you."

"Not going to happen."

Cole shrugged. "Henry wants you to call him."

As old military buddies we owed each other the courtesy of not losing touch. "I will. How is he?"

"The same."

Cameron and Henry had a love-hate relationship. But as brothers, they always came through for each other. They were opposites. Henry had thrown himself into running Cole Tea as CEO, which had always been the plan. Cameron managed the company's philanthropic enterprises here and abroad. With them at the helm the business continued to thrive.

Their acumen was a resource I'd used in the past with my fledgling business CloudSource—the one that had never gotten off the ground. I was just too damn busy at Enthrall.

The practical side of security suited me better.

Heading back toward the car, I threw a wave at Cole.

Cameron called after me. "Faulkner will come for her."

"I know."

"Start strategizing," said Cameron.

"Already on it." I opened my car door and rejoined Rue.

"Who's that?" she asked.

"The kind of man who can dissect your brain while you're still alive." I navigated the Rover back toward the iron gate.

"Sounds painful."

"That's why we're driving away," I said. "To save you from that ordeal."

The iron gate swung open before us.

CHAPTER SIX

Shay

I PARKED CURBSIDE A FEW HOUSES DOWN FROM CAMERON'S place, trying to come to a decision.

He was right. No one could offer protection the way I could. Rue could stay with me temporarily.

I headed for Malibu.

Along the Pacific Coast Highway, I glanced over at Rue. "Warm enough?"

She'd folded her arms across her chest. "Are we just going to drive around all night?"

"No, that's not the plan."

"Just take me home."

"You forgot to tell me the house is being sold?" I asked, glancing over at her.

She glowered at me. "How about asking if there's somewhere I want to go?"

"We are not going back to Pendulum."

"At a friend's, then."

"Do you really want staff from Pendulum turning up on your girlfriend's doorstep? They are looking for you. There's no doubt."

I'd noticed the silver Lexus following us a while back, and now the car no longer discreetly tailed us. The driver was flashing his lights for me to pull over.

Faulkner had not only inserted a tracker into Rue's collar but somewhere else on her.

At least I hoped it was him.

I'd implemented driving maneuvers to shake off any car that might have followed us from the club. I never would have driven to Cole's place if I'd suspected we were being tracked.

"Who gave you that watch?" I flashed Rue a wary glance.

She traced her fingers over it. "My master."

Of course, Kaison Faulkner had made a contingency plan. He was a lawyer and a good one at that. He could accuse me of kidnapping.

Faulkner also knew her value in the scene. A beauty like this would garner all kinds of favors for him. If he loaned her out. Placing a tracker in her wristwatch would have been a decision made before taking her to Pendulum.

Because of the danger there.

Fucker.

"How do you know him again?" I asked.

"He's one of the guest Doms at Majestic."

A house where newbies went to learn about the scene. Kaison had probably seen her from across the room and wanted her immediately.

We were flashed again by headlights.

Carefully, I navigated the car off the PCH and onto the strip of asphalt reserved for Gladstones parking, a beachside restaurant that would be closed by now. I could try to lose him, but he might be so full of rage he'd attempt to run us off the road.

Rue studied me. "Why are we pulling over?"

I put the car in park. "Faulkner."

"He followed us?"

"Yes."

She turned to look back at his car. "How?"

"Stay here." I got out of the car to confront him.

He was already out of his Lexus—his tuxedo disheveled, a pissed off expression matching his swagger.

We both kept our headlights on to illuminate the setting where shit was about to go down.

Waves crashed on the rocks nearby.

This place was a popular venue for lunch, followed by a walk along the beach afterwards. Now, the parking lot was deserted.

With a click of my fob, I locked Rue in the car and then continued toward Kaison.

"You were the plague doctor?" he said brashly.

"Have no idea what you're talking about," I answered casually.

"You have my submissive."

"She's taking a break."

"Didn't know you were a member of Pendulum."

"This is a dangerous road, Kaison." I glanced back at the PCH. "People die on this highway."

"I've been tracking you."

"Correction, you've been tracking Rue. It was a cheap trick to put it in her watch. She doesn't know you're following her. That's unethical."

"Can never be too careful."

"But you can at Pendulum?"

He stepped closer so we were face to face. "What the hell were you thinking?"

I knew there was no avoiding the truth. "I was asked to extract Rue."

"And you're taking Rue to this phantom friend?"

"How long have you known me?" I said. "I have better shit to do than this."

"I need to speak to her."

"Not a good idea."

Faulkner's jaw tightened. "I want to hear it from her that she's okay."

"I was merely asked to extract her. That's all I'll say."

"She's above the age of consent."

I straightened my back. "Pendulum? What the hell were *you* thinking?"

"No one enters without it being fully explained so they know what to expect." He narrowed his focus. "You've played just as fucking hard."

"We're old enough to know our limits and the limits of others. Rue's still learning."

He clenched his teeth. "I took her there for her sake."

"I'm sure Majestic appreciates that."

"They know?" He looked concerned. "How?"

I turned to walk away from him.

"I'm not letting you drive away with her," he said. "Rue's my responsibility."

Rue threw a friendly wave at him through the window.

"Does she look threatened to you?" I asked.

"You would do the same," he said, softening his tone. "Make sure she's safe. You wouldn't let some asshole wander into Chrysalis and kidnap her."

"She came willingly."

"I don't know that unless I talk with her," he bit out.

"You know my reputation."

"Do I? It's all super-secretive at Enthrall. Exclusive. Impossible to get into."

"Kaison, your connection to Pendulum sets you apart."

"Is that why I'm not permitted to join Chrysalis?"

"That, and your cocaine habit."

He looked pissed off and then relented. "What kind of man would I be if I let you drive off with her?"

"Someone who gets this situation."

"I will follow you all damn night if that's what it takes."

Exasperated, I weighed how much of a pain he'd be if I didn't placate him.

With a reluctant nod, I unlocked the car with a click of my key fob and gestured for Rue to join us. "You have five minutes," I told him.

Rue shoved open the car door and slid out of the passenger seat. She hurried over to us. A twinge of jealousy hit me when Kaison dipped his head and kissed her as she leaned into him.

"You okay, babe?" he asked.

She looked up at him with affection. "I'm fine."

He hugged her. "What's going on?"

Rue looked at me. "Am I in trouble?"

Kaison forced a smile. "Getting back into Pendulum might not happen."

"That's a tragedy," I mumbled.

"Why?" she said, clearly upset.

"Leaving the way you did reflects badly on me," said Kaison.

Rue let out an exasperated sigh. "I have to go with Mr. Boring here."

Faulkner looked amused. "You don't know who he is?"

She turned to look up at me. "Who are you?"

Faulkner answered for me. "Shay Gardner. Head of security for Enthrall. And a Dominant."

She blushed as she studied me carefully.

"Yes," he said. "Only he doesn't train subs. He just uses them and throws them away."

That made me angry but I didn't show it.

Kaison looked triumphant. "Subs crave him but soon learn a lesson."

"And why is any of this important?" I said.

We both knew why; because he thought I was moving in on his submissive. He was trying to let her know I was a bad match for her, that things would turn out unpleasant.

He wasn't wrong.

"Come on, baby," he said. "Let me take you home."

"She's coming with me," I said.

"Don't I get a say?" Her long lashes fluttered at him.

I ran through all the reasons why this wasn't my problem.

But Kaison would probably take her back to Pendulum if I didn't intercede.

"Get in the car," I said.

Rue chewed her lip thoughtfully. "You have to ask permission from my master."

Smugness settled on his face. "See how that works?"

Rue flirtatiously stepped forward and peered up at me. "Unless you're my master now?"

"You know nothing about him," snapped Faulkner.

"I'm a good judge."

"He won't take you to Pendulum," he added.

"But he can get me into Enthrall." Rue brightened.

That was never going to happen.

Even so, I went with, "I'll consider it."

"You don't have the balls to defy my mistress," she teased.

There was only one way to get a handle on this; *on her.*

I towered over Rue and commanded her. "Take off your watch. Give it to him."

"Why?" She glanced at Faulkner for reassurance.

I stepped closer. "Do I look like I'm negotiating?"

In a flurry of movement, Rue slipped the Rolex off her wrist and handed it over to Kaison. "Were you tracking me with this?"

Annoyed, he shoved it into his pocket.

Defeat didn't look good on him.

Rue faced me, looking spectacularly alluring.

She'd turned obedient, responding perfectly to my crafted illusion that I was her new Dom.

"Get in," I ordered her.

She hurried back toward the passenger seat of the Rover.

"There'll be consequences for this," Kaison muttered under his breath.

"I can handle them."

"She's sold, Shay. You should have put in a bid."

Glancing back at him, I added, "Delete all the footage you've taken of her. Or I'll delete you."

"As if I'd take any," he said, confirming my suspicion that she'd been more to him than he was letting on.

I rejoined Rue in the car.

"Change of plan," I told her as I drove us out of the parking lot.

"Where are we going now?"

"That was not me giving you permission to speak."

"Like I need it." She sunk back into the leather seat.

"Rue," I snapped.

"Yes, sir." She reflected obedience. "Sorry, sir."

"Better."

She turned to look out the back window at where we'd left Kaison standing.

"Eyes forward," I snapped.

And Rue obeyed.

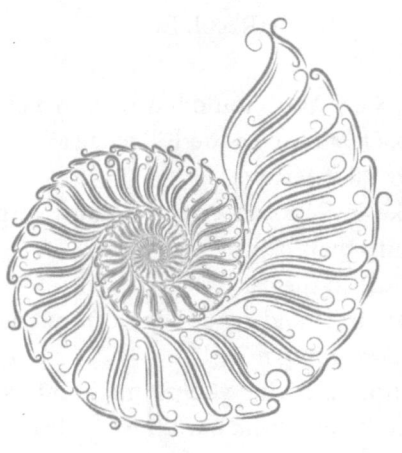

CHAPTER SEVEN

I STILL COULDN'T BELIEVE I'D BEEN PULLED OUT OF PENDULUM. Not after what it took for me to get in there.

Still, I consoled myself with the thought that this man might be able to get me into Enthrall—the premier club that was more difficult to get into than Pendulum, which was saying something.

My Domina was making my life hell by ordering him to watch over me.

Shay would probably never forgive me for that.

We'd driven away from Gladstones and within ten minutes pulled up to his beachside home.

I'd been pleasantly surprised to see the inside was as swanky as the location. After he gave me a quick tour to make me feel welcome, I felt comfortable enough to find my way around this four-bedroom two-story home.

Shay led me around as though I was an expected visitor and we'd not met under weird circumstances. Like he'd not seen me half-naked and secured to a ceiling. He was polite enough to act casual.

He didn't flirt; he was all business. Like I was a job, and he was carrying it out to the letter.

Shay admitted the place had benefited from the talents of an interior designer. It was all marble and expensive light fixtures and did not include much personal stuff to reveal his personality or character.

I was now stealing time in his luxurious bathroom to freshen up. Just as he'd invited me to.

This evening had been a catastrophe.

I'd worked hard to get into that secret club—a place that wasn't supposed to exist. I'd pushed myself during training and flourished under the guidance of my Dom. I'd counted down the days until my entry into Pendulum.

Only to be forcibly removed an hour later. Even if *he* was devastatingly enigmatic, I hated Shay for it.

Still, if some part of me had wanted to be rescued by a knight in a tailored suit, Shay Gardner would be that man. Only, I'd come too far to fail as a submissive.

There was no doubt Shay was brilliant enough to have been hired to work at Enthrall and interesting enough not to be intimidated by Kaison Faulkner. With me though, he acted like this entire charade was a mistake.

At some point, we'd have that talk. I could see it looming on his pursed and very judgmental lips.

What he couldn't know was I about to unleash my redheaded self onto an unsuspecting Shay.

I just needed to rid myself of this constricting bodice.

After my shower, I wrapped myself in a towel and sat on the edge of the tub. Grabbing my phone from the corner table, I spent a few minutes searching for more info on my mysterious captor.

Even though he came with Carrie's approval, I scoured the Internet for anything that would give me more details on this man.

There wasn't much. He kept his life private. His social media was locked down. The most compelling discovery I made was that Shay was an ex-Navy SEAL.

That detail had me pressing my palm to my chest to slow my racing heart. This explained his confidence, his alpha swagger. And his impressive physique. He was someone who had faced off with the worst danger.

Imagining Shay in a uniform was sexy as hell.

Pushing up, I stared at my reflection in the bathroom mirror, talking myself out of having a panic attack for being in the same proximity as the man who'd rattled Kaison.

Shay. The man infamous for keeping everyone in line at Enthrall. His reputation was everything. Apparently, he was into dark kink.

So, this is what you look like.

Wiping the smudged makeup away, I tried to erase the tiredness.

Maybe everything wasn't so bad.

Because I was here.

With him.

After a few minutes, I'd pulled on one of Shay's T-shirts. This, along with a pair of boxer shorts he'd given me to wear. It had been a relief to rid myself of that tight bodice.

I was shaken from my thoughts by a knock.

"Got everything you need?" Shay called through the door.

"Yes, thank you."

Just knowing he was on the other side made me giddy. *God,* he was so damn sexy. Masterful and capable of anything. Capable of walking into a place like Pendulum and stealing one of their own.

I wondered if there would be repercussions. Hopefully, Kaison would smooth that over. Make it easier for me to go back.

A shiver ran up my spine as I recalled the way Shay stood over me in the dungeon. What he'd done to me on the way out had been perfected dominance. I wondered if he knew how wet he'd made me. The thought he illicitly removed me from that private sanctum turned me on to the point of distraction.

I ran Shay's comb through my hair. I'd put so much product in it tonight the strands clumped.

I wanted to get another chance to seduce this man.

Or at least make him like me.

I could see us being friends. Maybe more if I could persuade him to see me differently.

I had less than twelve waking hours to work on him.

Smoothing out my hair, I let it tumble over my shoulders.

I'd needed this break from work.

My next shift at Cedars wasn't until Friday. Maybe I'd be able to persuade him to let me stay for a few days. Now this, I could get used to.

Finding a blue bottle of cologne, I sniffed the delicious scent that matched the man downstairs and spritzed it over me.

Breathing him in, I inhaled the scent like I was absorbing the man himself, and then blinked at my own reaction.

Wow.

If they'd tried to bottle sex they'd succeeded. Shay was a walking pheromone. I didn't stand a chance.

"Join me downstairs," Shay called through the door.

It made me jump.

"I will." I felt a flutter of excitement from being summoned by his sultry tone.

Leaving the bathroom, I walked barefoot along the hardwood floor, heading towards the sitting room. My pulse quickened at being in the same space as him.

Passing the kitchen table, I glanced at the open laptop.

My Instagram page was on the screen, photos of moments captured by me. My life played out in full color. Endless squares went on for years.

Me on Laurel Canyon's hiking trail. Selfies taken at the Hollywood Bowl. Partying with friends at The Reserve. Me in uniform at work. In a mini-dress entering Bar Sinister.

The last one taken was of a redhead heading out for the night in a masquerade mask. That Burberry trench coat a giveaway that

I was barely clad beneath. A bite of my lip in that photo was me anticipating what lay ahead at Pendulum.

Shay had wanted the upper hand.

I knew anyone could see them, but this was another level of scrutiny.

The sliding glass door was open. A fresh salty breeze reminded me he lived on the coast.

I heard the sound of crashing waves and seagulls squawking.

Stepping out onto the lanai, I saw the sandy beach and the autumn night sky. Moonlight glinted off the ocean's surface, making the setting seem magical.

A blue surfboard leaned against the wall. Reaching out, I ran my hand along its edge, feeling that familiar longing to take it out onto the water. Just like I'd done with my dad on the weekends.

Those precious days were now over.

Once again I felt that sinking feeling. Time had stolen my happiness.

"Hey," a voice grabbed my attention.

Shay was relaxing on a lounger with a can of Budweiser in his hand. He'd changed into ripped jeans and a white shirt. Sleeves rolled up revealing his impressively toned forearms.

A breeze messed with my hair. I brushed it away from my face.

Shay was so damn hot in those jeans. His feet were bare and resting on the table in front of him.

"You've been researching me?" I came out and said it.

He raised his beer. "Want one?"

"No, thank you."

"We have wine."

I clocked the fact he'd said *we*. Did someone else live here? "Did you enjoy looking at my social media pages?"

"You've stepped inside my inner circle," he said, his voice husky. "I need to know who and what I'm dealing with."

He brought the beer to his mouth and took a few gulps, then easily squeezed the can. It folded like paper beneath his grip. Even his hands were huge. Chances were another part of his anatomy was equally as impressive. I let myself enjoy that fantasy.

He placed the destroyed can on the table. Like a symbol of what he could do to his enemies.

Then he gave me a heart-stopping smile. "You look good in my shirt."

"The bodice was cutting off my circulation."

He went to smile and then stopped himself, merely revealing that charismatic quirk of a brow.

I looked out at the deserted beach. Other than the waves the place was quiet. It felt like we were the last souls on earth. And I felt safe with him.

Life couldn't touch me.

This is temporary.

He and I would never be more. I was merely the girl he'd rescued. The fact he had checked out my social media accounts made sense. He had to make sure I wasn't a risk to either Carrie or him.

His gaze traveled over my body. "Want a sweater?"

"No, I'm fine."

"If you need anything, let me know," he said.

"I want you to take me back."

His expression went from amused to serious. "On your knees."

It was as though he'd flipped a switch—that rare moment of kindness morphing into dominance, causing me to freeze.

"Rue?"

I hurried forward and dropped to my knees, bowing my head and avoiding eye contact, shivering with a delicious sense of obedience. My body flooded with arousal and I was overwhelmed with sensations I couldn't define.

It was like I'd been out at sea for weeks and finally glimpsed the lighthouse, that moment where I escaped this gut-wrenching grief—all that had gone before that hurt me, dimming in my heart.

The sounds of the ocean were a backdrop to this glimmer of peace.

I felt the warmth from his touch on my cheek, his fingers

trailing through my hair, twisting a strand, making my scalp tingle. His thumb glided to my mouth and brushed over my lips.

My eyes fluttered at the way he touched me, the way he wasn't scared of silence.

He patted the seat beside him. "Up here."

Rising, I sat next to him, resting my hands in my lap, feeling like my life was spinning on a different axis. Spinning back into control.

"How do you feel?" he asked.

How did I feel? Like I was in the presence of a true master—a man who'd stormed into the fire to retrieve me like I was important, like I meant something. This man was the kind who would find you if you got lost and bring you back from the brink of danger. He would be unfazed by any challenge.

"Tell me more about you," he said softly.

"Nothing much to tell."

"Any siblings?"

"Just me."

"I'm an only child, too," he offered up. "You used to live in that big house in Beverly Hills alone?"

"Yes, I didn't mind. It's got all the memories. Dad's law office was a few miles away. Mom was a surgeon. She worked at Cedars. They had me when they were in their forties after going through fertility treatments. When I was born, they were very protective."

I was rambling.

He made me that nervous.

I cleared my throat. "A year after Mom died, Dad was in a car accident."

He gave a look of commiseration.

"I can't afford the mortgage on my salary. I don't get my inheritance until I'm twenty-five."

"I see."

"I've been staying at Majestic." I continued to bleed words of misery.

"You're there for submissive training?"

"Yes. I signed a contract to keep me there for a month." I stared off and followed the flight of a seagull. "It's impossible to break it. It's at least one hundred K."

"That doesn't sound right."

"It was the only house that would take me." I raised my chin. "Enthrall wouldn't even consider me."

His frown deepened. "Don't move in with Faulkner."

I stared off toward the ocean. "Your place is beautiful."

"Actually, it's not mine."

"You rent?"

"It belongs to a friend. I'm staying here while I...find somewhere else to live."

"These are not your things?"

"My stuff is in storage. All this furniture comes with the house."

"Are you divorcing?"

"No."

It was impossible not to crush on this guy. The way he kept that wall up. Not letting me close. As though protecting me from what lay behind that steely glare.

He shrugged. "My last relationship didn't work out."

"What was her name?"

"Jake." He slid into an endearing smile as though amused at my misconception.

Somewhere in the far reaches of my addled mind I recalled Kaison mentioning Shay broke hearts. Also, that Shay took on submissives.

"Bi?" I asked softly.

"Yes."

"Is Jake in the scene?"

"Yes."

"So you've also had female submissives?"

A devilish bite of his lip. "Yes, of course."

It was the way he spoke those words, like the vibration of his tone was an invitation.

"You're into pain?" I asked.

"Especially while driving on the 405."

I laughed at that. Everyone in this city hated that congested freeway.

"You?" he said.

"Just endless pleasure," I admitted.

"Endless?"

A ripple of chemistry flickered between us, as though his voice had the ability to enter me, flickering all the way down there.

"Merely pleasure," he mulled that over.

"If it pleases my master."

Shay ran his thumb over his lower lip. "I can see you've had some training."

He had this way of turning me on with merely a tilt of his head. That cute smirk was more of a suppressed grin.

It sent me reeling.

The way he wielded his quiet power like a leather whip promising to kiss my skin.

Just the thought of him doing anything to me made my body flush. He caught my reaction, staring as my nipples beaded, giving me away.

He reached for another can of beer and pulled the tab, cracking it open.

"Why exactly did you check out my social media?" I said to douse this fire.

"Are you hungry?" he said, ignoring my accusation. "I can cook you something."

"No." My stomach was in knots. "Did you do a background search on me?"

"I was courteous enough not to be secretive about it."

"How much do you know about me?" Shay couldn't know *everything*. "That doesn't seem fair."

"We keep one face for the public and our true self hidden."

"And what is my hidden self?"

"You're still finding your way."

"I suppose that's true."

"It's the hidden part I'm interested in."

I met his gaze. "You probably know I'm an RN."

He took a swig of beer. "At Cedars, right?"

I went with his line of questioning. "I work in the ICU, but I've applied to transfer to a different unit."

"Why?"

"Change of pace."

"Whatever you decide to do you'll be great at it."

"You don't know that. I'm a little nervous."

"That's natural, but you have above average intelligence."

"How do you know that?"

"You scored high on your SAT's."

"How much digging around did you do!"

"As much as I felt was necessary."

"For what?" I smirked at my cheekiness. "You like to get to know your submissives before you take them to Enthrall?"

He gave me a look. The one that told me it wasn't happening.

Shay leaned forward and rested his elbows on his knees. "Your Domina sent me to retrieve you. To keep you safe. That's exactly what I'm going to do."

I looked away, frustrated. "You made me believe…"

He set his beer on the table. "I can't be held responsible for your imagination."

"You pulled me out of Pendulum. Do you have any idea how hard it is to get in?"

"Actually, I do."

I wagged a finger at him. "You don't get to sabotage what took me weeks to prepare for."

"You weren't prepared."

"You don't get to order me out of a scene because you don't approve. I'm sure you've done worse."

"As I said—"

I stood up. "You're manipulative."

"I fulfilled a commitment, which doesn't involve discussing 'the scene' with you."

"Seriously?"

He pushed himself up and towered over me. "You flew too close to the flame. Just be glad there was someone there to prevent you from flying directly into it."

"You don't get it," I snapped.

"I know Pendulum was important to you. Maybe when you're older you can go back, when you're capable of making adult decisions."

"That's not fair."

"You're not trained well enough for Pendulum."

"You don't know that."

"You were trembling when I entered the dungeon. I saw no sign of arousal."

"Until you walked in," I said, sounding breathless.

I let that sink in.

No games. Just me letting him know this mutual attraction couldn't be denied.

He glowered. "Your behavior is intolerable for a submissive."

"We're having a conversation."

"Did I invite you to?" He glowered back. "Just because you have a pretty cunt doesn't make you ready."

I slapped him hard across the face.

He didn't flinch. He just nodded as though he'd been expecting it.

Shay looked at me calmly. "Go to bed."

"What does she have over you?"

"Carrie?"

"Yes."

"Not a thing."

"My training was going too slow." I shrugged. "Carrie was concerned my fantasies are too demanding."

"A valid concern."

I'd not meant to reveal this.

That's what this man did to me—sparked feelings I normally kept suppressed. He made me defensive. Made me want him to like me like this. Made me want to know what it would feel like if he fucked me.

I imagined him in uniform when he was a SEAL. The kind of bravery he must have shown. The things he'd seen. The things he'd done. Shay was so damn tall and rugged and oozing sex appeal that he made me wet whenever I was around him.

My dream guy.

I didn't want to lose him, now that I'd found him.

Which made no sense.

For some inexplicable reason, I was jealous of anyone he'd dated. More than this, I was jealous of all the women he'd take to bed after I walked out of his life.

"Are you going to use silence?" he said.

"You don't know me."

"I know enough." His demeanor remained self-assured.

"They won't let me back in," I whispered.

"Pendulum?"

"Yes," I said, my tone was bitter.

He blinked as he processed that. "There's other places."

"Enthrall?"

He closed the gap between us, yanking me forward against his chest. He held my wrists behind my back, gripping them hard.

Capturing me…his body firm and heated against mine. My breasts were crushed against his chest, my nipples thrumming.

He's going to kiss me.

Why else would he be holding me like it was inevitable. Like it was the only thing that would help us understand each other. Help us bridge this age gap. His breath on my lips felt like he was breathing life itself into me.

The way he held me so tightly I couldn't escape, dominating me, caused a flurry of need in me, the arousal making me giddy.

Silence.

"Shay," I muttered his name as though it would anchor me.

Reading his expression made me want to disappear. I was seeing myself from his perspective. A misguided twenty-something. The spoiled brat who'd manipulated Kaison into getting me in.

I hated Shay for ruining my fun.

His lips glided over my cheek and lingered near my left ear. "Me not fucking you is the best thing that will ever happen to you."

My mouth glided toward his and nipped his lower lip. "I disagree."

He didn't flinch. "If you think for one second you're enough for me, you're delusional."

"You're trying to put me off you."

"I'm trying to protect you."

I didn't want to believe that. Didn't want to think of myself as someone he'd had to save.

A waste of his time.

His cock was hard between us; inviting and terrifying in size.

"Want to see my dark side? Go ahead and kneel." He let go of my wrists. "First, you might want to consider what my fetish is."

"What is it?" I whispered, needing to know and at the same time terrified of what he might say.

Yet I needed to hear him say it.

He quirked a brow. "If you have to ask."

I leaned in so close that our lips almost touched again. "You don't scare me."

"Bed. Now."

My heart rate became hectic, my body shivering. "Not when you just gave me the ultimate tease."

"This isn't a tease. It's a warning." He picked me up and threw me over his shoulder.

Discomfort traveled through me at this awkward position. He carried me down the hallway, my body crushed against his.

I heard him kick open a door and he entered a bedroom, flinging me onto the bed. Then he turned and walked away without saying another word.

He slammed the door on his way out.

This craving was a curse. A sick joke nature was playing on me. Because my body was yearning for him like a flower yearns for the sun—only to shrink again when the heat becomes overwhelming.

I'd have to face him in the morning. See that expression of contempt he wore when he set his sights on me.

I heard the sound of a TV down the hallway. From the commentator's voice I could hear he'd turned on the Lakers game. The squeak of shoes on the basketball court and spectators cheering gave the sport away.

He'd literally sent me to bed like a petulant teenager.

I rolled onto my side and reached for my iPhone, searching for any kind of distraction that would take my mind off him.

CHAPTER EIGHT

Shay

R ED HAIR BLOWING ACROSS HER FLUSHED FACE. HER FULL *mouth moving but no words flowing…*

A strobe light burned though my eyelids.

I'd been dreaming of *her*—the girl with the freckles.

The silent alarm had triggered flashing lights.

I'm at the beach house.

A cold sweat covered my body. I shook my head to clear it and then glanced at my watch: 6:35 A.M.

I climbed out of bed and pulled on my pajama pants, not caring about the shirt.

Walking barefoot, I padded toward Rue's room to check on her. She wasn't there, and I noticed her sheets were so ruffled it looked like she'd had a restless night. I felt a stab of guilt for me being the reason. I checked the en suite bathroom, finding that empty, too.

I stepped up to the security panel out in the hallway. A few punches on the keypad and I'd deactivated the strobe.

That familiar headache was back, followed by regret for drinking too many beers the previous night.

A breeze wafted in through the patio door.

Someone had opened it from the inside. Rue?

Sliding the glass door open further, I looked for her on the patio. Not finding her, I leaned over the banister to scan the beach. Footprints in the sand tracked all the way to the ocean.

That's not good.

Sunrays reflected off the water.

Way out there, a female surfer with a curvy physique was balancing on a blue surfboard and shredding a wave. It looked a lot like *my* surfboard. It was Rue in a T-shirt, the same one I'd given her last night. It was soaking wet and clinging to her. She could have been a cover model for *Surfing Magazine*. All wild and sexy and elegant as she rode the wave in, taking my breath away.

But she shouldn't be surfing alone.

I'd gone from pissed off to relieved and impressed. Relieved that some idiot hadn't broken in, forcing me to end the bastard.

Fully awake now, I suddenly remembered my life had imploded. That's right, I was here in Cameron's swanky beachside home because I'd sold my Brentwood house.

It was a place I'd lived in for years, but I had to start over again.

The beach house was meant to be a stopover—only I'd not found anywhere else to go yet.

There was something unresolved in my mind.

The soft sand down below had once looked inviting, but now it triggered a memory. *Not so fun when sand is in your fucking mouth.*

A sandstorm.

Unrelenting heat.

I fought the memories, dragging my mind back from the Middle East and reorienting, looking around for something familiar to grab to ground myself.

Rue, just focus on her.

Folding my arms, I continued to observe her out on that

surfboard. Now that I could see she was safe, I didn't want to look away.

She was simply mesmerizing.

At one point she looked toward the house and saw me watching. She leaped back onto the board and shredded another wave.

Drawing in a deep, cleansing breath, I realized how I'd neglected the ocean. How I'd been too inwardly drawn. Rue reminded me of myself before I'd joined the Navy.

A life full of choices.

Having a beautiful woman stay overnight wasn't exactly a burden.

She wowed me.

Eventually she waded out of the sea, carrying the surfboard up the beach, beaming with happiness. She hurried up the steps, her hair soaking wet and her cheeks flushed, dripping water. Her expression showed the adrenaline rush she was still feeling.

Last night she was sultry and stubborn and all kinds of alluring. This morning, Rue was earthy and sexy in a clinging T-shirt, now dangerously close to my type.

The type of woman I didn't know I liked.

Through the damp shirt I saw a belly button piercing; a ruby stone through the silver.

"Don't recall you asking permission to surf?" I playfully chastised her.

She was still my responsibility.

Rue smirked. "Good morning to you, too!"

I tipped my chin toward the ocean. "How long have you been surfing?"

"My dad taught me." Sadness shimmered in her gaze. "How often do you surf?"

"As often as I can."

"Why didn't you join me?"

Because watching you riding the waves was enough.

It was what my soul needed.

"Too early for you?" she quipped.

"Not too early to spank you."

She laughed and it rippled across the air like music.

"Didn't you notice the alarm?" I asked.

"I was like 'What the hell is that flashing?' Thought it best to get out before you stopped me."

That made me grin.

God, I'd missed this kind of banter. Missed waking up with company.

I took the surfboard from her and rested it back against the patio wall. She'd be tracking sand into the house.

"Wait in the kitchen," I told her, and went in search of a towel.

When I returned with a large towel, Rue was sheepishly dripping water on the tile floor. Like I'd once done when I didn't care about the small things. Before I'd been left to watch the sunrises and sunsets alone.

I ignored the fact she was naked beneath that see-through shirt.

I used the towel to dry her hair, squeezing her soaked locks. Having her tanned freckled face turned up to mine caused a shudder of awakening to run through me. It was as though these seconds were destined by some universal force. Maybe this was what I needed. Time with someone who I wasn't intimate with, taking the pressure off me to be more.

The reddish strands deepened in color as I dried them.

Her soulful beauty seemed untouchable. I could stand here all day just drying her hair and feeling the rush of our connection.

Like a meditation.

From the way Rue slipped into subspace I knew she felt it, too.

I admired this rare creature who stared back at me with a look I knew so well. She needed to be nurtured and told she was adored—shown that, too, with everything a man could give.

She had entered subspace simply by feeling cherished.

Her body seemingly thrummed beneath my touch as though electricity was passing through her and into me.

She pressed her palm against my chest.

I let her keep her hand there.

We felt the kind of chemistry that heats your flesh and sends you reeling with an unmatched high. I continued to rub her down, dragging the towel over her back and along her waist, and even though I avoided her breasts, her nipples became pert.

Last night at Pendulum she'd willingly offered herself to a stranger. So how bad was this intimacy now? That's what my ego asked as I fought to pull away.

She'd been rescued from that place and was now in the arms of a man she knew she was safe with.

That was the difference.

I wrapped the towel around her shoulders and walked away—mainly so she wouldn't notice how hard I'd become.

"Coffee or tea?" I asked, over my shoulder.

"Tea, please."

"Sure."

"We should surf together."

That comment made me turn around to face her.

Her gaze raked over my bare chest. "See how much we have in common."

I changed the subject. "Would you like toast?"

"That would be nice."

I walked over to the counter and placed a few slices of bread into the toaster, then set about filling the kettle and preparing two mugs.

Two mugs.

How long had it been since I'd made breakfast for someone else? Three months, two days, and twelve hours. I'd been living alone all this time. Here, in what was meant to be paradise.

My heart had felt like a rock lodged in my chest.

This morning was the first time that ache had lifted.

Having someone else here was good for me.

Rue dragged the wet T-shirt over her head and threw it into the sink, then shimmied out of the boxer shorts—unabashedly showing off her nakedness. She used the towel to finish drying herself.

It was like a gift from God saying, "Come get your reward for doing absolutely nothing."

Think of yourself as a big brother.

Someone she can be her authentic self with, someone she can continue to trust.

"I'm starving," she said.

It was refreshing to be around someone this relaxed and comfortable with her body. She moved around the kitchen as though not fazed by the man who was told he was intimidating.

Not so good was me being triggered to do more than just make tea and toast for my sensual house guest. "Cover yourself up."

She wrapped the towel around her body, then rose onto her toes and looked out the window. "People can see in?"

"Exactly."

The kettle whistled just in time. I brewed two mugs of tea.

Within minutes, I'd buttered four slices of toast and slid a plate with two of them over to her.

Rue joined me at the kitchen's central island, blowing on her drink to cool it.

She had too many freckles to count. It would be easy to try, to just stare at her face. Maybe lean over and kiss a few. Nip her ear. Tip up her chin and move my lips over her naturally pouty mouth.

Sink my teeth into her neck.

"Do I have something on my face?" she said, breaking my fantasy.

"A crumb." I touched my chin to show her where that non-existent crumb could be found on her blushing cheek.

I reminded myself that she was sacred, a female to be worshipped from afar—not someone to fantasize about.

"Shall I drive you back to Majestic after breakfast?" I asked.

"Okay."

"You don't seem happy about it."

"They're conservative."

"How?"

"Carrie believes in easing us into the scene. Nothing too intense."

"What kind of intense are you looking for?"

She gave me an amused glance. "You met me at Pendulum."

I changed the subject. "Where do you live when you're not at Majestic?"

"I was staying there for training and then I was getting my own place."

"That's good." I sipped my tea. "Has your dad's house already sold?"

"Yes, not long ago."

"So, you were in denial?" I asked, because that's where she'd had me take her first.

"I still have the key."

She missed her father—I could see that.

"Once it's sold you can't go back," I said softly. "Rue, your dad's not there. Have you ever thought about grief counseling?"

"No, have you had therapy?"

"Me? No, I don't need it. I just don't think about what haunts me."

"Something haunts you?"

I diverted our conversation. "You're okay to go back to Majestic?"

"I knew Carrie would be pissed I'd snuck out to Pendulum. I signed a contract with her."

"How long is your contract?"

She shrugged. "How do you know Kaison?"

I went to answer and then saw the trap.

Rue waved her slice of toast at me. "Exactly."

"I know how to navigate the scene."

"You ruined my night." She lifted her mug and took a sip.

"They have questionable consent at Pendulum."

"Most of us can't get into Enthrall."

She was right, of course. The best place to attend was the most difficult to get into. The elite training and therapeutic specialties weren't open to everyone.

Anyway, none of this was my problem. In less than a few hours she'd be out of my life.

"Tell me more about Enthrall?" she said.

"Never going to happen, Rue."

"Why?"

"Because I said no."

"If anyone can get me in it's you."

As much as I enjoyed this banter with a hotheaded sub it would only go one way if it continued—I'd end up spanking her.

Hard.

"Do you have a submissive?" she asked.

I scratched the back of my head. I didn't want to lie. Still, it was a conversation not worth having.

Rue slid off the barstool and came around to my side. "This is you making it up to me." She kneeled, peering up with those soulful eyes begging me to play along.

It made me wonder how kinky her predilections were.

Mine were probably too edgy for her.

"Master."

My dick responded before I could warn it this wasn't happening.

I wanted to throw away everything I knew to be true…that I was meant to be her savior. The man who'd removed her from danger.

Only right now, *I* was the danger.

My cock was trying to persuade me to give her what she wanted. What she clearly needed.

"Get up," I snapped.

Rue dragged her teeth over her bottom lip as though that would work.

I pointed in her bedroom's direction. "Go get dressed."

She let the towel drop.

Her breasts were round and firm and pert—the kind any man would have a hard time looking away from. My imagination was generous enough to provide a preview of how it would feel to circle her nipple with my tongue...*sucking.*

How delicious it would be to knead her breasts and pinch her nipples between my fingers. That's what her proximity did to me—had me running through what felt like a good idea.

It wasn't.

I sat on the barstool, holding myself back.

Rue reached for my PJ bottoms, her fingers sliding past the crotch. She pulled out my cock, gripping it tightly.

All I had to do was give the order to have her stop.

She was stroking me up and down with a firm hand. Leaning in, she licked the tip with her tongue, rimming with such accuracy all I could do was watch. We maintained eye contact as she ran her tongue all the way up my length.

"Enough." I gritted my teeth, digging deep for some sense of control.

"Relax," she whispered.

My inner voice silenced me, letting Rue deep-throat my dick. The pleasure felt raw and addictive; like she was trying to suck an orgasm out of my fucking soul.

This is what I need.

Rue moaned, tears streaming down her cheeks as she took me farther in, her head bobbing furiously. The sensation of her throat closing around my tip sent a jolt of bliss resounding through me.

I gripped the countertop with one hand and buried the other in her locks, directing her pace.

She groaned loudly and the sensation rippled around my girth.

Still gripping her hair, I eased her off my length, pulling her head back and holding her there suspended in that pose, her lips wet and mouth shiny.

This was a pleasure I had to ignore.

Coming in her mouth was a mistake I wasn't prepared to make.

Rue gave me a questioning look.

"Up!" I slid off the barstool as I dragged her to a standing position, still gripping her locks, which must have hurt but she didn't seem to care.

She just let me guide her along the hallway and into my bedroom. Maybe she assumed I was going to fuck her there.

I led her into the bathroom en suite.

Shoving her inside the shower, I joined her there and reached for the faucet, turning it to cold. The shock of freezing water hit us both as I held her beneath the spray.

Now this should chill us both back into reality.

My left hand slid from her hair to her throat, and I held her still. With my right hand, I reached for the soap bottle and flicked open the lid with my thumb, squirting the white liquid over her body. With the bottle returned to its corner, I set about rubbing the soap over her, washing off sea water and sand as my fingers trailed over her flesh.

"It's too cold," she complained, gasping.

"This is what you get when you defy me."

She was one step ahead, her fingers on her clit, thrumming herself. Furiously flicking, finding a rhythm.

The imagery was erotic.

It was so damn hot a lesser man would have come right away, hot seed spilling onto this beauty's abdomen.

I was not that kind of man.

Hell, I'd trained at Chrysalis for the darkest kink…had submissives taking turns riding me. I'd stayed the course during a session until enough had come on me to impress even the most seasoned of Doms who had witnessed the erotic scene.

This, this was easy to endure.

I was the fucking king of edging.

I moved her hand away from her clit.

She moved it back, her need so raw I knew refusing her release would be cruel. Holding her by the throat still, I allowed Rue to pleasure herself.

"Master," she begged for permission to come.

With a nod, I gave it to her, allowed the climax to sweep over her, possess her. As she traversed the waves of bliss, her mouth grew slack and her expression dazed.

I continued to hold eye contact with her as she moaned at the height of her orgasm.

By holding her at length like this, I was punishing myself.

Denying myself...

There was no other way.

When I let go of her throat, Rue collapsed against me and shuddered through the rest of her release. Her warm nakedness pressed against me, skin to skin, like we belonged together.

I stepped away, keeping my hands to my sides, letting her recover without touching her. I couldn't let her know she'd had any effect on me.

"Good girl," I said, soothing her.

I pressed my lips to the top of her head. "Now get the fuck out of my bathroom so I can take a hot shower."

She was breathless and boneless under my command. "You don't want me to...?"

My cock agreed with her suggestion.

"No." I turned my back on her.

I heard her step out of the shower, her bare feet padding along the tile. Maybe she grabbed a towel on the way out.

Resting my head against the shower door, I fought this craving, telling myself I'd done the right thing in sending her away.

I couldn't carry any more blame.

CHAPTER NINE

Rue

WE DROVE HELL-BOUND TOWARD MAJESTIC.

If Enthrall was rumored to be like a palace in the Hollywood hills, Majestic was more like a private home in boring suburbia. They didn't even begin to compare.

The PCH was quieter this time of morning, the traffic easier to navigate up the 101 eastbound.

Tucked away on Hillcrest Avenue in the heart of Glendale was the ugliest manor on the block—Majestic, the place where new submissives were initiated into the scene. The play was strict but safe.

Trees lined the driveway that led to the secluded house of pain—with submissives as the main act. The guard outside gave a nod of approval.

When we arrived at the manor, Shay parked his Rover out front.

I imagined Carrie had warned the staff we were on our way, maybe even given them Shay's license plate number. Everything was arranged ahead of time when it came to our security.

Shay unclipped his seatbelt and read a text on his phone. He peered up at the house. "Carrie's here. She's on a call. Wants to talk with me."

"Lucky you."

"She'll be out in five," he added.

An awkward silence ensued.

I tried not to fidget. Sitting beside one of the hottest men I'd ever known was making my toes curl. What we'd done in his shower this morning…what I'd done more specifically in front of him still made my body thrum.

It was hard to look at him now. Knowing he'd watched me get myself off and then merely thrown me out of his bathroom like our intimacy meant nothing.

This guy could just growl an order and make me wet.

I miss you already.

Even though I don't know you.

"The architecture is…interesting," Shay said, making conversation.

I let out a frustrated sigh. "My punishment will no doubt involve some kind of cleaning."

"You'll settle back in."

A comment like that came from those who didn't know what happened here. It was fun at first but after a while it was just the same routine over and over—submissives were spoiled but not allowed to dabble in anything risky.

"What goes on in there?" he said, scanning the windows.

"Sometimes we wear uniforms," I said. "I get punished a lot. Have to bend over the teacher's desk…"

He shot me a glance. "Don't say anymore."

"Why, that your fantasy?" I nudged his side. "Me having my bare ass spanked because I failed a test?"

He arched a brow. "Want to know what my fantasy is?"

"Yes," I said breathlessly.

"You, passing the 'shut the fuck up' test."

I folded my arms in a huff.

"Well done, you earned yourself a passing grade."

"You don't need to wait."

"I told Carrie I'd deliver you safely and that's what I intend to do."

"You realize how patronizing that sounds."

He glanced at his watch.

Just say it. Ask him.

I rallied the words. "Can I…see you again?"

"You mean like a date?"

"Yes."

"I don't think that's a good idea."

I looked out the window, trying to hide my embarrassment.

"Listen, Rue, can you refrain from sharing what happened this morning?"

"You mean the part where you ordered me to suck your dick?" said Rue sarcastically.

"I'm serious."

"What kind of person do you think I am?"

"I like to think a decent one."

"I know I'm not your type."

"It's not that exactly. You're…"

"I'm what?"

"Look, I think you'll eventually see that staying away from Pendulum is a good decision."

"I bet you did some risky things out in Afghanistan."

"Did you Google me?"

"Yes, there's not much there—other than your military honors."

He looked eerily calm. "That's a no-go subject."

"Why?"

He looked at me. "You don't want that in your brain."

"If it would help you to talk, I'm here."

"That's like trying to stop a boat from sinking when it's lying on the ocean bed."

"I'm sorry," I whispered.

"It's what I signed up for."

My heart ached for him. Reaching out, I laid my hand on his. He turned his over and held mine.

If silence could bring meaning…*I will find you.* If a touch conveyed emotion…*find me.*

Even though we were strangers.

He looked off toward the door and pulled his hand away. I followed his line of sight.

Carrie had opened the door.

I'd thrown myself at him and he'd rejected me *again.*

He moved in circles I coveted, his access to elite societies around the world enviable.

I'd never be part of that crowd.

Panic settled in my gut at the thought that he was my only chance at sexual fulfillment.

I turned in my seat to look at him. At his beautiful, rugged face. At the man who made me feel seen. I imagined he'd do anything to see his submissive flourish.

"I know you like me."

Shay went to say something, as though finally ready to admit his attraction.

Daring emotions shimmied brilliantly between us.

Fading with the passing seconds.

"Why not me?" I whispered.

"That's not what this is."

"It's you getting a favor lined up from Carrie in case you need it."

He looked amused. "You can be sure I don't need anyone's help."

"Then what is this?"

"Why does it have to be something?"

"What does that mean?"

"You've probably been searching for a safe space to explore your predilections."

"How do you know that?"

He hesitated and then said, "I recognize myself in you."

I needed a few seconds to recover from this profoundness.

"Why can't we stay in touch?"

He raised his hand to wave to Carrie. "This is what it's like to have a man place your needs above his. The world can be a good place. Not everyone is in it for themselves."

"I'm never going to see you again, am I?"

Shay reached for the door handle, hesitated and glanced back over at me. "It doesn't mean you're forgettable."

"I don't want to say goodbye."

"Honestly, I'm not the kind of guy you date. I'm the kind you call when your boyfriend's being an asshole and needs to be taught some manners."

"Or when you need to bury a body."

"Hope that's not a rumor."

"Maybe it is."

"Only in the line of duty." He winked.

His look sent a shiver through me.

Carrie tapped on his window, snatching away his attention.

Stealing him from me.

Shay exited the car and left me sitting in the passenger seat. I felt a wrenching in my stomach at the loss of his presence.

He set off toward the front porch with Carrie. They shook hands like they were agreeing on a deal. He towered over her, looking every bit like that dashing Navy officer who could handle the most sinister enemy. From his body language she didn't intimidate him at all.

That's all I was to him. An agreement followed through on.

Acting like I was fine with having others dictate my life, I stepped out of the car and headed toward them, hiding my desperation for fulfillment.

Ironically, the only person who could deliver it had turned his back on me—quite literally, as they continued their conversation.

Neither of them had any right to dictate anything I did in my life.

I raised my chin and joined them with a stony face to hide my misery, trying not to appear insulted that I was too old for this crap.

For God's sake, I was a nurse and had performed more life-saving activities than either of these two. I'd worked too many nightshifts in the ICU when we'd been short staffed and I'd had to juggle an impossible amount of tasks.

Yet these two were acting like I was too naive to make my own decisions. All because my going to Pendulum seemed like a mistake.

If Kaison would have me back, I'd resume my training with him. Maybe get another shot at Pendulum. Only I'd make sure Carrie was out of town.

Shay Gardner had wasted his time.

And mine.

The man who'd turned my life inside out was heading back toward his car, not even acknowledging me. That tall swagger of confidence a reminder I wasn't appealing to a man like him.

Watching Shay drive off down the pathway, I doubted he even looked in his rearview mirror.

I was already forgotten.

CHAPTER TEN

Shay

"**T**HAT PHOTOGRAPHER'S BACK. HE'S PARKED OUTSIDE *again*." Richard turned his computer screen to show me the security camera angle.

There he was…our stalker, sitting in his car, seemingly waiting to snap a money shot with a long angle lens.

Fucker.

"I'm on it," I said.

"Can't you just go down there and tell him to piss off?"

"Having something on him first is more effective in the long run."

He leaned back, frustrated.

"We're running his plate number," I said. "Getting something we can use."

"That's why you're paid the big bucks, I suppose."

"I suppose."

Funny he should mention the big bucks. He was now the Director of Enthrall and Chrysalis, so he was being paid a near fortune. The promotion from Assistant Director had been good for him. He mirrored Cole's fashion sense. Richard looked so-phisticated in that Prada suit.

Not too much of a stretch for a Harvard grad who'd once come from money—then lost it all when his father had wrecked the family both financially and personally.

You'd never know that, though. Richard was always upbeat.

He stared at me. "You look…different. Wanna talk?"

"Nothing to talk about."

He was referring to my beard, which was neatly groomed but he still wasn't used to it.

He studied me for longer than necessary and then relented. "Coffee?"

"Sure."

I sat down in the chair opposite his desk while he got up and ambled over to his Keurig. Lifting the pot, he poured two mugs of coffee and then carried them back, handing me one. The scent of rich vanilla beans and toffee filled the room.

It reminded me that I'd missed breakfast.

Wrapping my palms around my mug, I said, "His name's Darryn Amara."

"Our trespasser?" He glanced at the screen.

"That's who the car's registered to."

"Hold on a sec," said Richard, leaning toward his iMac and typing on his keyboard. "Got to reply to this."

While waiting for him to answer another email, I brought out my phone and entered Enthrall's portal, sweeping through pro-files. I scoured the faces of our submissives, looking for any that might have red hair.

Someone with the look that would get my mind off Rue—a few hours of carnal pleasure would strike her from my memory.

I'd tried everything else.

Three weeks had gone by since I'd last seen her. I couldn't get the woman out of my mind since I'd dropped her off in Glendale.

Not finding a redheaded submissive's profile, I tried to distract myself by looking around Richard's second floor office.

It hadn't changed much over the years. He'd added a few eclectic items to his shelves, sports memorabilia, mainly from the New York Giants. A silver submissive collar held in a glass box. A whip given to him by Cameron Cole hung on the wall.

It made me wonder if the crop had significance. Perhaps it was used on him in that session with Cameron that had saved his life.

Enthrall contained secrets within secrets.

Most of them I was in on.

Thanks to his wife Andrea, Richard's framed photos on the right wall showing him doing risky shit hadn't been updated. He'd pulled back on trying to kill himself.

Always a good thing.

Recently, I'd had a better insight into depression, my empathy so much more refined because of it. Though I doubted *that* kind of therapy would work on me.

I'd never been into self-harm, but I was damn good at self-punishment. I pushed that thought aside. No time for self-pity.

The framed photo of Richard swimming with sharks sent a shiver through me. I was up for adrenaline-pumping adventures as much as he was, but swimming with sharks was a hard *no* for me.

Because I wasn't a fucking idiot.

But *God* if Richard wasn't one of the best men you'd ever know; which was why Cameron considered him his closest friend and ally. And why we were all as close as brothers.

I fucking loved everyone here. These were the kind of people you could rely on. There was no bullshit—just straight talk.

"Are you going to tell me now?" Richard took a sip of his coffee.

"Tell you what?"

"A few weeks ago, you asked me to get you into Pendulum."

"All squared away."

"Wanna tell me why you were there?"

At the time I'd told him it was on a need-to-know basis—mainly to protect him from any fallout.

"You weren't there for pleasure?" He studied my reaction.

"No."

Richard sat back. "Will you be going back?"

"No."

"Didn't want to say it at the time, but you're high-profile."

"I wore a plague doctor mask."

"Nice."

Then I recalled Faulkner. "One other person knows I was there. I can handle him."

"Okay, well if you need anything more just tell me."

"I appreciate that."

Richard turned back to his computer screen. I assumed he was worrying about our stalking photographer.

"It's time to build that fence around the property," I said.

"Cosmetically it won't look good."

"We can get Scarlet on it. She has superb taste."

"Maybe an iron gate." He relaxed a little as though relieved to find a way to secure Enthrall without threatening the looks of the exterior.

Having our security compromised was a nightmare. We assured everyone the utmost privacy. Our clients were too important for us to fail them.

"How's Andrea?" I asked.

"Great, she's filming in Italy. I fly out in a couple of weeks to join her."

"You're always taking vacations."

"Making up for lost time." He grinned.

Being married to a Hollywood sweetheart suited him. I'd never seen him so consistently happy.

"How are you, really?" he asked.

"Great."

He didn't look convinced, peering over his mug to study me. "Have you spoken with him?"

Richard was talking about Jake, aka De Sade. He could tell my breakup with him was still affecting me.

"Haven't given him much thought," I lied.

"He still cares about you."

"Why are we talking about him?"

Richard hesitated and then said, "He's here."

My back stiffened. "That's fine."

It wasn't.

It was bad enough having him at Chrysalis, but here? An interesting choice on his part, and it made me feel both annoyed and intrigued.

Richard looked uncomfortable as though wanting to share more.

"Have I come up in conversation?" I asked casually.

"No." He tilted his head. "Yes."

"The subject?"

He hesitated to answer.

"I don't think about that anymore." *About us.*

Richard didn't seem convinced. "Right. Good. Well, he's here with Rylee. Thought you should know in case you bump into them."

Glancing away, I tried to fathom why I'd allowed myself to believe in something that wasn't possible, thinking that I could hold down a relationship with anyone.

Because life was crushing and trusting myself wasn't easy.

Anyway, I should be happy for them...*for him*, but all I felt was concern. "Which chamber?"

Richard got up from his seat. "Don't go down there."

I rose and my chair scraped along the hardwood floor, making an aggravating noise...the kind that frays nerves.

The kind that sounds unhinged.

"Don't interrupt them, Shay."

I gave him a look of annoyance. "I'm the cool-headed one."

Moving over to the wall, I rapped on the secret doorway. The camouflaged entrance popped ajar.

A soft blue glow lit up the way.

Without looking back, I went through into the dusky space and descended the twisting stairwell.

I made my way down to the lower level.

With each gut-wrenching step, I second-guessed myself. Not quite sure why my brain thought this was a good idea.

It was my heart leading me. It always got me into trouble.

I'd learned to shut down my feelings in Afghanistan. It was what we all did, shielding our souls from the horrors we saw and the ones we merely imagined going on around us.

When we returned home, opening ourselves up again was a problem.

Forgetting all that chaos.

It took patience to reach us. Most people couldn't get past our walls. Most of us refused to give them the privilege to try.

De Sade had been one of the few I'd allowed in.

He'd been so close to the center of me.

Reaching the hallway lined with the luxuriously designed dungeons, I took a few seconds to try and talk myself out of this.

This self-inflicted pain was unnecessary.

I liked it down here, usually.

All the chambers were different. All of them fit for the clients who spent time in each one.

Jake was in one of them, flaunting his identity as De Sade— the sick fuck who liked to see his subs squirm in both pleasure and pain. Being with him was the risk they chased after, the fear factor that came with a session with a grand master.

For me, self-hate had no room to flourish when he was handling the scene. That's how he'd gotten me to open up to him. That's how De Sade had broken down my walls—with sheer violence. The kind of energy that felt painfully familiar, as though the only way to find myself was to go back into that warzone.

Some part of me is still there in that Middle Eastern desert.

I'd become addicted to De Sade's cruelty, his skill, for the relief it brought. Even though it was unhealthy in the long-term. I knew that. Of course, I did. That level of debauchery was just so alluring.

A queasy feeling in the pit of my stomach told me he was close.

A light shone above Chamber Eight, a warning not to proceed further. A session was in progress.

Chamber Eight was the room you took your submissive into when you wanted to feel closed in with them. The space was intimate and the toys geared towards punishment.

I walked a few steps back down the hallway and turned the handle to the adjoining chamber, pausing for a beat to reconsider.

And then I stepped inside.

I strolled towards the one-way glass that showed the shadowy figures on the other side, peering through the window into their private sanctuary. They couldn't see me, which was best for everyone.

Yeah, they were back together.

Rylee, De Sade's ex-wife, knelt before him in a submissive pose. The stunning brunette had drawn everyone's attention back when she was single. Back before she'd caught De Sade's eye.

She was the kind of beauty any man would crave; her long silky black locks falling over slender shoulders, her Persian features regal and breathtaking.

She was fiery, too. That's what he'd told me. Her temper sometimes got out of control—and I think he liked that about her. He was attracted to her insatiable hunger for life and her ability to stand up to him, forcing him to up his game.

He had her on her feet now.

He walked her backwards until she met the padded table behind her. She slid onto it and splayed her legs. Jake didn't miss a beat, leaning in and devouring her pussy, his mouth wide as his tongue explored every crevice of her sex. Her thighs trembled with the pleasure, her throaty groans echoing in that dusky chamber to lure him on.

He held her stare. The look of passion between them was undeniable.

De Sade had looked at me like that, once.

She bucked her hips, demanding more of his mouth, bringing her legs up to spread them wider. She wanted him to fuck her.

I wondered if he would.

His wedding ring was back on his left hand. When the divorce proceedings had first begun, he'd removed it.

Funny how life can implode so quickly, being so incredible one second and in the next you're struggling to come up for air. Struggling to make sense of where you went wrong.

Letting him walk out my door was where I went wrong.

Could I have stopped him? If I had asked him to stay?

He used his hands on her as though reading her mind; teasing her nipples and then playing with her clit—giving her his all.

I heard the click of a door opening. It had come from behind me.

I turned to see Lotte standing there, our pretty Dominatrix wearing a warm smile, kindness emanating from her eyes.

She glanced through the window and then looked back at me, polite enough not to give me a look of pity, her big, vibrant eyes highlighted by her new pixie cut.

I wanted to tell her that the hairstyle suited her, only my throat constricted with emotion.

"I like you with a beard," she said.

Rubbing my scruff self-consciously, I gave her a wry smile. She came closer and stood beside me, turning to peer through the glass.

Even dressed in high-heeled boots, Lotte wasn't close to my height. But she was still a spitfire. Everyone knew to behave around her.

"I was never here," I whispered.

"Of course."

I stared at them. "They're back together."

"What gave you that impression?" She winked at me.

De Sade and Rylee were now fucking.

Making me wish I'd taken Richard's advice not to come down here.

Jake was pounding his ex, and it was wild and dirty and raw.

She looked like a porn star. My little dig at her made me feel better. Wouldn't say it out loud, though.

I wasn't usually a jealous man, but De Sade was one of the best-looking men I'd ever fucked or lived with.

Or fallen in love with.

I should have told him that.

Maybe it was a good thing Lotte was here. Richard had probably sent her to stop me from ruining everyone's day.

I was breaking the rules.

I'd like to break this glass.

Lotte touched my arm. "Look at me."

I turned away from the window and faced her. How many times had we seen each other through difficult times? I'd drawn on Lotte's kindness over the years and her give-no-fucks wisdom.

"It's going to be okay," she said softly. "Remember what you once told me. You'll look back at this moment with gratitude. Because the universe will give you something better. What happened was merely a preview of things to come."

"And you believed me?"

She punched my arm. "Yes, and it was true. And it will be true for you, too."

My focus settled on De Sade again, on the lovers still entwined.

Memories sprung up to remind me how much fun we'd had on those lazy Sundays, watching football together, him talking me through the plays. He would call the action because he'd once thrived as a quarterback in the NFL. A player for the ages.

Right up until he was injured and had to retire.

The late-night swims where we moved over to the Jacuzzi and talked until midnight. Days and nights and weekends flashed before me, mine to keep.

He never surfed, though—never wanted to learn. Another memory was piqued for some unfathomable reason—the image of Rue riding a wave.

I needed the surfing. That would clear my mind.

"You know I love you." Lotte tried to break my trance.

"I know."

I hated showing any kind of vulnerability.

"I'm sorry to do this." She clutched my arm. "That photographer is back."

Half-distracted, I glanced toward De Sade. "Richard told me."

"I didn't know what else to do," she said, her voice wavering.

My attention fell back on her. She looked harried—why had I not realized?

"Come outside," she coaxed.

We left the chamber and I fell into step beside her. "What's wrong?"

"I sealed him inside the elevator." She walked faster toward the stairwell.

"The photographer? The bastard tried to access the building?"

"Yes, can you imagine?"

"Well done, you." I opened the door for her and gave a reassuring smile. "Can't wait to meet him."

CHAPTER ELEVEN

Shay

I F YOU WANT TO KNOW HOW YOUR DAY CAN GO FROM BAD TO worse, find yourself wasting time in the Cedars-Sinai ER on a Friday night.

I sat around waiting for the results of a wrist X-ray to come back, but at least it wasn't mine.

Two hours ago, twenty-something Darryn Amara had to be wrangled from Enthrall's elevator. Once out, he'd been reluctant to hand over his camera. With some not-so-gentle coaxing he'd eventually let me look at the photos.

I'd deleted them.

Then I'd handed the camera back. I'd confiscated his phone's SIM card, too—rolling my eyes as he complained that he'd incurred "untold physical harm."

I'd not used that much force. He was just a fucking pussy.

Now, I had the displeasure of sitting in this private room beside him, feeling a headache looming. I'd taken Tylenol but it hadn't kicked in yet. Even though I was "hangry" and agitated,

I was able to keep my calm. An art I'd mastered long ago when keeping your head literally meant life or death.

We'd notified Dominic, our acting council, so we were already lawyered-up, wanting to make sure Darryn didn't go that route—not because we couldn't deal with his attorney; we just hated the attention.

I wasn't the only moody bastard in the room.

Sporting a grumpy attitude, Darryn lay on a gurney next to me, the curtain drawn on his private consulting room.

Cedars always felt chaotic; at least it seemed that way every time I'd visited this state-of-the-art hospital. Cameron had worked here once. The profession really had lost its shining star.

He'd been hailed as the Carl Jung of our generation. His leaving psychiatry was a tragedy—even if he still consulted now and again.

Cameron had thrown himself into the family empire and the company had benefited from his acumen. His sense of adventure would never fade. There was always some new venture on the horizon for him.

It was easy to think of him now as I dealt with this crisis, drawing on thoughts of what he might do, centering myself.

Just as I had when bullets had been flying over my head halfway around the world. Those were the darkest nights of our lives.

Compared to that experience this was a walk in the park, which was the point, I suppose. Things would never get that bad again.

Maybe it was the smell of ammonia that was triggering me, the scent of cleaning agents along with the noise and bright lights—whispers of doom and gloom emanating from behind treatment room curtains.

Harried staff worked their asses off.

Darryn's nurse had gone to lunch. Before leaving, she told us another RN would cover for her. We continued to wait for someone to swing back around with his X-ray results.

"Thanks for this, mate," said Darryn. "Bringing me here, I mean—though it's the least you could do, right?"

His English cockney accent added to the sinister aspect of his profession. A job that had him breaching others' privacy in the worst kind of way. His clothes looked rumpled. Probably from sitting too long in his car while spying.

I ignored his last comment.

"How long have you worked as a paparazzi?" I asked.

"No comment." He flashed a smile that revealed yellowed teeth. "How long have you worked at that club?"

"No comment." I sat back.

"We'll both agree to keep those secrets, then." He looked smug. *Fuck that.*

"Who do you work for?" I snapped.

Again, he shrugged.

I'd find out, though I wouldn't tell him that. Alerting him to the elite team I'd hired would spike his interest and turn Enthrall into an agenda.

"How the hell am I meant to pay for this?" he mumbled.

"Doesn't your kind of work pay?"

"I'm freelance."

"Ah."

He held my gaze and that was my cue.

"We'll pay the bill." I raised a hand. "Not that you deserve that courtesy."

"Very generous of you."

"If you ever return to that location, it'll be more than just your wrist you'll injure."

"Point made, mate."

"Stop calling me mate."

"I saw Tori Crawford entering your club." He looked triumphant. "Now that would cause a stir."

"Right. A tall blonde in L.A. Don't see many of those around these parts."

His head crashed onto the pillow. With his photos deleted he had no proof Tori had ever visited us.

"How much would you have made off that photo?" I arched a brow. "Of the anonymous blonde?"

He looked frustrated. "Thirty."

"We'll give you thirty."

"Seriously?"

"Sure. As long as you agree to stay away."

He studied me, maybe to see if I was serious about the money. Maybe he was wondering if he could get more. A lawsuit we could handle. We'd win, of course. Darryn had trespassed and we'd captured his entry on our security footage.

He'd long been intrigued by our club and his zoom lens could do a lot of damage. But he was the kind of man you could pay off.

"You'll have to sign an NDA," I told him.

"Where's the fucking pen, mate?" He smirked.

A nurse burst through the curtain. "Mr. Amara," she said brightly, her face instantly familiar.

It was Rue, looking as vibrant as I remembered, her full figure curvy in her dark blue scrubs. She had her hair tied back in an unruly ponytail. aby

Her face fell when she saw me.

Then she blushed.

Refocusing her attention back on Darryn, she spoke to him about his wrist. Something about him only sustaining a strain, the X-ray report revealing nothing broken.

I couldn't take my eyes of Rue while she talked with Darryn. She had the kind of beauty that drew unwanted stares.

How long had it been? Three weeks? Yet it had been easy to recall her freckles and the way her pouty mouth quirked up when she was amused. The memory of her was imprinted on my brain like a photograph.

Now, her lips were curved in a not-so-amused smile, her expression annoyed as she gazed at me.

In truth, she was more breathtaking than anyone's mind could possibly recall.

This bright, young woman I'd rescued from Pendulum a few weeks ago was apparently flourishing here. Rue had come across as a thrill seeker. It made perfect sense to find her working in an ER, enjoying the adrenaline rush.

"Do you know each other?" asked Darryn.

Probably because Rue's blue eyes were throwing daggers my way.

"Hey," I greeted her warmly.

She ignored me and turned back to Darryn. "I'll bring your discharge papers for you to sign." She laid an advice sheet on the table next to his gurney and glided it his way. "How do you two know each other?" she asked, making it sound casual.

"We go way back," said Darryn.

"Like hell we do," I mumbled.

Darryn raised his wrist to show her. "Do friends do this to each other?" There was nothing to see.

She glared at me and turned back to Darryn. "He tried to ruin my life, too."

"Enough!" I shot to my feet.

"Whoa!" Darryn's glare hopped from me to her and back again.

"Are you in any danger from this man?" Rue asked him while pointing at me.

"You tell me, sweetheart."

"For God's sake," I snapped. "Darryn, get out of that gown and get dressed. I'll drive you home."

He looked amused. "You just want to see where I live so you can send me a restraining order."

"You're not as stupid as you look," I said.

I rounded the end of the gurney and approached Rue, guiding her out of the ER.

I released her arm as we walked away, putting some distance between us and Darryn so he couldn't overhear. That would be the kind of nightmare I couldn't get back in the bottle.

I directed Rue to a more private area down the hall. "Darryn is paparazzi. Anything you say will be used against us."

"Like I care," she snapped.

"I'm serious."

"He looks harmless."

I was sure he had clocked her name on her badge. I didn't want to scare her with that bit of knowledge, but it would be easy for him to dig around and maybe even link her to Carrie.

"What happened to him?" she asked.

"He took some photos of a client. Then he tried to break into Enthrall to snap some more. I'm here for damage control." I glanced over my shoulder to make sure he hadn't followed us.

Rue rested her hands on her hips. "Did he trip coming out of the elevator?"

"Looks like it."

"I'm surprised he's not suing you."

I suppressed my frustration. "That's why I'm here—to prevent any chance of that happening."

"Everyone who comes into contact with you ends up in a mess."

"That's not fair," I said.

She poked my chest with her finger. "Mind telling me why I have a lifetime ban from Chrysalis?" Her fingernail was sharp.

It hurt but it was the kind of discomfort that ensured our connection. Her touch caused a frisson throughout my body.

Two magnetically drawn people caught in a stand-off in the hallway.

The world fell away.

Half of me wanted to grab hold of her throat and dominate the impertinence out of her.

The other half knew better.

The sounds around us became distracting, buzzers and phones and loud conversations.

"You never thought to warn me you'd be here?" she said.

"I had no idea," I shot back. "You told me you were leaving the ICU. You didn't mention where you were transferring to."

"I think I did."

"No, I would have remembered."

Because I remembered everything about her in fine detail. And may have replayed a scene or two just for my mental viewing pleasure; memories of her between my legs back in Malibu were a particular highlight.

Rue's freckles were still kissable. Her red locks made her blue eyes vibrant. She was cute in scrubs, too. I had this urge to lean in and plant a kiss on her cheek.

Which was insanity.

She was just so damn pretty.

Seeing her again felt like a miracle.

Rue's ID badge had RN after her name. "You're here permanently?"

"You catch on quick."

My eyebrow arched at her sarcasm. "So do you."

"Fuck you."

I threw a calm wave to a security guard who was watching us. Rue threw him a fake smile to let him know she was fine. Though one wrong word from me and I was sure that would change. She'd probably enjoy watching me being escorted out.

Walk away.

Forget her.

Say goodbye.

I didn't need any more drama to add to this day. Yet all I could do was admire the woman standing before me. Admire her bravery and her ability to take on what was clearly a challenging specialty.

I imagined Rue was an anchor in this sea of chaos.

For me, she was impossible to turn away from.

"You look…" *Just as beautiful as when I last saw you.*

Didn't say it though.

I'd dropped her off in Glendale and then driven away, though my thoughts had turned back time when I'd allowed myself those rare moments to think of her.

Her jaw tightened. "Imagine my surprise when I arrived at a private party at Chrysalis with some friends, and I was turned away at the door."

"That would have been embarrassing." I shrugged. "Wouldn't try that again."

"Shay Gardner!"

"I was protecting you."

"From what?"

"Clearly now's not the time."

"I'm not allowed back into Pendulum either!"

"Consent is dubious there."

"You do realize that's my kink."

That sounded vaguely familiar. I think she'd told me that while staying with me overnight. Still, she didn't know the consequences of what that meant. Not really.

"If you're going to explore you must do it in a place that has boundaries," I said. "Majestic is a good fit. The place protects you from exploitation, so all the pleasure flows your way."

"You have prevented me from entering any club."

I made it look like I was trying to recall if that was indeed true. It was.

I'd put calls in, but I'd had her best interests in mind. She was too wild to let loose in any of them. *And* I might have warned Faulkner to stay away, too. He wouldn't have the consideration to master her with the dedication she deserved.

"Faulkner's refusing to train me any further."

"Really?"

I could tell she didn't believe me.

I was a gentleman when it mattered. I'd made it my business to watch over vulnerable subs.

Rue was simply too erotic a creature. Her adventures needed careful orchestration. She was stunning and wild and authentic in ways I'd only touched on and she was all the things this world could destroy.

Someone had to look out for her.

Or was the truth too selfish to contemplate? That I'd let my jealousy get in the way and not wanted anyone else to have her.

Own her.

If I were to admit this, I'd really be an asshole.

I hadn't just done this for Carrie. I'd done it for me, too, if I were honest.

Rue being dominated at that level, being possessed entirely by another. That was only going to happen when she was able to grasp the consequences of that level of surrender. She had to be psychologically prepared to go that deep.

"Don't like hospitals?" she asked, probably because of my quiet musing.

They weren't exactly fun houses. "How do you like the ER?"

"You don't get to behave like we're friends."

"Frenemies, then?" I gave her a heart-stopping grin.

Rue sighed and then glanced down at her phone. "I have another patient coming in."

"Right, of course." Though I stood looking at her as though letting her out of my sight was a mistake.

"How have you been?" she asked softly.

"Me? Fine."

"You don't look fine."

God, I really must look like crap considering Richard brought up my appearance earlier. I caressed my beard, feeling bristles beneath my fingers.

"It makes you extra fuckable," she said, gesturing at my beard.

My cock stiffened.

Little minx.

I knew just how to rein in my dick by saying, "How's your Domina?"

"I've not spoken to Carrie in weeks."

"Sorry to hear that. Why?"

"The place just wasn't a good fit."

"Why?"

"After going to Pendulum without permission, I was forbidden to orgasm for two weeks as punishment."

"That's not good." I cringed.

"Ya think! Anyway, what do you care? You're in her camp."

"I just did her a favor."

"How about doing me a favor and pissing off. I'm busy." Yet she stood there looking up at me as though waiting for me to say more, quietly begging for something. For affection, maybe? Or approval?

"I got my own place," she said, breaking the silence again. "A one-bedroom apartment opposite The Grove."

That was her way of letting me know she'd put some distance between her and Majestic, her way of letting me know she was independent.

"Great location."

"I like to go to the Farmer's Market."

I gave a nod. "They have a Barnes and Noble."

"I really like the shops."

I knew what this was—it was us refusing to part ways.

Staying away was the kindest gift I could give her. No one needed a man like me in their universe.

"Look after yourself, Rue." Saying goodbye felt like a strike to my chest and beyond, right into my cardiac muscle.

A familiar feeling of self-loathing followed.

She closed the gap between us. "Lift my ban."

I looked away as I tried to think of an excuse that would appease her. "You can't afford the membership."

"I've never hated anyone as much as you."

"I'm flattered."

She went to leave and then hesitated. "Have you ever heard of a place called Hillenbrand?"

"In France?" A shiver went up my spine. "Yes, why?

Just hearing the name made my pulse quicken. Nestled in that secret den of iniquity in an exclusive location in Paris, subs were used for pleasure.

"It shut down," I said sternly.

"Seems you heard wrong."

Cameron and I had flown over to France and visited that palatial manor. We'd rescued Mia from there when things got as bad as they could get. I'd shoved that memory away. We'd done some dark play to get her out.

I vaguely recalled a short-lived breakthrough for me personally.

A childhood trauma that had been set free. I'd let go of that crap about my dad not loving me enough.

Rue clicked her fingers in front of my face to get my attention back on her.

I stared down at her. "You better not be thinking of going there?"

"First class ticket to Paris." She pressed a fingertip into my chest again. "Flying out on Monday. And you can't stop me."

"Why Hillenbrand?"

"They specialize in exhibitionism."

And there it was, her fetish shared with no sign of shame.

"That's the least of what they'll have you do."

She folded her arms. "Good."

"Did Faulkner get you in?" I gritted my teeth at the thought. "Is he paying for this?"

"No, it's my money."

Either my ears were ringing, or those monitoring alarms had sliced through my last nerve. Guilt, my old enemy, the brother of regret. It either suffocated you until you were useless or inspired you enough to do the unthinkable—go against my well-meaning scheme to keep her away.

"I think we can do better than Hillenbrand."

She studied me carefully. "You don't mean…?"

"Actually, I do—"

"You're lying."

"Enthrall. Monday. Noon. I'll text you the address. Don't be fucking late."

"You're serious?" She blushed wildly.

If she'd been bluffing about flying off to France, it had worked.

"Change of mind?" she teased.

"Yes, I'm offering you something far better than Hillenbrand," I said, my voice husky.

"What is that?"

My jaw tightened, my thoughts spinning with what I'd do to her. "You have one minute to decide."

Stopping her from flying to France was going to take some

finagling. But that's what I was good at—throwing the occasional smoke bomb and bringing out the mirrors. Going all Svengali on a woman to make her believe whatever I wanted.

Just keep her safe.

"Can you handle me?" She licked her lips.

There was no doubt our kinks were aligned. If I wanted it, we had the potential of becoming an erotic yin and yang...a blending of two souls who yearned to sin.

If Rue wanted to misbehave to that extent, I could oblige with an erotic fire and brimstone show that would ironically keep her protected. I'd have her burning up with so much sensual passion she'd forget she ever mentioned Europe. That place didn't deserve an angel like her.

Rue moved closer and pressed her breasts against my chest. "What's a better offer than Paris?"

"Pack for a week," I told her.

"Immersion?" Rue shuddered, eyelids closing for a beat and then opening again, her blue irises brightening with all the possibilities.

"Run along now."

"I still hate you," she mumbled.

"Your brand of hate is intriguing." I pivoted to walk away. "It gives me something to work with." The loss of her body against mine felt like *a thing*. I already missed the warmth of her.

I headed back to the ER to deal with that annoying British photographer.

Rue couldn't see that I was smiling.

CHAPTER TWELVE

Rue

I WAS ON TIME.

My canvas duffle bag had been packed for a week-long immersion. I'd chosen a few bodices that I thought might work, along with my best underwear of lace and silk.

I'd brought my best attitude, too. I was going to rock this week and come out as a permanent member of Enthrall—win my place alongside the other elite submissives. Money couldn't get me in because it was way out of my league, but being chosen as one of the first-class novices was a possibility.

Per the instructions, a chauffeur-driven SUV had picked me up from my apartment and brought me here. The driver had taken the long way instead of a direct route. Something had told me he had used defensive tactics to make sure we weren't being followed.

Perhaps just in case someone from Majestic—or even Kaison Faulkner—was keeping track of me.

Shay had advised me to wear a cocktail dress, something suitable for a black-tie event, which had intrigued me. Though I knew a first impression was everything.

Finally, I found myself within the walls of Enthrall after being dropped off discretely at the side entrance.

I'd gone with my Dolce and Gabbana feathered mini-cocktail dress in the hope of impressing my new Dom. The man with the fire in his belly.

The hottest master I'd ever met.

I couldn't wait to see Shay again…have him guide me. I'd been unable to think about anything else since I'd seen him at the ER on Friday—the day he invited me here.

The day my life changed.

The thought of entering a dungeon with him made my skin feel hot.

With my hair tumbling around my shoulders and makeup highlighting my features, I felt pretty—and ready for anything he might ask of me.

I'd spent the last hour with Mistress Lotte, signing forms and going over my limits.

Afterward, I'd been told to wait in the staff lounge. The swanky décor of blue velvet couches and comfy bright colored chairs lent a luxurious, relaxed air to the place.

I remained standing in the center of the room, waiting.

My chest tingled with excitement for what would come next as I waited in an elite club that everyone in our community coveted. If you weren't connected or invited, there was no getting in.

The lounge door opened.

In walked Shay, looking all kinds of masterful in a tailored suit and tie and silver cufflinks. His beard complemented his rugged suaveness.

I did my best to hide my reaction—the way he made me shudder, the way he made my skin tingle.

My imagination flourished with thrilling ideas of what might happen.

Shay merely took in the room and me with it. Probably to make sure we were alone.

He kept his distance.

I wanted him to kiss me for the first time and was terrified he wouldn't. That stark contradiction proving all thoughts led back to him.

Second guessing myself…

Dropping to my knees, I bowed my head, the skirt of my dress billowing around me. The small petals that decorated the material were something I could focus on.

I felt a frisson of anticipation marking this moment as I waited for him to come closer.

The silence made me uneasy. He was merely standing before me, not saying anything, his hands tucked into his trouser pockets, as though assessing.

"Look at me," he finally said.

I peered up searching for a cue.

"Ready?"

"Yes, sir."

As ready as you'd expect from someone who'd virtually begged for this.

"You've left Majestic?" he asked.

"Yes."

"What do you make of Enthrall?"

"I thought there might be more guests."

He shrugged. "You signed your life away?"

"Not technically."

He smirked and it looked so damn sexy. "Did you complete the list?"

"Yes, sir."

"Anything resonate?"

"Lady Chatterley's Lover."

"What did you like about the book?"

"Not much." I recalled how her husband had encouraged her to have a lover. "It baffled me how she could love two men at the same time."

He looked thoughtful. "I see."

Lady Chatterley's husband was a war vet, unable to be intimate with his wife due to his severe injuries from battle. So, he'd let her have another man.

"I couldn't do that, though," I admitted. "I would have found a way to be with my husband."

"Very honorable." Shay's tone became serious. "Contraception?"

"Lady Chatterley?"

He looked amused. "No, you."

"I get the shot. Every three months."

"You reliably take that?"

"Yes, of course."

"I have to ask, you understand?"

"Shall I call you Master?"

"As I'm not your Master, no."

"Then what?"

"I've gotten you in, Rue. That's it. Don't expect leniency, either."

A chill caused the hairs on my forearms to prickle. "But I thought…"

He raised his chin. "His office. Now."

"The director?"

"Follow me."

Shay pivoted and led me out and along the hallway, his words firing my confusion. If not him, then who?

I only wanted it to be Shay. I just had to choose the right time to insist on it.

He stopped before a door and gestured for me to go in.

"Is it Richard Booth?" I asked, breathless, turning to look at the door like danger might greet me on the other side.

"Sir, to you." Shay turned the handle and gestured for me to go in. "Don't fuck it up."

Exhaling slowly, I entered the room. Turning sharply, I saw that Shay wasn't coming in with me.

Then I faced Sir. The one with all the power.

He was handsome in a sophisticated way. His dark blonde hair had golden tints probably from being out in the sun, since he was tanned. I could sense all kinds of privilege bouncing off his tall, toned body. His irises were bluer than mine—all seeing. All knowing.

He had a striking face that was hard to look away from.

His sharp suit looked tailored.

Richard Booth leaned back against his desk with his arms folded. "You're late."

Hurrying forward, I stood in the middle of the room and assumed *the* pose—back straight and arms behind my back with my wrists together, elegant and feminine.

"You're very pretty," he said.

"Thank you."

"We care more about your personality, though." He shrugged. "You can't use your beauty to manipulate."

"I'm not expecting special treatment."

"Special treatment," he echoed.

Silence filled the room.

Tension was served up with a heavy dose of domination.

I felt the kind of fluttering a submissive craves, as though a spanking was imminent. The promise of a punishment that would make me cry, and then make me come.

Richard grabbed a file, opened it and read what was inside. My file, I assumed.

His brows arched with curiosity.

I'd always been good at reading people. My profession relied upon my ability to gain rapport quickly and navigate human behavior. Here, now, my gut told me this man wasn't impressed.

Having been trained by Faulkner, albeit briefly, I was prepared for a moment like this; though that schooling had been unique to Pendulum. There, flirty and dirty and totally slutty were pleasing attributes.

Maybe that would work here.

Lifting my hem, the material billowing around my hands, I revealed I wasn't wearing any panties.

Richard peered over the file.

"I assumed…"

"You assumed?" he said flatly.

"I'm here to impress you."

"If you want to do that, talk about Chaucer. Quote Marcus Aurelius."

"The Roman emperor?"

"Yes."

"I remember reading something about him that creeped me out."

"You don't think he was one of the greatest philosophers who ever lived?"

"Why is this relevant?"

"It's relevant if I say it is, Rue."

"I've signed the forms. Doesn't that mean I'm in?"

"It means you've made yourself known to me."

It was the way he'd spoken those words that elicited a sensation inside me like a kundalini awakening.

"Your work and personal life have been arranged so that you can devote a week to us?"

"Yes, sir."

"Any health issues you failed to mention?"

"No, nothing like that." I hesitated and then said, "No, sir."

"Blood work is good," he continued to read. "No sexual diseases." He just came out and said it without embarrassment.

I watched his expression turn dark.

He looked up at me. "You trained as a submissive at Majestic?"

"Yes, sir."

He glanced back down at the file.

"What does it say?" I asked.

His frown deepened. "How long were you at Pendulum?"

"A few hours."

"You don't commit well to submissive training, Rue."

"Have you spoken with Shay about me?"

Richard's glare became intense.

"Master Gardner," I said, correcting myself.

"What can he add?" He slapped the folder closed.

Maybe it was a secret that Shay had visited Pendulum. One thing was certain—it was bad form to reveal who you saw at any of the clubs.

I went with, "What happens now?"

"God, you're chatty."

"I can show you I'm serious about joining Enthrall."

He opened the file again. "I'm taking another look."

"If you have questions…"

"I'm searching for something that might impress me."

I reached beneath my hem and thrummed my clit with a flicking finger. Pleasure surged between my thighs. It made me desperate for more.

He was the gatekeeper—the man who had the final say. Impressing him was imperative. He'd expect my readiness for eroticism.

"What kind of master are you looking for?" he asked calmly, like I wasn't playing with myself in front of him.

"I was hoping that Master Gardner…"

"What are you doing?"

My finger paused but didn't leave that throbbing nub that was hard and needy beneath my lingering touch. "I want to impress you."

"By touching yourself?" he sounded surprised.

"Yes, I thought…"

"Without permission?"

Richard walked over to the corner and pulled the papers out of my file, pushing the pages into the top of a shredder, destroying the forms. He threw the empty folder on his desk and brushed his hands together as though he felt glad those papers were gone.

I hoped he'd made a copy, or at least scanned my paperwork into an electronic file. I'd spent time on the application and answered the questionnaire. Given over the kind of intimate details I didn't want to repeat.

"Rue," said Richard, "you've not shown any indication you're ready for this level of play."

My stomach twisted in knots. I disagreed but knew better than to contradict him. A man with this much power wouldn't tolerate it.

"You're requesting high-grade sexual scenarios."

"It's a higher level than most subs want...I know that," I explained, pressing my hand to my chest. "I don't know what I'll do if I don't get it."

"Seek fulfillment elsewhere, perhaps?"

That's what I'd previously threatened to do.

My throat tightened. "This is Enthrall."

"Even we have our limits."

"I'm only asking for..." I wondered if Shay had mentioned me going to Hillenbrand. "I'm a..."

"Exhibitionist," he said. "I read that."

There was no shame in it for me. "Yes. And at Chrysalis you have parties where..."

"What goes on there is private."

"Of course, I didn't mean anything by it." Glancing right, I studied the framed photos on the wall, searching for a way to divert the conversation, or at the very least save it.

One photo was of a man swimming with sharks. In another, a man was rock-climbing without a harness. The photo on the end was of a man skydiving.

"Is that you?" I asked.

Richard's gaze never left me. "I'm the one asking the questions."

His harsh tone seared into me.

No wonder he'd attracted the likes of Hollywood icon Andrea Buckingham, an actress who'd starred in a movie about BDSM. It made me wonder if that's what had attracted them to each other.

"You have a great reference," he said. "Your last master highly recommends you."

I'd not wanted Faulkner to know I was coming here. It made sense though, asking what kind of submissive they could expect.

With all their high profile clients they had to be thorough. Maybe he'd been the one to tell them I'd left Pendulum.

A mark against me.

"I'm here because of Master Gardner," I said, unable to keep the fire out of my tone. "He says I'm ready."

"Is that not for me to determine?" Richard looked affronted.

"My body. My fantasies. If you can't handle them because I'm a woman…"

He glanced at my pussy. "Cover yourself."

I let the hem drop and it fell below my knees.

I've blown it.

I could see he was annoyed. "I didn't mean to be disrespectful."

"You may leave." He gestured to the door.

"Master Gardner's paid for my membership," I added quickly.

Richard's face wore an irritated expression. "I'm a busy man."

"No more talk of Chaucer, then?" It sounded funny to me.

"I doubt you've ever heard of him." He glanced at his watch. "Look at that, it's 'fuck off 0'clock.'"

How was it possible to admire and hate someone at the same time? This man was hard to read. If only he wasn't so damn handsome—his confidence was off the charts.

Richard strolled closer and towered over me. "Want to know why it's a no?"

I bit the inside of my cheek.

"You didn't kneel?" He raised his hand sharply. "It's too late now."

"I just spent the last hour signing everything," I blurted out.

"You might be one of Faulkner's worst subs."

"That's not true." I flinched, realizing he was testing my resolve. "What do I need to do to prove I'm ready?"

"If you have to ask."

Lowering myself as elegantly as possible, I kneeled and spread my arms out before me in a submissive's pose, letting my hair tumble before me.

Even though he'd warned me it was too late.

I'd done everything wrong. Misread the room. The interview had begun as soon as I'd stepped over the threshold, only I'd failed to see that.

This…this was how I was meant to begin.

I was unsure of how much time passed. Ten minutes, maybe? My body was reacting as though unaware I was failing—arousal soothing my sense of doubt.

I'd have stayed like this for hours if ordered.

"Rise." Richard's voice broke through the quiet.

Pushing up, I avoided eye contact with him and hesitated as though these last moments could undo my mistake.

If I could just find the right words.

But I couldn't.

I headed for the door and clutched the handle, turning back to him. "I liked Canterbury Tales."

"Chaucer's best-known works," he said approvingly. "So you have read him."

"Marcus Aurelius not so much."

Richard gave a nod. "Impress the all-mighty one and you're in."

Who?

"One chance."

My mouth went dry. I had a feeling I knew who he was talking about. The one man everyone respected. And everyone feared.

A man who could destroy a submissive.

Outside in the hallway, Shay was waiting.

He tucked his phone in his pocket. "How did it go?"

"He wants me to see…"

Shay gestured for me to follow. "On your knees. You'll crawl the rest of the way."

CHAPTER THIRTEEN

Shay

"I_s IT HIM?" ASKED RUE, LOOKING AROUND THE ECLECTIC chamber.

"It's him," I said.

Richard agreed it was best we have the ultimate assessment. Make sure Rue was ready for the unique level of intensity she'd requested.

Only it wouldn't be in this manor.

I had just made the difficult decision to officially close Enthrall.

We'd begun locking the place down and were completing a rudimentary walk-through to make sure everything was secure.

I wasn't going to look at it like we'd lost this battle. It was more about us coming back stronger. More secure. Enthrall had evolved into an extraordinary establishment and we had to change with the times.

Once the iron gate was constructed, we'd reopen.

Enthrall had once been a well-kept secret. A few famous

clients had hinted of its existence and now Enthrall's exclusivity had become compromised.

I had access to the live security footage of the perimeter on my Smartphone—could check to see the way was clear before anyone arrived or left the manor.

"Will it happen here?" Rue broke the silence.

She waited in the center of the room on her knees, looking exquisite in that pink dress. Even though she wasn't mine I was still proud to show her off.

Putting some distance between us, I leaned against the side of the Saint Andrews cross, reminiscing about what I'd done within these burgundy walls with De Sade.

The day before he'd gone back to Rylee.

I wouldn't have chosen this room, but Cameron had told us to meet him here. Maybe he'd noted how much time I'd once spent in this chamber. It wouldn't surprise me.

"Are you going to share me?" Rue whispered.

"Silence."

I let my mind speculate as to what they would have done to her at Pendulum. It would have been the kind of experience no training could prepare her for. And Hillenbrand, that place would have destroyed her. Though something told me she wanted that.

Her self-destructive side needed protecting. She nursed the kind of pain that nudged her into making interesting decisions.

Rue bit her bottom lip as though sucking on a delicious thought.

Yeah, it's not what you think.

This could be one of the most profound experiences of her life. Because of him.

Cameron Cole strolled in with his usual intimidating presence, his gaze focusing on Rue as though that's all it would take to get a feel on her. To read her soul.

I studied her, too. A redheaded goddess on her knees, lush locks falling over a freckled face. Too pretty, really. Too precious. Too fucking perfect for a man like me.

I liked it rough and could endure hours of passion with a lover. I'd probably break her on day one—in every conceivable way. Enough to have her blissed out but not enough to have her fall in love. Not when she saw the real me. The cold-hearted man who let no one in.

Though part of me could see the value in spending more time with her.

Her beauty was alluring.

The first time Rue saw Cole was at his palatial home in Beverly Hills. He'd probably not seemed intimidating, not with that puppy by his side and his easygoing nature, which she had observed from afar.

Here, Cole would be a different man.

Shrugging out of his jacket, he then removed his cufflinks, tucking them away in his pocket. He rolled up his sleeves, revealing muscled forearms. The way he removed his tie was all business—taking his time as though winding up a clock. All fine precision and mindful focus.

He swaggered around like he still owned this lion's den.

As the founder and former director, his brilliance was still needed here. Cameron may no longer rule but his opinion remained sacred.

Over the years, I'd seen him tackle every conceivable situation. Take on every challenge without flinching.

He was the grand master of control.

I waited for Cameron to do his thing. Make sure Rue was ready.

"The gate will look good." Cameron quirked a brow. "You made the right decision."

"We have to have more security in place before we re-open."

He nodded in agreement.

I motioned for Rue to come toward us. She rose and scurried over to Cole, kneeling before him.

"Look at your master," he ordered.

I went to correct him. "She's not my—"

"We are assessing your suitability, Ms. Asher," he said, ignoring me. "Under the watch of an elite master."

"Sir, did you just say Enthrall is closed?" she said, glancing at me with uncertainty.

"To the public, yes," Cameron replied. "For now."

Rue's frown deepened.

Silence lingered; long enough to cause her to fidget.

"I'm ready," she said.

"You're not ready for me, Rumer Katy Asher," he said, his tone sinister.

She tried to read his meaning.

Cameron walked over to a chair and sat, leaning back and crossing one long leg over another. "Let's go back to the beginning. All the way back to your childhood."

"Wait." Rue pushed to her feet. "What is this?" She looked from him to me and then back to him. "What's happening?"

Cameron was unfazed. "Our first session."

"Like therapy?"

"What were you expecting?" he said.

She blushed. "I don't see why this is necessary."

"It's all relevant, Ms. Asher," he said.

"I don't need a psychiatrist," she blurted out. "I need a place that respects me. Respects my desires…without judging."

Cole uncrossed his legs and leaned forward. "Interesting."

She looked uncertain.

His gaze narrowed. "You left Pendulum under questionable circumstances."

Rue glanced at me for support.

"You broke the rules," he said coldly. "Changed your mind? Let down your master."

"Well, I…"

"Why should we trust you?" he added. "Here at Enthrall?"

She swallowed. "I did leave Pendulum under unusual circumstances."

Cameron frowned. "So you're banned from Pendulum?"

She shot a desperate glance my way, silently begging me to defend her.

Rue could reveal I'd visited Pendulum. That she'd met me there. That it had been me who'd removed her.

She hadn't overheard the conversation I'd had with Cameron about me rescuing her from there.

Cameron looked thoughtful. "I'm saying no to Enthrall. For now."

She blinked. "Why?"

Cole pushed to his feet, hinting he was leaving.

Session over.

A *what the fuck* expression flashed over her face. "I understand every aspect of what I'm asking for. I will be placed in situations that push my limits. Maybe fucked by more than one man. Punished and pleasured and…"

Cole tucked his hands into his pockets as he continued to study her. Doing his thing; mind-fuckery on the highest level.

"I'm ready for anything," Rue said, her tone pleading. She licked her lips. "This need is so strong I'll die from it if it's not sated."

"I would ask you to kneel again," Cameron said coldly, "but we only ask that from *our* submissives." He grabbed his jacket and tie off the back of a chair and headed for the door.

Rue stared at me with a confused expression.

"Wait here," I told her.

I followed Cameron into the hallway, trying to get a read on him.

Cole's brand was an acquired taste, decadent and without limits and strangely necessary. It could be a shock to the system even when consumed in small quantities.

I suppose it could be argued that if he didn't send you reeling, he wasn't doing *his thing*.

"She's exquisite," he said, as though he'd not just sent off an emotional nuclear bomb in there.

He reached into his pocket and brought out his cufflinks,

reattaching them to his cuffs, tugging on his shirt sleeves afterwards.

I hoped Rue wasn't crying. I hated tears—hated the idea of having to comfort her and this memory of Enthrall being her last.

"Thoughts?" I asked, jaw tight with exasperation.

One thing I knew was to expect the unexpected. He was still able to unsettle me.

"She's lovely," he added. "Ethereal."

"Obviously, but I meant as a submissive."

He blinked at me as though confused.

"That's why we're here," I snapped, due to the fact I was still rock hard and needed to get back in there.

Cameron seemed to take pleasure from my impatience. Or maybe his dark side got a kick out of me standing here with a boner.

"She'll make a stellar submissive," I said, needing to hear him say it.

"She is extraordinary."

In those few words he'd defused the chaos inside my mind. Reassuring me I was seeing her potential. That I'd not just projected what I needed to see.

She was real.

Authentic.

A woman who deserved to be cherished by someone.

The kind of beautiful we'd be honored to have.

"Is she ready, Cole?"

He looked thoughtful. "She's interesting."

"In what way?"

"Is that Tom Ford?" He looked me up and down. "Looking good, buddy." He waved his hand in a circle. "You're consistently mercurial."

I shook my head, refusing to be distracted. "Are you going to share your thoughts on her?"

"How have you been sleeping?"

"Fine."

"Periods of insomnia?"

I let out a frustrated sigh at this change of subject. "I get a lot of reading done."

"You know, depression is a signal, not a malfunction, Shay."

I caressed my brow. "You've told me this."

"You need a break," he said.

"I'm taking one… soon." Once the breach here was contained.

"That's progress."

That was me looking to the future and we both knew it was something I did with reservation. "Look, Rue needs to be protected," I said. "She's threatened to fly off to Hillenbrand. This is about her. Can we please make it about *her*?"

"Her threats won't work on me."

"I know," I said, trying to remain calm.

He smiled, one of his warmer gestures reserved for his closest friends. "Let's fence again soon."

"Sure." I stepped closer to him. "I take it Rue passed your test?"

"Did she pass yours?"

"How do you mean?"

"She never sees herself as falling in love because she's scared to. That kind of risk is terrifying. Sound familiar?"

He'd read in her file about the tragic death of her parents—a year apart. It was something that would shake anyone's reality.

"You think she's acting out?" I asked.

"Her fantasy is a place her mind can hide in, perhaps."

"Is she ready for her fantasies?"

"She will seek them out irrespective," he said. "Providing a safe environment is essential."

"Which is why you and I are standing here."

"Right." He looked thoughtful. "She needs to be loved entirely so she can learn to trust life again."

"Exactly."

"She's a rare erotic creature. You're lucky to have her."

"I'm merely escorting her into Chrysalis."

He squeezed my shoulder. "Of course you are."

"Yes, Cameron, I am."

"Work on finding a Dom for her, then. If there are doubts."

"That's what I intend to do."

I wouldn't let him rile me up. That much I'd promised myself. But here I was, frustrated with him. "You thought De Sade would be good for me, too, but look how that turned out."

"What did you learn from that experience?"

"You mean my relationship?"

"Whatever you choose to call it, yes."

"I was open to a certain level of commitment."

"Which brings us back to Rue."

"I'm not sure I even like her," I muttered.

That was a bald-faced lie but the sound of it was reassuring.

He gave a nod as though understanding my dilemma. "You've never brought a submissive here."

"I'm doing this for her."

"You dream about her."

Was that meant to be a question? "How could you possibly know that?"

"Because you just confirmed it."

"I hate it when you do that!" I snapped.

I'd been around him too long for this bullshit to literally work every single fucking time.

I watched his reaction, and then said, "My gut's sending all kinds of signals."

Waiting for him to react was like waiting for the death blow.

"What do you want?" he said softly.

Her, maybe?

I just couldn't say it.

Couldn't get to a place where I gave myself permission to have her. Because my track record was shit and hurting her was an agony I didn't want to inflict on her.

"Shay, you have a chip on your shoulder. Not a bad one, you just figure all women want a man with a private island. They don't.

Most women are romantic. They want to find love. To be loved. To feel safe. Fulfilled."

"I want to get her out of my system. I know that."

And if I fucked her maybe that would do it.

"Don't throw away this opportunity to heal. To grow, even."

My throat got tight. "I did all my growing up in Kabul."

"Kabul," he whispered. "I remember."

He had gone through hell, too.

"Do you remember?" he said softly. "Remember that day?"

"What?

God, I was a bull in a china shop with any matters of the heart.

Because I was a SEAL in a designer suit. But a SEAL, no less.

Cameron stepped closer. "Listen, if ever you feel ready to see someone let me know."

"Someone?" I knew what this was.

Cameron was hinting there were shadows within me I needed to explore with a therapist. Subconscious residue from Afghanistan.

"Henry is having success in that regard," Cole said. "He asked me to share that with you. He told me to tell you—"

"No," I said quickly. "I'm fine. Don't need anything like that. I'm perfectly capable of sorting all that out in my head."

I hated thinking about it…

Sand everywhere. No privacy. Constant gunfire. Friends who disappeared from my side.

The mountainous regions of Afghanistan.

A reconnaissance mission.

A lion emerging from a sandstorm.

Henry's life being threatened.

A decision had to be made.

And I made it.

"Where were you just then?" asked Cameron.

"I'm here where I need you to be," I snapped.

His raised an index finger to indicate he was about to say something profound.

"What?"

"There will be pain before there is peace," he said quietly, then turned and walked away.

Trying to decipher his words, I watched him leave.

Why did Cole always have to come up with a brain tease?

Either way, he'd left the decision regarding Rue up to me.

CHAPTER FOURTEEN

Rue

L EFT IN THE WAKE OF CAMERON'S PRESENCE, I ASKED, "Were you able to get him to change his mind?"

Shay held out his hand for me.

I hurried forward, my fingers curling around his, instantly feeling a shiver of delight. This close proximity was everything I needed.

Maybe I could change their minds.

Maybe there was still time.

Shay had stood beside Cameron Cole the entire time and held his own, showing just how commanding he can be.

"Are we leaving?" I asked, as we entered the elevator.

He punched the button for us to descend.

I gazed up at him. "It would have been nice of you to warn me about him."

He ignored the comment. When the elevator door slid open, he gestured for me to exit ahead of him.

I was too overcome now with emotion to talk—I merely clung to Shay as he led me toward a door. We weren't even leaving via the front of the building. He was sneaking me out the side door like he didn't want to be seen with me.

I paused when I saw the limo. A faint memory. I'd heard that's how submissives were picked up from the airport in Paris before being driven to Hillenbrand.

Only we were in L.A.

I didn't want this to be goodbye.

As we strode toward the waiting car, my thoughts spiraled out of control with how I would handle his rejection.

"I forgot my overnight bag," I said.

"It's in the trunk." Shay opened the rear door for me.

I knew my worth. Even if they didn't see it. Even as doubt made my stomach clench.

Ducking my head, I climbed into the car, scooting all the way to the other end.

Shay leaned down. "I meant for you to sit on this side. I'm not a complete caveman."

"You're coming with me?"

"Yes." When he climbed in beside me, my heart lifted at not having to endure the journey alone.

His sensual cologne reminded me of what I was about to lose. *Him.*

The car jerked forward and pulled around the front of the grand manor.

I admired the exquisite brickwork of Enthrall, ornate windows holding secrets behind their one-way glass, the stone entryway where guests came and went because they were deemed worthy. All the possibilities of what I could have had now slipping away.

We drove away from Enthrall and my fantasies were dashed on the rocks of uncertainty. These could be the final moments I'd ever spend with Shay.

I'd fallen for him, there was no denying it.

He settled back and crossed one leg over the other casually, seemingly unaware of the war going on inside my mind. Negotiating with him was useless.

I would never be part of his elite circle.

Anger rose in my belly. "I was destined to fail."

"Fail?"

"Did you enjoy it? Watching him put me in my place?"

"No. What makes you think that?"

"I thought…"

"You exited the building respectfully. You were calm and remained contained considering the circumstances."

"That was a test?"

"Everything is."

"I didn't tell either of them that I saw you at Pendulum," I said bitterly.

"They know I was there, Rue."

"They were waiting to see if I betrayed you?"

"Discretion is essential."

My hands were shaking. "But you're taking me home?"

I felt like my emotions were taking a wild ride on a roller coaster.

Shay reached inside his jacket pocket and pulled out his phone, entering a text. I tried to read it, but he stopped me with a warning look. Then he went back to sending more messages.

"Let me out here," I said, suddenly feeling the need for air.

"Relax," he said calmly.

Leaning back, I resigned myself to the fact he had all the power. And each moment with him was precious.

And there was still Hillenbrand.

He glanced up from texting. "What's going on in that mind of yours?"

His voice was a spark that ignited every cell in my body—our chemistry combustible.

When I didn't answer, Shay shoved his phone back into his pocket.

"Turn around," he ordered.

"Why?"

"I've not seen any evidence you're an elite submissive.'"

I spun round so that my back was to him, every nerve on edge.

Glancing over my shoulder, I saw a strip of black silk in his hand.

He secured it around my head, covering my eyes, giving it a tug to ensure nothing could be seen through it.

I heard a soft rustle of movement.

It had sounded like he was sitting back where I couldn't touch him.

My body thrummed with each passing second. All that had gone before, all the training, all the time as an ingnue revealing its worth.

Since the first time I'd seen Shay at Pendulum, I'd desired more time with him. Fantasized about what it would be like to be *his*.

But after the interviews with Richard and Cameron, I'd given up hope of it ever happening.

He didn't speak. I could only hear the purr of the engine and the sound of cars passing by.

I resisted the urge to ask where we were going.

I knew.

My flesh tingled in anticipation, nipples hard against my dress, my sex throbbing with longing.

I'd fantasized about this.

Over the last three weeks, I'd brought toys to my sex and pleasured myself with thoughts of him.

This man.

Replaying again and again the limited time I'd had with Shay at Pendulum.

My reverie unfolding like a brilliant dream coming true. Awakening to a new experience. I could see through the erotic looking glass—the one I'd pined for since first learning pleasure came in so many forms.

If all those involved with my admission into Chrysalis truly honored my vision, then life would never be the same.

My delicious ruination was guaranteed.

All I had to do was surrender. Trust that my new Dom had the skill to take me all the way into the depths of depravity.

Sexual bliss.

I wanted to ask what would happen next, what was the reason for this blindfold.

But I knew better.

I tried improving my pose as I mentally gave myself over to the adventure—offering him my mind and body and soul.

"We need to improve your form," said Shay.

His firm hands brushed over my spine as he directed me to sit straighter, as though I was a dancer and he was my instructor improving my pose.

I felt the sensation of his fingers tipping up my chin.

My lips pouted as though a kiss might even find me. The promise of his lips on mine.

Sharp pinches to my left nipple made me flinch, sending jolts of exotic pleasure into my breasts. I felt the slow gliding up of material as my hem was hoisted above my thighs.

If the driver turned around, he'd see me. See my sex exposed and wet.

"Whatever Faulkner had you doing," Shay said in a stern tone, "I'm going to have to correct it." He eased my thighs farther apart. "We have higher standards at Chrysalis."

"Permission to speak, sir."

"Permitted."

"It's happening?" I said breathlessly.

"How wet are you?" he whispered fiercely.

"I'm wet for you."

"This pleases me."

Then I remembered the driver would overhear.

He might even sneak a glance in the rearview mirror. See Shay dominating me. The thought of it was so arousing.

"Your safe word?" asked Shay.

"Cadence."

Firm fingers found their way along my crevice, the tips

entering me, penetrating deep. His fingers found a rhythm and began a dizzying thrusting pace causing my muscles there to clench against his exploration.

I drew in a sharp breath, inching closer and closer to release.

He was driving me into the very center of euphoria as his thumb circled my clit.

"Harder," I said.

"It's unacceptable to demand anything from me." He withdrew his fingers.

I fell back against my seat, my body going into shock at the loss of his touch.

His teasing had left me needy and desperate.

Shay rested his fingers against my lips. I obeyed his offering and licked the tips, licking my arousal from them.

He withdrew his hand.

Then nothing.

I felt a stark chill between my thighs from the loss of his ministrations. I could still taste myself.

I imagined he'd sat back and was observing how well I kept my pose after his stimulation.

It was a challenge not to move or grind against the seat.

Feeling desperate for release, I focused on pleasing him. Obeying even what was not spoken.

We continued our journey like this, me proving I was ready.

I was being taken into his world.

The air around my body felt electrified, as though the oxygen itself was about to ignite.

I might ignite.

With trembling toes pointed down like a ballerina, I tried to keep still, balancing against the rocking limousine.

Showcasing myself. Showing I was willing to do anything for my new master.

Please him. Inspire him.

Be everything he'd ever wanted.

Finally, I felt the limo glide to a stop.

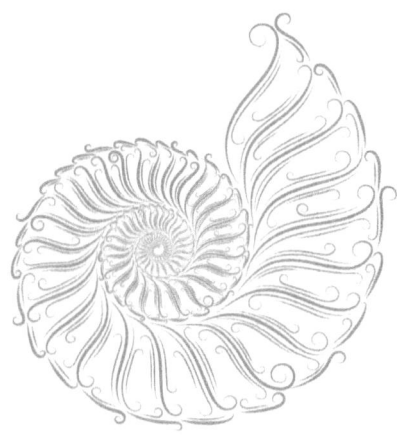

CHAPTER FIFTEEN

I FELT THE TUG OF THE BLINDFOLD AS IT WAS REMOVED FROM my face.

I'd been ordered to kneel on the cold marble floor.

Peering up, I stole a glance at the enormous chandelier.

I'm in Chrysalis.

My heart soared.

In front of me was a wide, elegant staircase that curved up to another story.

Master Shay was to my far left talking with a beautiful Domina with bobbed hair. She looked classy in a lovely Chanel suit.

"Stand," said a female voice from behind me.

It happened in a flurry of movement—three submissives easing me out of my Dolce and Gabbana mini-cocktail dress, while another at my feet unclipped my shoes and removed them.

Soon I was standing there completely naked, bathed in the light from the chandelier above.

Shay and the dominatrix looked on with seeming approval.

A box was placed before me on the marble.

One of the submissives reached into it and removed a strappy black bodice. All three worked around me.

Within minutes I looked like one of them.

Strips of black latex fit around my form, hiding nothing. My nipples were covered in pasties, and my thong was so fine it showed everything.

I wondered if Shay had texted them my shoe size. The high heels they slid onto my feet fit perfectly.

Everyone left the foyer.

Except for one submissive who kneeled before me with a square velvet box in her hands, her head bowed, dark locks falling over her face.

She lifted the box up and Master Shay took it from her.

He handed it to the Domina and she held it for him as he took off the lid. Then he reached in and removed a sparkling ruby collar.

For me.

I trembled as my master stood behind me and placed it around my neck. A click and it was secured around my throat.

"How does it feel?" he asked.

"Like it belongs," I whispered.

"Because it does." He brushed a strand of my hair away from the collar.

"Thank you, sir."

"You've already met Mistress Lotte," he said. "She will give you the grand tour. You have permission to speak to her."

I met her kind gaze. "Is this Chrysalis?"

"It is, yes," she said. "How do you feel about that?"

Emotion welled in my throat and tears stung my eyes.

Mistress Lotte held a form in front of me. "Is this your signature?"

"Yes."

"You consent to stay here for one week?"

"Yes, mistress."

"Verbalize what you understand about Chrysalis."

"It's a B&D manor."

"We're so much more than that, dear." She gave a nod to Shay. "I'll take it from here."

"I'll be back, Rue," he said. "You're in good hands."

"When will you be back?" I suppressed the panic in my voice.

"Soon." He strolled away.

My heart rate sped up as I watched him leave through an ornate door. Maybe he was just stepping out for a few minutes.

"Right," said Lotte. "Let's show you around."

This had to be one of grandest manors in the world; it was like a palace. Lotte gave me the full tour, showing me everything from the vast ballroom to the luxury spa.

We stepped outside and she pointed to the impressive swimming pool. "You can swim if your master permits."

"Thank you."

"Careful out here," she added. "We have peacocks."

"Oh, cool."

"Not when the fuckers chase you," she said. "Master Booth thought they'd add a fantastic touch to the place. I don't even know if he's aware how territorial the males can be."

"Have you ever been chased by one?"

"You mean chased by a large cock across the lawn?" She laughed. "Once or twice."

She made me giggle.

We headed back in and continued down the hallway, crossing the foyer again.

"We're not going farther than the Harrington Suite," she told me. "The area beyond that room is forbidden to you for now."

"What's down there?"

Lotte stared off in that direction. "It's for VIPs."

Accommodations for the rich, maybe?

We ended up in the kitchen, where she brewed us tea in a Union Jack patterned pot. "I know what you're thinking," she said, as she handed me a teacup.

"Oh?"

"This is just us getting to know you, Rue. We need to

understand your limits and your expectations. Make sure you're ready for the intensity of what we offer."

"I appreciate that," I said.

"Once we've established what your boundaries are, we will plunge you into your first session."

I nodded and she gave me a warm smile. "Let's show you the dungeons."

Running my fingertips around my collar, I felt a shudder of delight pass through me.

"From here you crawl," she said.

I dropped to my knees, honored to continue like this by her side.

"After the dungeons," she said. "I'll show you your room."

CHAPTER SIXTEEN

Shay

P UTTING SOME DISTANCE BETWEEN ME AND CHRYSALIS THIS afternoon was a good idea.

Mainly because of that small matter of the submissive I'd left in the foyer with Lotte. The one dressed so seductively, I'd had to walk away.

Just fucking say her name, asshole.

It's not like thinking of her would change anything.

Rue.

Her first twenty-four hours there would be all about her orientation and finding her way around the manor.

The shock of her meeting with Cameron Cole would soon wear off.

I was merely the conduit for her access. As promised, I'd delivered her into an elite society that she could flourish in.

The rest would work itself out.

Even so, I missed her upbeat energy and her inquisitive nature. I had a surge of jealousy when I thought about seeing her with her new master.

I'd left Dominic and Lotte back at Chrysalis to deal with those decisions. Our senior Dominatrix and head of legal could more than handle it.

Not thinking of Rue was the way to go.

I turned the Rover onto Princeton Street and searched for the house I'd driven Darryn Amara to on Friday.

This was a nice neighborhood.

My gut had told me something was off then, but I'd just not had the time to personally investigate why. Now, my radar was turned all the way up on full alert.

Santa Monica was a popular tourist trap—close to the beach and with enough decent restaurants and entertainment to keep both residents and visitors here. This city attracted the wealthy crowd when it came to real estate.

I'd brought Darryn here straight from the ER. He'd told me he rented a house along with some buddies.

He'd wanted me to believe he lived in this charming Spanish bungalow on a tree-lined street off Wilshire. I mean, sure, the photogs got paid well for their exclusive shots but him living in one of the most expensive neighborhoods didn't add up.

He just didn't strike me as a Santa Monica kind of guy.

I'd watched him walk up to this house and then head round the back, not entering through the front door—which was why I was here now carrying a bag of groceries as an excuse to visit. With a sprained wrist, he might find shopping difficult. So it was a conceivable excuse. Maybe it could also be construed as me giving a fuck.

I headed up the pathway toward the front porch.

A young guy answered the door.

"Is Darryn here?" I raised the paper bag. "I wanted to drop off some things for him."

He raised a hand to refuse the groceries. "Who?"

"Darryn Amara. He gave me this address."

"This is my dad's place."

I cringed at how this looked and took a step back. "Darryn's not a housemate?"

"No." He looked annoyed. "What's this about?"

"I have the wrong address."

He closed the door a little. "Looks like it."

I'd literally watched Darryn head round the back of this house, but I wasn't going to share that with this young man and creep him out.

With rent so high it wasn't unusual for a homeowner to lease their guest house at the back of their property, make extra cash to try to keep up with L.A.'s exorbitant rates.

Though that didn't seem to be the case here.

With a background check I'd have the legal name of the owner. If they were covering for Darryn, I'd find out.

I strolled back to my car.

Darryn's asshole status had just been upgraded to threat level one.

I climbed back into the Rover and checked my watch. It was just after 5:00 P.M.

Going back to Chrysalis was a possibility, but the thought of seeing Rue brought a sense of uneasiness.

Especially seeing her dressed like an elite submissive with that collar around her throat.

Like she was mine.

I started the engine and pulled away from the curb, turning onto Wilshire and driving toward the PCH, which would take me back to Malibu...and home.

CHAPTER SEVENTEEN

Shay

A 5:00 A.M. RUN ALONG THE BEACH: *CHECK*

An hour at the gym: *check*

Now, stealing time at the gun range before heading to Chrysalis. I raised my pistol, steadying it with my other hand, and pointed it down range at the target.

Bang. Bang. Bang. Bang. Bang.

Just don't think about her.

The sub I'd left back at Chrysalis yesterday.

The woman I'd escorted inside with so many possibilities ahead of her. Lottie would watch over her, give her all she needed to feel comfortable that first night there.

Why was saying her name so challenging?

I believed a night apart would give me time to think.

Time to work out which Dom might be a good fit.

It wasn't like I was falling for her, the ingénue I would have to face this morning.

I was about to provide her with a new master.

Anyone but Faulkner.

Just not me.

What I had with De Sade was one thing, but with Rue it would become an obsession—that much I knew. She was just too damn mesmerizing not to distract me from my work.

My job needed focus. It was about keeping everyone safe. Everyone out of harm's way. I was too busy and too important to Enthrall and Chrysalis to let myself get involved on that level of intensity.

All roads led back to me when it came to security.

After engaging the safety, I set the gun down and then punched the button to zip my target toward me to take a closer look at my aim. The bullets had brushed the edges of the bullseye.

Rue was affecting my focus.

I could do better, aim better, but I just wasn't in the mood to prove it to myself.

I checked out of the range, leaving the gun behind. The rule of thumb at Chrysalis was that all weapons were banned and, apparently, mine was also included in that protocol.

Within minutes, I was speeding back towards the elite Bel Air manor perched on a hill. Enthrall may be closed but Chrysalis remained open.

For now, anyway.

A year ago, we'd installed a wrought iron fence around the property. The scanner automatically read the tag on my car window. Seconds later, those impressive iron gates swung open.

I drove up the private road and crested the hill, that vast palatial manor coming into view. It blended easily with the other multimillion dollar properties that were scattered across the area.

Parking out front, I let the valet know I'd be keeping my keys.

I wasn't staying.

Not for long, anyway.

Heading around to the rear, I admired the well-tended acreage and dramatic view beyond the garden. The impressive swimming pool reflected the morning sunlight.

I kept a look-out for one of the many peacocks we had here.

One especially needed to avoid them during mating season—they could be territorial fuckers sometimes.

I'd gone around to the rear of the manor because there was a decent view of the breakfast room. Which meant I could observe *her* before going in.

And there she was.

Rue sat alone.

Bright sunlight bounced around in there, too. It caught the highlights in her hair. Tangling my fingers through those silky locks was the kind of pleasure I'd never know again.

Rue had proven she was loyal, too.

She'd not betrayed me, refusing to tell Richard and Cameron that she'd met me at Pendulum. That kind of loyalty was rare and impressive. Especially since what she'd stood to lose was everything she'd always wanted.

God, she was so damn beautiful. The way she peered from underneath long lashes toward the other end of the room, as though imagining me there.

This ache in my chest worsened, as though I'd already lost her.

Already let her go.

The next few minutes were inevitable.

Rue wrapped her hands around a coffee mug, looking forlorn and staring at the place I should be sitting as though she was trying to conjure me out of the ether.

Rue.

Her name left my lips like a curse or a prayer or a plea.

She'd fallen for me.

That much was true. I'd seen that look too many times. Watched it fade. Witnessed love being drawn back in real time because of something I'd done.

I was the problem.

The guy who pushed lovers away.

This was a preemptive shove.

An early strike.

After the fallout of a breakup came the crushing truth—that

person would no longer be in my life. The best way to deal with it was to disconnect. That was something I was good at. Throw in a little ghosting and you had your classic extraction.

Withdrawing all access.

"Get it over with, asshole," I muttered under my breath.

Then I halted at the glass door.

Rue's Celtic ancestry had given her that windswept appearance. Like she'd just strolled over the moors and was emerging out of the fog.

For some reason, that felt cathartic.

She looked ethereal.

Like a rare creature.

Did she have to look so damn vulnerable, too?

I might be a dick at times, but I was also a gentleman when it counted. I'd share my thoughts and not leave anyone guessing. Get it over with quickly.

A swift strike.

I rapped on the glass to get her attention, throwing a friendly wave when she looked my way, startled. She brightened when she saw that it was me, leaping up and hurrying over to unlock the door and open it.

Then she hesitated as though not sure whether to hug me or not.

My body stiffened. "Listen, Rue."

"Come in."

I stepped inside and closed the door behind me, turning to face her.

She knelt quickly and stretched her arms forward in a subservient bow, locks of her hair tumbling like a red sea around her.

Exquisite.

Obedient.

Wistful.

Her bodice was elegant, as were her feet in those strappy heels. She looked out of place dressed like this so early. Though the curve of her ass was inviting.

No, not out of place. She was exactly where she was meant to be.

"Up," I said.

She pushed to her feet and rose elegantly. "Permission to speak, sir."

"Of course." It was a stupid rule.

Especially in this scenario.

She beamed. "Didn't want to start breakfast without you."

I glanced over at the long table. "You shouldn't have waited."

At the opposite end of where she sat was a placemat set for me. A teacup. A glass of orange juice. An empty plate for a breakfast yet to be brought in.

"Rue…I really care about you."

Her expression wavered as though she sensed what was coming.

I reached out and rested my hand on her shoulder. This was best done gently. My words needed to be softened for effect.

I tried to ignore the warmth of her skin beneath my palm, a tingling that found its way into my fingertips. Not an unpleasant feeling, just one that was unexpected because this should be easy, really. This should be all business as usual. Switching out one master for another should elicit a thrill for her.

A knock on the door.

I flinched with frustration.

Dominic strolled in with an equal measure of confidence and arrogance. As Chrysalis' resident attorney he had authority here. Cameron liked him so that's what mattered. He trusted him.

For the most part, Dominic managed Chrysalis when Richard wasn't present. He and I had butted heads more times than I could remember. But the subs adored our gay council. Beneath that severe exterior lay a man who really cared.

Even if he was bossy and interfering.

"Nice of you to join us," he said in that condescending manner that grated on my nerves.

"Actually," I said. "I was going to come find you."

Maybe it was Dominic's intuition, but he glared back with a silent *don't you dare back out now*.

With a flick of his fingers, two submissives hurried in each carrying a tray. They set the silver platters filled with breakfast selections on the table.

"No expense spared," I bit out.

"Remember where you are," he said. "Doms are treated like kings."

Which was his way of sliding in the knife to let me know withdrawing from this responsibility wouldn't be easy.

He knew me too well.

Dominic had a good reason to be pissed off with me. Last night, I'd dropped off a submissive and then left.

I'd probably be banned from ever having a submissive here again.

"Leave us," snapped Dominic.

The subs scurried out. They were responding well to their training—and they both deserved better than to serve breakfast to a man like me.

"Rue signed the contract," said Dominic firmly. "Just needs your signature."

Clearly, he'd not gotten the memo.

I wasn't "the one."

Dominic genuinely cared about her. He took pleasure in making sure she had everything she needed—from her wardrobe to her meals. He treated Rue with dignity, giving her the kind of love I was incapable of.

From within his jacket, he whipped out a piece of paper and laid it on the table where I was evidently meant to sit. It was the contract that would bind us together.

I didn't want to look at Rue.

Didn't want to see her hope fade.

"I'll take a look at it," I told him.

"I want them back." He set a fountain pen beside it. "The pen and the contract."

"As I said, I'll take a look." I strolled to the other end of the table, pulled out a chair and sat.

Dominic walked over and pulled Rue's chair out for her—just like a gentleman should for a lady. I was being an asshole of epic proportions. She didn't deserve this cold attitude from me.

There was no other way.

I pushed to my feet and grabbed a spoon, scooping up some scrambled eggs and what I assumed were vegetarian sausages for her. I placed some buttered toast on the side of her plate with my fingers, which earned a look of horror from Dominic like I'd just handled a live bomb.

I might be rough around the edges, but I knew etiquette. I just couldn't be bothered. I licked the butter off my fingers to prove it. Rue needed to see that I would never be good enough for her.

"Serviette?" Dominic offered.

I grabbed one off the table and placed it over her lap.

It was too damn early for these rules. These expectations. This fevered need to suppress what I wanted to do to Rue whenever I was in the same room with her.

This was me protecting her.

Couldn't everyone see that?

I placed the plate in front of her. "There you go, sweetheart."

My stomach grumbled. That vigorous run along the beach had left me hungry. Up until this moment I'd been too distracted to be able to eat. My body was demanding food despite my reservations.

Dominic gave a nod of approval. "Are we set, Mr. Gardner?"

"Sure thing." I gestured to the door. "Cheers."

"Thank you for this, Master Dominic," said Rue, making up for my rudeness.

"You're very welcome, my dear," he said.

"Yes, thanks for breakfast." I gave him a thin smile. "Next time, can you bring coffee instead of tea?"

There was no way they wouldn't be serving Cole's family brand of Earl Grey. That wily psychiatrist had a way of sneaking into my psyche.

With a nod from Dominic to prove I outranked him, he strolled out with his head high and superiority brimming.

"Settling in?" Seemed a reasonable way to start a conversation.

"Yes." Rue reached for a piece of toast. "Lotte told me you'd be back this morning, first thing. And here you are."

She'd been worried.

Yes, here I am.

To deliver the bad news.

"Do you like it?" She tugged on her bodice.

As though coming out of a dream I admired her again, letting my gaze roam over her. The snuggly fitted bodice, embroidered with what looked like emeralds, looked stunning on her. It was easy to stare at her curves. Take in her button nose and the way her blue eyes popped in contrast to the waves that tumbled over her bare shoulders. Those freckles were a curse because it felt like an invitation to kiss them.

I could spend hours pressing my lips to those delicate freckles like a mad man chasing the stars.

"You look beautiful," I said at last.

If Dominic had tried to appeal to my earthy side, he'd succeeded by dressing her like this—though at 9:00 A.M. it seemed ridiculous. I'd been fighting an erection since arriving.

"Are you cold?" I asked, admiring the way her naked shoulders looked in that bodice but at the same time concerned the air-conditioning might be set too low.

She blinked as though struck by my concern, her face lighting up. "I'm fine."

No, she wasn't.

I rose, shrugging out of my jacket, and made my way down to her end of the table. I wrapped it around her shoulders and she slid her arms into the satin-lined sleeves, smiling up at me. It swamped her.

I went back to my chair and sat there feeling the distance between us. Dragging the contract over to me, I scanned the legalize all the way down to where my signature would have gone.

I nudged the fancy fountain pen away.

"I signed it," Rue piped up.

"I can see that."

"Dominic says any feelings we have this morning are natural."

Dominic had told her that, but the message was for me. "What else did he say?"

"To share something personal with you so we can get to know each other better."

I reached for a slice of toast and mulled over whether I was in the mood for these mind games. I bit into the slice, the taste of butter and bread hitting the mark. I dabbed my mouth with the napkin.

I really was hungry.

"Shall I go first?" she said softly.

Lifting the teapot, I poured hot liquid into a teacup. "They don't have mugs?"

"He told me you'd say that."

I lifted the cup to my mouth and carefully took a sip. The golden liquid tasted refreshing. We were drinking Cole tea—I'd imbibed enough of the stuff to recognize its luxurious flavor.

"This is fucking ridiculous," I said, lifting the cup like an idiot with my pinky out.

Three gulps and it was empty.

Looking over at Rue, I couldn't stand the space between us. It was like we were royals or something, or we couldn't bear to be close. Whoever had made this a thing back in the day deserved one of those bullets I'd wasted this morning when my aim was off.

I got up and brought my plate over to her end of the table, along with my annoyingly small teacup, and set it down. "Mind if I join you?"

She looked amused. "No, of course not."

I went back for the teapot and poured the light brew into her cup to refill it. With a nod from her, I added milk.

Sitting much closer, we ate breakfast together.

"Were you working this morning?" she asked.

I didn't want to lie. "I needed to get a couple of things done."

"Anything I can help with?"

"No."

"Because that's how I'd like to proceed. I can help in any way."

"I have it handled."

"I'd like to see what you do."

"It's a lot of behind-the-scenes work." I didn't want to bore her with the details.

"Shall I start?"

Dominic had set her up for this. His mind games were an attempt to persuade me to stay.

"Go on then," I said.

"Back in high school, a few years ago—"

That made my brows shoot up.

She went on, "I was being bullied by another student. She was relentless. Always cutting me off in the hallways. Messing with my head, you know? And no one could do anything about it so I decided to deal with it myself. I went to a spy shop and bought a small camera. The kind you can't see. You'd be surprised how small they can be." She demonstrated how she had clipped it on. "Like a button."

"I know the kind," I said.

"I synced it to my laptop."

"You recorded her bullying you?"

"And bullying others. Every time she approached me or someone else and said those things, I recorded her."

"What did you do with the footage?"

"I projected it onto the wall during one of our principal's speeches—her bullying me in bright Technicolor."

"What was the outcome?"

"We were expelled."

"Both of you?" I said, wondering if it was too late to hunt down her principal and have a few words with him or her.

"I was glad to be out of there," she admitted.

"How did your dad react?"

"He set up homeschooling."

"Not another school?"

"No."

"I'm sure he was proud of you." I leaned back. "I would have been."

"My being homeschooled disrupted his schedule."

"Well, you fought back. That was the right move."

Rue perked up. "Tell me something about you."

Okay, now is as good a time as any.

"I'm the worst kind of man, Rue."

"Why do you say that?"

Because I'm about to ruin your fucking day.

Rue pushed up from her chair and came closer. I turned my chair to face her, ready to take her hands in mine.

She went down on her knees before me.

This wasn't the first time she'd caught me like this. This time, she merely rested her head on my lap. My jacket swamped her small frame.

"You're not the worst kind of man," she said softly. "You do so much good. Everyone here adores you. They really do. I want you to know that."

I'd never really cared what anyone thought of me.

Except her, I suppose.

I ran my fingers through her soft curls, caressing her scalp.

"You've not met everyone," I said, amused.

"You know what I mean. The staff I have met. A few of the submissives, when they asked who I was with here. They are so happy for me."

I gave myself this moment to savor.

Comforting her before the impending guillotine of disappointment came down on us both.

"I have a secret," she whispered.

"There should be no secrets between us." Though soon that wouldn't matter.

It was easy to fall into a trancelike state from this intimacy with her merely resting her head on my lap. Rue's femininity flowed into me like a tranquilizer.

She looked up. "I want to tell you something."

"I'm listening."

"I sent money to Richard Booth to help pay for my stay here."

"Where did you get the money?"

"I asked my aunt for an advance on my inheritance."

That made me cringe. "I'm glad you told me."

"It's important you know that I'll pay my way."

"Rue, submissives don't need to pay anything. I'll get your money back to you."

"You told me I couldn't afford a membership."

"I was being an ass."

"I forgive you."

Brushing Rue's cheek with my curled fingers I said, "Rue, you're exquisite."

I'd taken this place for granted. Its freedoms. Its uniqueness to reach a person and pull them back from the brink. A sacred space in which to heal.

How could I deny her that?

If I took her on, it would mean losing a piece of myself, giving over my heart to this virtual stranger.

Holding on to my pain to relieve hers.

Even if she was here, now, I just couldn't be *the one.*

"I will be everything you want in a submissive," she whispered.

And there it was, that final strike to persuade me to find him for her quickly.

"Go lean over the table," I said firmly.

It was time to begin.

Eagerly, she pushed up and hurried over to the end of the table and rested her palms there.

She'd exchanged the only money she had for time at Chrysalis.

I'd told myself no other man cared as much for her as I did. After all, I was willing to set her free—this woman who in any other universe I'd have chased down and made my own.

I would find the man she deserved.

There was just one final matter to take into consideration. I needed to know what it felt like to be inside her.

I owed her that, at least.

And it would be for my sake, too.

Because soon another man would claim her.

There was no way I was leaving this room without knowing what fucking her felt like.

It would be a memory we'd both cherish.

I wanted this time with her.

Grabbing the fountain pen and sliding off the cap, I wrote along the dotted line of the contract: Master to be determined.

CHAPTER EIGHTEEN

L EANING OVER THE TABLE, MY BODY TENSE, I GLANCED OVER at Shay and watched him run the pen along the contract. He'd signed it.

When he got up and walked toward me, my fingernails dug into the table with anticipation. He stood behind me, being silent, as though waiting for something. I knew not to turn around. Not to speak. Not to do or say anything that would change his mind.

Shay eased his jacket off my shoulders and threw it further up the table.

Kneeling behind me, Shay eased my panties down my thighs. I stepped out of them, my butt exposed. His palm caressed my cheeks, sending a shiver along my skin, his hands sweeping over my ass—as though he was ready to mark my flesh with a slap.

He rose behind me.

I held my breath, full of dizzying excitement.

His hands moved over my bodice, exploring, and then he pulled my hair back from my face, taking his time, seemingly admiring what was his. He reached around to the front of my bodice, tugging it down and easing my breasts out.

Having freed them from the tight binding, he tweaked my nipples, kneading them, running a fingertip around the beading areolas. The rush of sensations caused me to inhale sharply.

He was examining the curve of my spine now, and then moved me into a more pleasing position by tapping my legs apart. Tracing along my cleft, he made an appreciative noise on finding me wet.

"Relax," he said. "No one will disturb us."

He didn't mention the long glass windows that anyone could look through and see us. Yet that thought made me feel a wave of excitement.

Shay redirected me to look forward.

"Brace yourself," he said firmly.

I steadied myself and waited for the first strike, assuming he was going to spank me.

I heard the sound of his zipper and then felt the sudden pressure of his erection nudging my folds, felt the stretching of my channel as he pushed all the way into my pussy. My shocked gasp revealed that I'd not expected this so fast.

He couldn't wait.

My thighs shuddered with the intensity of him pushing inside. Clenching his large girth, I moaned loudly as my body tried to accommodate his growing size, pleasure vibrating through me.

I wished he'd kissed me.

I replayed the way his lips had almost touched mine.

"We both need this," he growled.

"Yes, yes…sir."

That much was proven.

I felt him tug on my locks, twisting my hair and using it for leverage.

His first thrust had been a warning, and now he set about a violent pounding, going deeper.

I was flung against the edge of the table by the force of his frenzy, his hips crashing against me. The rising pleasure I felt was so intense I could hardly hold the air in my lungs.

It was like being taken from zero to a million miles an hour in less than a second.

The slapping sounds I heard turned me on even more.

He was rough and cruel and unforgiving and it was everything I yearned for. No holding back…just a man taking his pleasure out on me—and it felt divine. I reveled in the dizzying pressure of him riding me, feeling his other hand on my left hip, steadying me.

He made me feel like a queen.

We were together at last.

Shay was giving himself to me in the best kind of way. We were sharing ourselves, rising and rising into this easy bliss.

"I'm close," I cried out.

When he pulled out, I was on the verge of screaming my frustration. I felt him drag his tip all the way up to my asshole, wiping my own wetness there to prepare that puckered hole.

He walked away. The sound of a cupboard opening. He was back behind me and rubbing something around my anus. The coldness of lube.

Making me ready.

He plunged inside, pillaging what was his—me, his submissive.

The pressure of him stretching my asshole was too much and yet not enough. I cried out.

He slowed a little until I gave a nod to let him know he could go deeper, faster, take more of me.

"Come," he whispered.

He remained still, reaching around my body, thrumming my clit so well it could have been my own hand—his flicking hitting the spot with such precision he sent me hurtling toward a climax.

My moans echoed around us.

My thighs trembled and I took short, sharp breaths as I tried to keep still, tried not to come again until he gave the order.

He let go of my hair and held me in position with his two

hands on either side of my waist, his strong hold keeping me standing.

"Such a filthy whore," he rasped.

"Yes, Master."

"What have you learned?"

"To trust you," I blurted out, finding it hard to think. Or feel. Or know what was expected. My legs felt so weak—I was breathless and boneless and relying on him to hold me up.

Soon I was too far gone to form words.

He leaned toward my ear. "Time to come again."

He ground into me, hips twisting to bring maximum pleasure.

Letting go, I let myself become his completely, surrendering to the pleasure surging through my being—onward to the heights of ecstasy.

Hips striking aggressively, he emptied himself inside me and I felt a sudden warmth, cherishing our consummation.

He leaned against me as though needing a moment to catch his breath. We remained like this, joined, trying to catch the air in our lungs and steady our racing pulses.

When he withdrew, I felt bereft from the loss, as though he'd withdrawn more than just his cock, but something that connected us deeper.

Something intangible.

I turned to face him, maybe to hear words of solace or receive assurance that I'd given him all he needed. And I needed to see his expression. See that he, too, was changed forever.

I glimpsed a flash of kindness in him before he retreated behind that impenetrable wall.

He tucked himself away.

Then he eased my breasts back into their cups, my nipples feeling overly sensitive. He took my face in both hands and leaned in to kiss my lips.

I closed my eyes and waited for his mouth to press against mine.

Then nothing…

Shay broke away and kneeled, looking up at me. "I will make sure you have your erotic adventure." His tongue began circling my clit.

"Thank you, sir," I said breathlessly.

I wondered why he'd changed his mind about kissing me.

"Promise me one thing."

"Anything." I swooned at the way he'd clamped his mouth against my sex and suckled, drawing in my clit and pulsing it with a rhythmic tension.

Oh, God, it was lavish and sweet and intense. My mind began to drift, and then the ripples of an orgasm washed over me—an overwhelming rush of sensations.

Finally, he broke away. "Don't fall in love while you're here."

Don't fall in love?

Had he not seen the way I look at him? Or the way I responded to his touch? Or did he not remember he'd been the one to grant me access?

I owed him everything.

"I'll try not to," I replied, my voice shaky.

How could he not know I'd already fallen hard?

"If you find yourself feeling that way," he added, "tell me, so that I can make other arrangements."

"Other arrangements?"

Even the thought of it sent me reeling. But if he was trying to distract me with his talented mouth, he was succeeding.

He'd nestled back in, continuing as though those words hadn't been spoken. Licking and flicking me there, his tongue strumming me into oblivion.

Moaning through another orgasm, I collapsed, trembling, leaning against Shay, clinging to him and yearning for the sensation never to cease.

He pushed to his feet and towered over me. "Such a filthy whore."

Yet in his arms I felt adored and beautiful and sexy as hell.

"I'll be monitoring your progress," he said.

Wouldn't he be watching my progress?

A knock at the door startled me.

Shay pulled his jacket off the table and covered me with it, holding it around me as though assuming whoever was there might stroll on in.

"Yes?" he called out impatiently.

Dominic appeared in the doorway and headed toward the table. He was carrying a mug.

"One Tempest coffee." He set the mug down on a coaster. "As requested."

Dominic snatched his fountain pen off the table and glanced down at the contract. He stared at it for a beat. Then whipped the form up and carried it with him toward the door. "I'll await your decision then," he said sternly.

"Yes, Dominic, you will," said Shay.

Dominic turned and gave a low bow.

"Is the library available?" asked Shay.

"It is," he said.

Turning his back on us, Dominic walked out the door.

That same wall I'd tried to breach before came back up to surround Shay.

I tried to comprehend his pain.

"We need to get you out of this bodice and back into the submissive uniform. There should be no special treatment for you." He seemed to bristle with annoyance.

He was referring to what I'd been dressed in when I'd first arrived—that strappy number that revealed everything.

"You're no different than them," he added.

"I know, sir." Even as I replied I felt the stab of his cruelty. "I just want to please you."

"Then why aren't you on your knees?"

I lowered myself to the ground and stared up at him.

"Follow me." He walked toward the door.

CHAPTER NINETEEN

Rue

"**G**OT EVERYTHING YOU NEED?" ASKED DOMINIC.

"I'm fine," I said, taking another look around the library. "Does every submissive start here?"

"Everyone has a different path. Clearly, the powers that be believe these books will be helpful."

I moved toward the coffee table and picked a book off the top of the pile, *The Power of Now* by Eckhart Tolle.

I'd already been given reading material before I'd arrived. This could be done another time.

"When will I join the others?" I asked.

"Soon, I imagine." Dominic wasn't good at lying.

They were trying to keep me busy until Shay got back. That much was obvious.

"If you need anything just say so, dear."

Dominic left, closing the door quietly behind him.

I collapsed on the sofa, still reeling from what Shay had just done to me in the breakfast room. The aggressive fucking he'd given me over the table—it was like all his feelings were vented in one show of power.

Still feeling boneless, I shuddered through the residual pleasure. The world felt safe for the first time I could remember.

I was staying. That much was obvious.

There were so many pleasures waiting for me on the other side of that door.

I couldn't wait for Shay to return.

But being given a distraction until he returned wasn't so bad. This was one of the swankiest libraries I'd ever seen. Wall to wall dark wooden shelves were filled with books of every description, along with a few first editions.

The relaxed atmosphere was comforting. A lit fireplace crackled with orange flames; occasional sparks bursting out onto the hearth.

The warmth felt soothing. I relaxed on the cozy couch, surrounded by high-backed armchairs. Rugs covered the floor here and there, giving the space an eclectic feel with both masculine and feminine touches. A low hanging crystal chandelier sprayed sparkles of light from delicate glass droplets.

I was pretty sure I'd find some erotic literature in here, too, if I had more time to explore.

Suddenly I had an eerie feeling like I was being watched.

My gaze snapped toward the doorway.

A visceral sensation.

A tall, handsome man almost filled the doorway with his broad shoulders. His intense stare couldn't be ignored. Ripped jeans and a T-shirt downplayed the wealth his Rolex gave away.

He smirked. "So, this is where the exotic little sparrow is hiding?"

"Sir?"

I noticed he was wearing a wedding ring.

"You must be Rue."

Uneasiness slithered up my spine. Maybe it was the way he

was looking at me or the fact he knew my name. He oozed an intensity that reminded me of Shay.

"I'm Jake." He closed the door behind him.

My heart skipped a beat.

The infamous De Sade was walking toward me—the man who made all other sadists look tame. His reputation was gossiped about by many submissives I knew.

This was the man Shay had once dated, apparently.

De Sade came closer, gesturing for me to remain seated. "How's the book?"

"Haven't started it yet."

His smile widened and I knew in that moment why Shay had fallen for him. Jake had an easy charm and a confident swagger.

I hoped he kept his distance.

I didn't want any part of his brand of agony that others sought out. They called him De Sade, after the Marquis de Sade, a French nobleman from the seventeen hundreds who was into an equal measure of philosophy and perversion with gold standard pain.

This De Sade was now dangerously close to me. "Scared to explore?"

"I'm not scared."

"Let me guess. This is Gardner's way of keeping you busy while he's away." He winked.

"I don't mind." I pointed to the books on the table. "They look interesting."

"Yeah, but you can read them at home, right?"

"Master Shay will be back soon."

"Am I making you nervous?" It seemed to please him.

"I know who you are."

He raised his hands to gesture he'd keep his distance.

I pulled my legs up and hugged them, and then realized how vulnerable it made me look.

"You're the nurse?" He sat on the arm of a chair. "You are very pretty."

"Thank you."

"Is your hair natural?"

"Yes…and my pubes match if you're wondering."

"I was wondering about that, yes. Though I was polite enough not to order you to show me."

"You're not my master."

"And who holds that distinguished title, Rue?" He gave me a lazy smile.

"Master Gardner."

He tucked his tongue in his cheek as though he knew something I didn't. Then his expression turned hard. "If I order you to do anything, Rue, you will do it. Do you understand?"

"Yes, sir."

"Are you sure we're clear about that?"

"Yes, sir," I said. "Because your reputation precedes you."

He smiled again. "I'm intrigued. What do you know about me?"

"Not much." I threw in for his ego's sake, "You're a retired quarterback. Apparently, you were a rock star in your day."

"You make me sound old."

"How's your wife?"

He inhaled sharply. "Fine, thank you for asking."

"Was it the right decision to go back to her?"

"You're a spitfire. I like that." His focus intensified. "It would give me something to work with. If you were mine."

"I belong to Master Gardner."

He gave a slow, steady nod. "Sure about that?"

"Yes."

"At some point he will deliver you into the very competent hands of another Dom. I want you to be prepared."

"Maybe it was just you."

He rubbed his face as though tired of the conversation, or maybe he was tired of Shay's crap.

"Something wrong?" I asked.

"How many times has he backed out from training you?"

I reached for my teacup and took a sip. "We're just starting out."

"You don't have to do this."

"Do what?"

"I heard there are a couple of Doms willing to own you. Want me to bring them in?"

"Why are you saying this?"

"Because I care about Gardner. I also care about you. I want to see him happy. I want to see *you* flourish. If you're unsure you can handle his lack of affection, then it's better to back out now."

"We've already agreed."

"On?"

"There won't be an emotional attachment."

He looked amused, shaking his head.

"I'm fine with it," I added.

De Sade caressed his chin thoughtfully. "How does that make you feel?"

"Doesn't matter. It's what he wants."

"That's what he *thinks* he wants."

"Are you suggesting you take me on?" I held my breath, terrified of the answer—and cursing myself for asking.

"Have you ever passed out due to pain?"

"No."

"Would you like to?"

"No."

"Then you'd be a bad fit for me as your Dom."

I exhaled slowly. "Men like you get a kick out of scaring subs like me."

"And what are you like?"

"It's in my file."

"You're asking for the extreme, I imagine?"

"How would you know?"

"I'm a good judge."

"I have to read this." I pointed to the book that lay open by my side. "Before he gets back."

"Is that my cue to leave?"

I cringed inwardly at how badly this had gone. This man had influence here and I was making an enemy of him.

Being the enemy of a self-proclaimed sadist was never a good thing.

De Sade rose off the chair and came closer, towering over me. His presence made the room shrink—and spin.

"I'm here for you, Rue. I know what it's like to fly too close to the sun."

His cologne reached me; something dark and mysterious with deadly undertones so damn alluring. Discreetly, I inhaled another whiff of him as though under his spell.

If Satan had a twin, it would be De Sade.

"I'm here strictly for Chrysalis training," I said. "Not to get involved with anyone. Not like that."

"Look at me. Now tell me you don't want to feel *his* affection?"

I tore my gaze away from his and tried to convince myself this wasn't important. That being in this place was what I wanted more than anyone in it.

Even though Shay had a way of making me feel special, like he and I were connected on a deeper level. It felt as though he had already stolen a part of me. His passion for life matched my own in every conceivable way.

But I knew...*knew* that my being in this room and Shay not being here was the answer I'd feared. Tears stung as I realized that this was what De Sade was trying to tell me.

I peered up at him, trying to hide my pain—hiding a feeling of dread that he was right.

He smirked. "That's what I thought."

"You thought what?"

"You showed Shay how much you need him. That was the beginning of the end."

"You want him back? Is that it?"

He looked surprised. "I'm not that much of a sadist."

My face flushed brightly.

"Though I will say this, once Shay knows he can trust you, you'll have his loyalty." He looked thoughtful. "If he gives you more, cling to those moments. They don't last." De Sade stepped back and headed for the door. "If you need anything, little sparrow, I'll be around."

"I've never needed anything from anyone," I called after him.

De Sade paused after opening the door, turning to look back at me, his gaze sweeping over me one final time.

And then he left.

I slumped back against the sofa as though I'd been hit by a lightning bolt.

I knew if De Sade couldn't keep a man like Shay, I didn't stand a chance.

CHAPTER TWENTY

Shay

I MADE IT BACK TO CHRYSALIS IN RECORD TIME.

Having Rue there waiting for me felt exhilarating. I may not be a permanent fixture in her life, but we could explore a few of her fantasies—activities that would take my mind off these chaotic thoughts.

I'd self-analyzed and with some introspection felt prepared to give her over to another man for pleasure—because that's what she'd asked for in her file. The specifics a turn on for any red-blooded Dom.

Taking her this morning in the breakfast room was the first time I'd been able to find some sense of peace in months. That was worth holding onto for a while.

A day or two, maybe.

Right up until the moment I'd have to let Rue disappear into the heart of her fantasies. Chrysalis was the place where erotic dreams came true.

She would fit right in.

I'd have her fitted for a new bodice for the ball—something

spectacular. I'd never been more thrilled to show off a submissive as exquisite as her.

She'd never be mine, but we could play for a while.

Rue was by all accounts settling well into Chrysalis. Soon, she would be exposed to the hard-core activities that went on behind closed doors...the kind she wanted—a new level of debauchery.

Those filthy games were always enthralling.

For the rest of the day, I'd focus on *her* entirely.

Prepare her for more.

My team was keeping this place safe; although I still micro-managed. I'd hired the best and they had security covered—which meant I could indulge.

Strolling through the foyer, I glanced up at the hidden cameras. They weren't in every room, but there were enough of them to monitor the movements of those inside. I'd replay the footage later and check to make sure our submissives were obeying the rules.

I headed down the hallway, and my back went stiff when I saw him.

Jake was leaving the library. My gut tightened in response.

He'd been in there.

With *her.*

He saw me. There wasn't even a hint of guilt on his devilishly handsome face. A surge of jealousy rushed through me as I walked toward him. That he'd even considered approaching Rue.

I stood in front of him to cut him off.

Jake looked too damn relaxed for someone who'd just violated my wishes.

He raised his hands in defense. "It's not what it looks like."

"You talked with her?"

"I was checking on Rue, yes."

"Dominic's watching over her. I have it covered."

"I wanted to make sure she's settling in."

"What did you tell her, Jake?"

"Honest answer?"

"You have no right to interfere."

"I care about you. This is me making sure you don't mess things up again."

"Again?" I seethed.

"Yes. Now if you'll excuse me." He turned to walk away.

I grabbed his bicep. "What do you want?"

"For you to be happy, Shay. That's all." He looked down at my hand on his arm.

"I don't want you near her." I released my grip. "We all know your brand of fuckery is an acquired taste."

"Nothing sinister went on in there."

"You better not have touched her."

"Fuck off." He banged my shoulder as he continued down the hallway.

"I know what you're like," I called after him.

Jake pivoted. "You pushed me away. Don't you dare pretend otherwise."

"You went back to your ex."

"Rylee and I worked through our differences. That much is true. Things are good…considering the circumstances."

"You walked out on me."

"Because you wouldn't let me in, Shay."

"Not true."

"I know this place is important to you, but you put it above everyone, including yourself and your own needs. You can't continue like this."

Chrysalis was my life. These were my people. I continued to mull over the facts as I stared him down. "I gave you everything."

"Your 'everything' is compromised."

"You seem to enjoy the security I bring to this place. It gives you the freedom to be a sadist."

His brows shot up. "Until you see what *you are* you'll always be broken."

"You just come out and say it, don't you?" I felt a stab of fury. "You have no filter, Jake."

"Something happened on that mission south of Kabul. You need to talk to Henry about it. He was there."

"Nothing happened." I stepped back. "It all blends together anyway."

"You need to tell someone. Let it out."

"Let what out?"

"Whatever it was that changed you."

Gesturing my frustration, I raised my hands. "Everyone came back changed. I'm no different."

"You are."

That would have shaken me if it were true.

"I'm sure Cole would have mentioned it by now," I shot back.

"He probably knows you're a lost cause."

Is this what everyone thought of me? Someone who couldn't be fixed to their level of acceptable?

"You never knew me," I said.

"That's just it, I knew you too well." De Sade softened his tone. "Look, when a quarterback takes the field, he needs his teammates—"

"This isn't a sports metaphor, is it?" I hated those. "Anyway, I was a SEAL. We take camaraderie to the next level."

He sighed. "Look, what I'm saying is…the game of life can't be won alone."

My shoulders dropped as I mused over his ability to get through to me.

"Some introspection might be useful." He pointed at me. "And never knock a sports metaphor."

"Just tell me you're okay," I said softly.

"I miss you, but I can't look back. I can't go back to feeling starved of…" He let his words trail off, a pained expression on his face.

"I gave as much as I could."

"The person you're with deserves all of you."

I didn't want to deal with this now.

My afternoon was tainted; he always had this way of bringing me down.

"Rue's too special to be ruined," he threw in.

"You don't think I know that?"

"You know she's desperate for love."

"She told you that?"

"Didn't need to…I can read it all over her."

"She's been briefed on what to expect."

"Seems like you're trying to instigate what you think is best for her while ignoring her desires."

"And how would you know that?"

"End it. Give her to Grantchester or someone who can fulfill her needs."

Fuck him and his opinion, even if I was about to lead her on.
Lead her into bliss.

Wasn't that enough?

My gut twisted at the thought he might be right. I'd planned a perverted afternoon with her that would leave us both sated.

But it was nothing close to what Rue was asking for.

"I'll always love you," he called back. "No matter how much I hate you." The charming smile he gave me was his way of defusing the moment and proving his point.

He always needed to have the last word.

Although the built-in variety of two switches seeing each other is naturally enticing, in my experience when rolls weren't consistently defined, a relationship would soon find itself on rocky ground.

I watched him go.

Then I turned my attention to the library door, beyond which I'd find Rue. Maybe she would be reading a book. Maybe she was holding on to the hope we'd become more.

I reached for the doorknob, and then paused without turning it.

If I joined her in there and reset in motion what we began this morning, I'd be causing more heartache.

I didn't want to go in and see De Sade's truth in Rue's demeanor or have anything to do with the emotion that killed my desire. That useless one called love.

Hurting that young woman would be the worst thing I'd ever done.

And I'd done some terrible things.

Because of that, I'd kept myself so closed off Jake had felt locked out. Letting someone in was more daunting than warfare.

My grip slipped off the doorknob.

I walked away.

CHAPTER TWENTY-ONE

I'D SAT IN THE LIBRARY FOR HOURS TRYING TO READ AND HAD been unable to see the words—because all thoughts returned to *him*.

De Sade had tried to warn me, tried to get me to see reality.

A sob shook me to my core.

Shay had put me in here but wasn't following through.

He wasn't coming back.

I couldn't figure out why.

Pulling back on my emotions, I forced myself to calm down, not wanting anyone to see me like this. Being tearful on my first day would embarrass everyone and probably get me sent home.

Maybe I was still in the library because they were deciding what to do with me.

After pushing up from the couch, I realized there was nothing but grey ash in the hearth. It had died right in front of me.

I'd not even noticed when the last flame went out.

Bringing my pile of books with me, I carried them through the house, heading over to where I'd started this morning—the dining room. It was a reasonable place to look for Shay since it was lunchtime.

The private dining room was empty.

The table had not even been set for a meal. Peering forlornly out the window and looking beyond into the garden, I saw someone splashing in the oversized pool. A man wearing swimming goggles was cutting through the water.

Him.

I felt anger well up in me. He'd been out there the entire time.

Unlocking the glass door, I carried my books toward the edge of the pool and watched a naked Shay swim down the center using the butterfly stroke. Toned and muscular, his impressive body looked taut and tantalizing. A tattoo marked his right shoulder—a large bird over a trident.

He was a water Adonis snatching air, turning his head sharply from side to side, repeating this method as he swam fast and strong to the end, then flipping and swimming back to the other side.

He'd thrown his clothes on a lounge chair before diving in, setting his shoes and socks beside it. A towel waited for him. His dip in the pool had been planned.

He knew I'd been in that dreary library all this time, waiting for him. Yet he'd chosen to ignore that fact.

Ignore me, because clearly I was not his submissive.

Lifting one of the books from the pile in my arms, I flung it across the water at his head.

It barely missed him.

Shay stopped swimming, treading water, and stared at me. He eased his goggles up, sliding them to his forehead.

Got your attention now.

The next book I threw splashed a foot away from him.

He looked at me like I was insane. "What the fuck!"

That didn't stop me from throwing another. The book splashed and sunk.

"Stop that!" he yelled.

"I know what you're doing!" I shouted.

"Rue, stop it. Or I will—"

"Punish me? You're not around long enough to have any lasting consequence."

"I can see you're upset, so let's talk about this."

"Upset?" I held up the last book for him to see. "This one is signed."

"Carl Jung! Don't you dare!"

"You should have thought twice before ghosting me."

"I'm protecting you!"

"I don't need protecting. I need to be fucked...hard. I need what I came here for—immersion, bondage, S&M. The whole thing..."

"Rue, I'm serious."

I leaned over the edge of the pool. "Promise me you will deliver everything I am asking for. Or the book gets it." I raised it high.

He swam toward me and looked up. "We can discuss this."

"The time for talk is over."

"I will spank your ass until it's raw if you throw it."

I started to hurl it over his head.

"Whatever you want!" he yelled.

I lowered the book. "Don't lie."

Shay swam toward the metal stairs and ascended them swiftly. Then he padded toward me with a masterful swagger, water dripping off his impressive body, his cock half erect. That tattoo looked even more intriguing.

He held out his hand for the book.

"Say it," I demanded softly.

"Give me the fucking book." He snatched it from me.

Swallowing hard, I felt his rage like a burn that would scorch me—the kind that would leave scars. It was the kind of pain my flesh yearned for.

He looked fierce. "The punishment for this is extreme. Are you aware of that?"

"Yes, sir."

He stepped closer and reached around my waist, dragging me toward him. My chest struck against his hard, his heat burning through me. His grip on me was verging on painful.

His gaze held mine. "Your fantasies are for a more experienced submissive."

"I'm ready."

"Tell me you know what you're asking for."

"I do."

"Ask me flat out for it."

"I want what they do at Hillenbrand."

His expression became thoughtful. "Say it."

"I want to."

"Say it."

"It's in my file."

"Your file is gone."

"It's difficult to articulate."

I felt a stab of pain as he buried his hand in my hair and pulled my head back, his lips close to mine, his breath on my mouth.

"Still not convinced, Rue."

Being this close to him, feeling his body pressed against mine, I dared to hold his gaze, seeing right into his soul, past the tough guy attitude. I saw the man no one could touch, no one could hurt. That's what he tried to project, but I saw through that wall he had built around himself, right through to the other side.

I saw him.

His arrogance started to fade because he was showing how much he cared. That was his Achilles heel and he thought no one knew. It would have been easy for him to throw me into the scene, savor my fall into the pit of debauchery. Yet Shay held on to me, held me back, unsure if I truly wanted what I was asking for.

The hero behind the mask. A side he kept hidden.

"I don't want to be the man who causes you regret," he said quietly, as though realizing I could see the truth about him.

"I'll go back to Pendulum," I threatened, wanting him to throw his sense of responsibility away with those scattering leaves caught in the breeze, swirling around us with their autumn dance.

"They won't have you back," he said.

I was waiting for a kiss.

His lips hovered close to mine, as though he was teetering on the edge of pressing his mouth against mine and binding us together.

"You brought me this far," I said bitterly.

"You consent to me orchestrating your time here?"

"Yes." I was breathless.

"You consent to going beyond your fantasies?"

"Beyond?"

"Yes, Rue. I will take you farther than you have ever gone. That's why you're here, right? To be pushed over the brink?"

Tears stung my cheeks. Finally, someone saw me.

Understood what I needed.

He stepped back. "Meet me in the foyer in an hour. Wear something suitable for dinner at Imperial. Ever dined there?"

A rush of excitement flooded through me. "No, I've never been. I can wear the dress I wore to Enthrall. Will that do?"

"No panties."

"Yes, sir."

He gave a nod of approval. "We'll discuss your next session over dinner, and then go from there."

Shay walked away.

"Are you going to back out at the last second?" I called after him.

He turned to look at me. "The real question is...will you?"

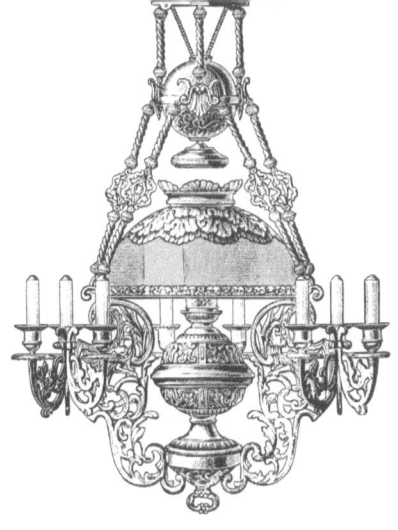

CHAPTER TWENTY-TWO

Shay

RUE WORE THE SAME DARK PINK DRESS I'D ADMIRED WHEN I'd taken her into Enthrall. The color complemented her sexy and sassy side.

As instructed, we'd met in the foyer of Chrysalis.

Her perfume wafted around me; the scent of submission.

She looked stunning waiting beneath our grand chandelier, those shards of light offering their blessing for what lay ahead.

Cole had thrown a million dollars at that central light fixture—and it looked like it, too. The thing was massive. It was the type you'd expect to see in a fancy hotel lobby. I still remembered the first time I'd walked in here and stood in awe, just staring up at it, waiting for Cole to appear.

He'd strolled toward me with arms open wide and a big welcoming smile and said, "What do you think? Not bad for your first day at work?"

It was his way of offering me the job.

And here I was, with another beautiful submissive before me, feeling like I'd always been part of this place.

Rue peered up at me with trust in her eyes.

Her ruby collar looked stunning.

I leaned in and kissed her forehead.

With Chrysalis, nothing was ever as it seemed. I glanced left down that long hallway, past the Harrington Suite and beyond Richard's office door, all the way down to those double doors and what lay secretly behind them.

The setting where all submissives were forbidden to go alone.

The place we'd return to soon.

She'd flourish there.

But first, this...

I escorted her out the front door.

Once inside the chauffeur driven limo, I'd placed a blindfold on the exquisite submissive, temporarily under my command.

Observing the way Rue went into subspace was a new kind of pleasure; seeing her completely surrender as she sat upright on the back seat, listening for my next command.

She had to be curious about our destination.

Thinking too much about our situation was a mistake. It wasn't about me. Or what I wanted or needed. It was merely me fulfilling a promise.

She could never be mine.

And, by the end of this, we would know who best fit the role of master for her by observing who she had chemistry with and how the Doms responded to her as well.

Sitting back, I studied Rue, her large breasts and curves emphasizing her femininity. Her hands rested in her lap.

I admired the many facets of Rue Asher, from talented surfer to competent professional who knew what it felt like to save a life.

A sensual goddess.

So many would get to appreciate her.

It would be selfish to get in the way of that.

I savored the journey that had us driving along the freeway, the limo picking up speed only to encounter that familiar slow crawl of L.A. traffic.

The driver had been instructed which exit to take off the freeway, the destination given to him before we'd left Chrysalis.

Within the car, music blasted from hidden speakers to set the dreamy mood; *Heaven Or Las Vegas* by The Cocteau Twins.

The time for questions was over.

When we arrived at our destination, I got out first, guiding Rue. She remained blindfolded. I rested my palm on the top of her head to protect her as she climbed out of the car.

Halfway along the path, Rue hesitated; no doubt feeling self-conscious that others may see her wearing a blindfold—see exactly what she was from her ruby collar.

With a firm hand, I insisted she keep walking. She gripped my arm as I led her forward, and I could tell she was listening out for others, listening for clues to where we were.

This was merely two friends having an evening of fine dining and good conversation.

Once we made it through the front door and were standing within the restaurant foyer, I whipped off Rue's blindfold, tucking it into my jacket pocket.

She blinked, adjusting to our surroundings, and then blushed wildly when she saw we were mere feet from the maître d'.

He'd caught our dramatic entrance but was polite enough not to react, gesturing for us to follow him.

Rue seemingly remained in subspace, even as we took our first steps into the dining room filled with guests, who were enjoying their Michelin chef meals while sipping cocktails.

Heads turned to look at her—Rue's beauty was that captivating.

A relationship would never have worked out between us in a permanent agreement. Someone this striking would end up belonging to an elite Dom. Their wealth and position would seduce her eventually, even if Cole tried to convince me otherwise.

The wealthy VIPs would end up stealing her away.

Keeping my heart closed was all I had to do for now—and keep Rue from going to Hillenbrand.

That was the plan.

With Rue's hand in mine, we followed the maître d around and between the tables. Wealthy guests dined in the center and around the edge of the room were generously sized booths seating those who wanted a little more privacy.

Even though I'd never met a woman like Rue who matched my ferocity for kink, I couldn't keep her all to myself.

That much was true.

She might be the only woman I knew who needed to explore her exhibitionism as much as me—a healthy obsession safe to explore at Chrysalis.

For anyone who dared to go that far.

Rue looked at me inquisitively as though asking, "*Why here? Why this fancy restaurant?*"

My fingers brushed against her flushed cheek. "I like the wine here at Imperial."

Honestly, I loved everything about this place.

My favorite Parisian-inspired dining room reflected grandeur and oozed opulence. From the luxurious Louis XV Rococo chairs and tables to the fine linen tablecloths, to the surrounding mirrored walls that reflected the guests.

Everyone came here for a fine-dining experience and dressed accordingly—the men in tuxedos and the women in elegant gowns or cocktail dresses.

It was a perfect place to bring Rue.

"This is lovely," she said, snuggling against me.

All the tension seemed to drain from her, her shoulders relaxing and her breathing returning to normal.

She was finally letting her guard down.

Conversations flowed around us, some in foreign languages, the clientele reflecting society's elite.

I kept my focus on Rue, gesturing for her to slide into the booth ahead of me. I joined her, settling behind the table with my back to the wall so I could view the entire place.

I smiled and tucked a strand of hair behind her ear. She was special and I wanted her to feel that way.

Our waiter appeared and handed us the wine list. I chose a vintage I thought she might like.

"Chardonnay," I said, pointing to the expensive bottle I would not have to pay for.

It would be both sweet and tart, a perfect blend.

We took our time studying the entrées.

Rue ran her finger along the menu. "This looks great."

I set my menu down and faced her. "When did you first discover you were into kink?"

She leaned back, seeming to think about it. "I went for older men because they were more experienced."

"Then you discovered Majestic?" I said.

"A friend mentioned she'd heard of the place. I pretended to be shocked, and then secretly applied."

She'd joined others who found a way to go deeper into the lifestyle, which was how she fell into training with Faulkner.

"How about you?" she asked.

"I assumed my exhibitionism was a fantasy never to be explored." I sighed to express my old frustration. "Until I came to Chrysalis as part of their security team. I was on duty at a party one night, jealous of everyone having an incredible time."

"You saw…things?"

"Everything you can imagine. The next day I approached Cole and asked to join as a member."

"He let you in?"

"Not immediately. I had to observe sessions with submissives first. Then, after that, I was given an honorary membership."

"Because it's expensive."

"I could afford it on what they pay me. I naturally fell into the lifestyle, and never looked back."

"I love that."

My fingers tapped the menu absentmindedly. "You were approached by De Sade in the library?"

"We talked a while."

"About?"

"He didn't tell me anything I didn't already know." She shook her head, amused. "How bad is a session with him?"

"He's a sadist. You'll leave a session with a permanent reminder of the experience."

"Like a scar?"

"He would call it a badge of honor."

"Where's yours?"

I arched a brow. "We don't talk about the details."

"Why?"

"It's forbidden." I lifted her chin. "If I were to leave a mark on you, where would you like it?"

"I'm drawn to jewelry…down there. I saw it in *Story of O*."

Just as I'd seen it on Carrie Quinn, Rue's Domina.

"A piercing?" I gave a nod. "That's extreme."

"With your initials on it."

I'd not expected that—Rue announcing her thoughts so blatantly.

It made my dick hard at the idea of having my name engraved into her labia ring, the kind of silver piece that proved ownership.

Still, we never went that far at Chrysalis.

To hide these arousing ruminations, I shrugged it off.

"Too much for you?" she teased.

Maybe one day I'd share with her how far I personally liked to go. What kind of kink I enjoyed. Maybe even share my sacred memories of the scene.

She licked her lips, meeting my gaze. "You're meant to choose my meal."

Just as her master would have.

My devilish nature rose to the challenge. "What other things should I be doing, Ms. Asher?"

"You can touch me?" She waggled her eyebrows.

"Your pretty cunt?"

"Shush." She blushed wildly.

"That's very daring, Rue."

She let out a sigh, the kind that hinted at boredom.

"We can do better," I said sternly.

Did the minx really have no idea what we were capable of here?

I looked toward the booth opposite of where we were sitting.

An elegant young couple was enjoying dinner. The dashing guy was dressed in a tuxedo and the stunning brunette beside him wore a formal gown. I imagined they'd come straight from the theatre. Or maybe this evening meant something special to them, perhaps a celebration. They certainly looked like they were into each other, having an intimate conversation while sipping champagne.

"Do you know them?" Rue looked intrigued.

I accepted the shallow sample of Chardonnay set on the table by our waiter. Swirling my glass, I then tasted the sweet wine and gestured that the bottle would do.

The waiter poured two large glasses for us and, seeing my nod, he walked away, heading back into the kitchen.

Rue was still studying the couple opposite. "What about them?"

They briefly glanced our way and then returned their focus on each other, two lovers enraptured. An artist would fall over himself to capture this cultivated vision.

"Crawl over to them on your hands and knees," I said to her, my tone dark. "Take a sip from his champagne. After you've gotten his attention, go beneath the table and pleasure him."

Rue's smile faded as she realized this was a command.

I glanced at my watch. "You have ten minutes to make him come. Then return to me."

"Now?" she asked, wide-eyed.

"Starting now, yes."

She seemed to consider her options. "What about his girlfriend?"

"We're down to nine minutes and forty-five seconds."

"Why are you doing this?"

"Why are you doing this, *sir*," I answered sharply.

"Sir."

"You wanted Hillenbrand. I've brought Hillenbrand to you."

"But this is L.A. You're going to get us thrown out."

"In that case, you will have failed."

"What happens then? You'll drive me home?" she said bitterly.

"Either you obey, or you don't."

"And if I don't?"

I glanced at my watch again, at the second-hand dragging time along with it.

"Comply. Or you won't meet the deadline."

CHAPTER TWENTY-THREE

MAYBE THIS WAS A PUNISHMENT FOR ME THREATENING to throw Carl Jung's book into the pool. Okay, it was a collector's item, but I never would have done it. I loved books too much. He didn't know that, though. How could he? We'd hardly spent any time together.

Shay was asking me to do something exhilarating and filthy and daring and all kinds of wrong.

It wasn't that he hadn't chosen someone who was devastatingly gorgeous. The thirty-something looked like he'd stepped off the cover of *GQ*. And the woman beside him was just as stunning.

They were glamorously intimidating.

He looked like a young Marlon Brando, all moody and handsome with an aura of unpredictability. She looked like a vintage princess, perfectly made-up with a flawless dark-skinned complexion and flowing hair.

Shay's demeanor had now become intimidating.

As soon as I stood up to make my way over to them, he'd

probably grab my wrist and pull me down. Maybe give me a dashing smile.

Though right now there was no sign of him changing his mind.

He was apparently waiting to see what I'd do, leaning back against the booth as his fingers trailed through his beard, possibly trying to imagine the scene.

Scanning the restaurant's patrons, I imagined what they would do when they saw me under the man's table.

Shay gestured to the waiter. "I'll tell him we're leaving."

"No." I rested my hand on his.

He was threatening to cancel dinner. Cancel me. I hadn't come this far to fail this early by tripping over my own gudddffear.

I had nothing to lose.

I wasn't brave enough to crawl—not in front of this type of crowd, even though it had been an order. That alone would draw immediate attention.

Elegantly, I rose and edged out of the booth, glancing back at Shay, making sure there was no doubt in his mind that he wanted me to perform an elicit act on a stranger.

His focus returned to Brando across from us.

I began walking slowly toward them.

Such an act—one I hadn't decided if I was going to commit— was socially forbidden. Yet I couldn't help considering it.

All I had to do was look into that man's soul to see if this was something he'd like. Something he might be into.

My adrenaline spiked. It felt like the rush you get before the roller coaster thrusts you down the first drop at a million miles per hour.

Glancing at their table settings, I could see they hadn't ordered their food yet.

The woman beside him stared back with curiosity. I weighed the chance she was about to throw her drink at me.

Or worse.

Far fucking worse.

I'd deserve it, too.

Leaving was an option. Walking away and waiting for Shay to join me outside. I had no idea where we were. We'd driven here with me blindfolded. I could be in the Hollywood Hills or somewhere in West Hollywood.

Someone might take a photo.

I'd never be able to return to this restaurant again.

Or even the planet.

I glanced around.

No one was looking my way.

I reached for Brando's glass and brought it to my lips, taking a delicate sip. He stared at me, not reacting. Up close his rare beauty was disarming, and hers was too. She had elegant features—high cheekbones and full lips. Gold eye shadow complemented her warm brown eyes.

Should I say something?

Ask his permission? Ask hers?

Offer myself?

The rush I was feeling was heady.

Hell, I'd come this far.

I sank onto my hands and knees and crawled beneath the table, my heart pounding with panic. Yet some part of me felt this was as natural as breathing.

My master had ordered it—therefore it would be done.

Underneath the table, I crawled closer to him, resting my hands on his knees, hoping he didn't kick me.

He widened his legs, causing me to pause. *This was happening.*

Kneeling between his open thighs, I reached for his zipper, prepared for when his hands came down fast on mine to stop me.

When that didn't happen, I slid his zipper down—again, expecting a reaction. I expected that woman to kick me away, or at least scream at me.

She was the ultimate threat to this intimate moment, and she deserved to be. This was her man, and I was doing the unthinkable.

At that moment, I hated Shay for putting me through this.

As though rising from a dream, I became aware of the chattering guests around us and the sound of cutlery clanking against dishes—the normal sounds of a busy restaurant. I heard no sounds indicating someone had caught me in the act.

That couldn't be possible.

Yet Brando was seemingly willing to let me take liberties.

Reaching into his pants, I drew his cock out and explored his length, admiring his girth, feeling him grow hard at my touch.

Heart racing, face flushed and body trembling, I leaned forward and ran the tip of my tongue around the head of his bulging erection, licking around his rim and feeling him swelling in my mouth.

Oh, my God. I was doing this in public.

My pulse was beating so fast it made me dizzy.

I took him deeper into my mouth until he was at the back of my throat, until all I knew was this—everything else had disappeared.

I'd obeyed my master.

Doing as he'd asked felt delicious.

My pussy throbbed with pleasure. If I touched myself, I knew I'd be wet.

But that had not been the order.

The command from my master was to have this stranger climax, to come in my mouth and not cease until that had been achieved.

Perfecting the rhythm, I was taking him as far as I could go, feeling his tip bash against my throat, sighing when he gripped my hair and controlled my pace. He was encouraging me to finish this rare gift, to go faster; wanting more from me, more of *this*.

Conscious of the timeframe, I sped up.

Head bobbing, I felt grateful for the partial shield of the tablecloth.

The shuddering of his legs hinted he was close, a small groan as he edged toward bliss. His rich cologne invaded my nostrils;

a heady scent of masculinity and something else. Something expensive.

"Don't spill a drop," said his girlfriend, her voice as soft and smooth as velvet, anointing me with permission.

This made me shudder with arousal and I was flooded with a stark joy that caused my flesh to ignite.

She wanted this for him, too.

Brando became rigid against me, his thigh muscles firm, and then I felt a slight tremble run through him. Using my hand in unison with my mouth, I aimed to deliver the best blow job he'd ever experienced, sucking so hard I'd send him into oblivion.

Accepting everything he gave me, I drank him down, swallowing as the warmth flowed and flowed until I'd drained him until his thighs ceased their trembling.

I wiped my mouth, hands shaking as I began to come down from my adrenaline rush. I'd pleased him. Pleased them both.

Gently and respectfully, I returned Brando's cock to his pants and zipped him back up.

Preparing to face all those people who might have caught the wayward guest doing the unthinkable, I eased out from beneath the tablecloth and stood, taking a look around.

No one was staring at me.

Diners continued their conversations, continued to savor their food seemingly unaware of the erotic scene that had played out in their midst.

Brando gave me a nod of approval, his soft smile hinting he was more relaxed, having been given the ultimate sensual gift. The beauty by his side played with the hair at his nape. She gazed at him with adoration in her eyes. Having allowed me to perform this for him, it was as though she had shared in the sensual performance.

This could have been a gift to him from her.

The intimacy between all three of us felt pure.

"Well done," young Brando said huskily. "I'll have a bottle of champagne sent over."

"Thank you, sir."

I walked back over to Shay with my head held high.

With a nod, he invited me to sit beside him again.

Face flushed, heart slowing its frenetic beat, I looked around us to make sure there were no strange glances our way.

"I can't believe I just did that," I said, still high from the danger.

"I thought I told you to crawl," came Master Shay's chastisement.

"Sir, I wasn't sure—"

"Never fail an order again."

My clit ached deliciously. "No, sir, I won't." I reached for my glass of wine, taking a long sip as a chaser to steady my nerves.

Shay reached for my skirt and his palm slid toward my sex, his finger caressing me there, as though testing my wetness.

"You performed to your master's satisfaction. Other than failing to crawl, you did well." His fingers brushed the swollen tenderness, spiking my arousal.

I widened my thighs. "What do I get as my reward, sir?"

He removed his hand. My clit pined for his touch to return.

"How do you assess your performance?"

"I pleased the couple and I was obedient, sir." I'd risked everything to do what he'd ordered.

I could feel my face grow warm again. I didn't want to look that way now, to see Brando and his girlfriend having second thoughts about what I'd done.

Shay clicked his fingers to get my attention. "You were still disobedient."

"If I'd have crawled—"

The waiter placed an ice bucket on our table which held a bottle of champagne.

"From the gentleman, sir," he said, glancing to the booth opposite.

"Pour two glasses," Shay said to the waiter.

The man proceeded to pop the cork and then filled two flutes with golden champagne. It bubbled and sparkled in the tall, delicate glasses.

"You may go," Shay told him, handing me one of the flutes.

The waiter scurried off.

Shay could be savage. I saw that now, with each word and each gesture of authority.

He'd subdued me by proving my powerlessness.

How did I get away with giving head in the middle of a busy restaurant?

Maybe I hadn't.

Maybe everyone here was too embarrassed to look my way.

"Master, I want to please you. Show you I'm capable of anything you ask of me."

"I'm not sure that's true," Shay chided, taking a sip of champagne.

I'd more than earned that expensive drink for him.

"I know this much," I told him. "You won't ask anything of me I'm not capable of."

"Sure about that?"

What I'd done for him had left me needy and wanting, my sex wet and swollen. My thoughts carried me back to those intimate moments beneath the table, stirring me into a frenzy of quiet passion.

Shay expected me to eat a meal and sip champagne and continue as if nothing had happened.

"So that's it?" I joked.

He opened his palm and there lay a pair of Ben Wa balls in the center of his hand.

"Put this in," he said.

I was desperate for his touch, for his approval. For him to see my rebellion was merely me getting a reaction out of his cool demeanor.

I took the gift from him and lifted my hem, discreetly easing the balls inside me, using a fingertip to shimmy them in deeper.

My fingers came away wet from my arousal. I used a napkin to wipe them.

Shay watched me. "How does that feel?"

"Really good," I said, sinking into the sensation. "Thank you, sir."

"Aroused?"

"Yes, sir," I said breathlessly. "Of course."

"Desperate to come?"

"Yes, Master."

He looked toward the center of the room, at a table where four gorgeous men in tuxedoes sat having dinner. From the way they conversed, I could tell they were comfortable with each other. They were an intimidating collection of alphas oozing confidence.

"See the gentleman with the tattoo on his hand?"

"Do you know him?"

Oh, God. I sensed it before he spoke the words.

"Offer him dessert," he said.

I smirked at Shay. "From the menu?"

"Not from the menu, no."

My face blanched at his meaning. He meant me. I was dessert. More specifically, my pussy was on the menu.

"Can I invite him to the restroom?" I suggested.

"No, I wish to observe."

My gaze snapped to the men, then back to my master.

If climbing beneath a table in a popular restaurant wasn't daring enough, going over and doing what he was asking was impossible. "You're setting me up to fail this time."

He crossed his arms. "Or am I setting you up to fly?"

CHAPTER TWENTY-FOUR

E VEN THOUGH I HAD FANTASIZED ABOUT SOMETHING LIKE this, I couldn't bring myself to leave the bathroom.

I'd been in here for five minutes.

Instead of stopping at the table, I'd walked by it to the restroom.

My reflection in the bathroom mirror revealed my conflicted emotions—I silently pleaded with myself to trust in Shay, to let him guide me in this fantasy.

I can do it.

My imagination played out what going up to that table would feel like or even look like, lifting my hem and saying those words, offering a stranger the kind of act that was forbidden, as though I was driven by an unseen force.

Yes, I was vulnerable, yet at the same time I felt nudged toward the sexual freedom I craved. But when it came to carrying out my master's order, I hesitated.

Even as I doubted myself, I reached into my purse and removed my lipstick, gliding the makeup over my mouth, pouting my lips and plumping them; wanting to look pretty for the one I would offer myself to.

Was I brave enough?

Daring enough?

I was certainly horny enough.

The Ben Wa balls inside me felt divine.

How could those men not respond with shock? How could I not be shunned and shouted out of the restaurant?

Shay was right. It all came down to trust.

Wait.

He'd driven me here blindfolded. What was the reason? So I wouldn't see the entrance?

It wasn't like I hadn't just been reckless.

I had literally walked to the other side of the restaurant and climbed under another couple's table. Not one person had looked my way in surprise. In fact, perhaps that couple had responded with approval because they had been in on the fantasy.

Or was something else going on?

There was only one way to find out if this whole thing had been staged. It sure as hell looked that way.

I felt ready to face the erotic danger I craved—face the risk that could see me fall into the center of a scandal as I played out an erotic fantasy here at Imperial.

Perhaps the name was a dead giveaway.

Enthrall always put their submissives first. Protected them and worshipped them.

Always.

Maybe this was my initiation ceremony.

It wasn't like I'd not demanded this—threatening to throw that collector's item into the pool like I was having a tantrum.

Carrying out Shay's order would decide my future, decide whether or not I was good enough to be part of his elite circle.

I was about to put that theory to the test.

I checked my appearance one final time in the mirror to

make sure I was no longer disheveled from that under-the-table adventure.

My body tingled all over, feeling fully alive.

I left the bathroom and made a beeline for the table where the four men were sitting.

My breathing was rapid and my pulse was racing.

The one with the tattooed right hand was classically handsome, but looked like a gangster. He studied me intently, emanating a presence that would make anyone intrigued but scared.

What I was about to say would either rock his world or destroy mine.

I was about to become the centerpiece.

What if passers-by peered in through the wide window? Being blindfolded had meant I'd been unable to see if it was two-way glass.

I tried to read the expression of the one I was meant to impress, and looked to his friends for a clue that would give away if they'd been expecting me. They merely offered looks of curiosity.

I glanced over at Shay to see if he was about to leap out of the booth and stop me—or if he looked pleased at how far I'd taken this.

He gave a nod.

Oh, God, I'm going to do this.

Reaching for my hem, I lifted it up, slowly at first, and then raised it higher. Each of them had a clear view of my pussy. I squeezed the Ben Wa balls tight within me as though it would help. It didn't—it merely sent me reeling with arousal.

This was exhilarating.

I glanced around the restaurant to see if anyone was watching. Then I saw my reflection in the mirror—my skirt hoisted around my waist revealing everything. I looked pretty, but oh so slutty.

The room fell still.

A few guests turned our way.

Just breathe...

Heady from the champagne gifted by Brando, heady from this

exposure, I tried to read the faces at the table before me—looking for a sign that I had gone too far.

"Look at me," said the one with the tattooed hand.

Which was a favorable response, I suppose, though I had nothing to compare it to. No point of reference for how things should go when doing something like this.

"Dessert, sir," I said, offering myself.

"My favorite," he said huskily.

My sex tingled with surging pleasure and he hadn't even touched me yet.

If I was breaking any laws, then so be it. I was beyond caring at this point. I was about to shock the entire room. All I knew was this exquisite sensation from showing this stranger everything I had to offer.

A woman's voice said, "She's beautiful."

Someone else approved.

"Raise your hem higher."

When I obeyed, the man's tattooed hand reached for my clit, flicking it. That's all he did, rested a fingertip upon that small bud and rubbed it fast.

It hardened beneath his touch.

I felt a jolt of arousal off the charts, causing it to swell and throb. I glanced down, realizing I'd leave his finger wet.

"Is that nice?" he asked, his voice gruff.

"Yes, sir."

"Then I think you'll like this." He nestled his head between my thighs and began devouring my pussy with his feverish mouth.

I felt another shock of pleasure between my folds, a lightheadedness that caused me to swoon, caused my legs to tremble. My body was alight with the sensations of him ravishing me.

I was doing this…in front of all these people.

My reflection in the mirror showed a girl swept up in the presence of a dangerous stranger, his dark hair silky to the touch, his head at my pelvis, devouring me.

I surrendered to him, to this, savoring the delicious

thrumming as his furtive tongue searched every crevice, his hands reaching around to grab my butt and hold my cheeks so firmly I couldn't escape.

Possessing me.

Owning my sex.

I glanced over at Shay to see his reaction.

He merely observed, as though gauging how well I performed. As though proving this was about my needs and my wants and everything in between that could lead to my freedom.

I'd given in to what my heart and soul yearned for, an exquisite experiencing of being desired, public humiliation that had morphed into erotic bliss.

I was the ultimate exhibit.

Shay left the booth, strolling masterfully with his hands tucked into his pockets, slowly, like a shark cutting through water, closing the distance until he joined our table.

He came up behind me and I fell against him, my back to his front. He wrapped his arms around me. Even as the other man continued to lavish licks and flicks between my thighs, Shay gripped me to him as though letting everyone know I was his now.

His to explore.

His to play with.

Shay eased the bodice of my dress down to expose my breasts, and then began playing with my nipples. Pinching and tweaking and tugging until all I knew was oblivion. With the material bunched around my waist, I might as well have been naked.

They were all staring now, everyone in this room, their expressions easy to read. Not shock for what they saw but a kind of awe—looks of respect and understanding, like they were sharing in my display as I was shown off and flaunted.

Solidifying the fact that Imperial was staged.

A moan rose in the depths of my throat.

The thrill of vulnerability was like a prayer from the heart.

Gently rocking against Shay, I let the sensations flow in and around me, carrying me into their very center.

Inside me the Ben Wa balls, outside, those tweaks to my nipples shooting down to where that stranger still flicked me with his tongue.

I swooned as the two men adored me…one feverish between my thighs and the other punishing me with the exquisite pinching of my nipples.

My face had to be flushed red—my cheeks were burning up; I felt the heat between my thighs, this rising orgasm close to claiming me.

I dared to study the faces of the other men around the table. They all wore lascivious expressions; as though yearning to taste me, too.

Peering down and seeing that man's mouth clamped to my sex was both terrifying and exhilarating.

"Master," I said, breathless.

"Come," coaxed Master Shay.

I rolled into the deep end of a climax that went on and on and on as my thighs shuddered and my body convulsed, as I became one with them both, riding a wave of pleasure that felt never-ending.

I was gasping, wrecked into nothingness.

I lay weakly in Shay's arms as my orgasm finally began to fade.

Shay spun me around and I fell back against him, self-consciously easing my bodice up to cover my breasts, my hem having fallen around me.

As if such a thing as modesty mattered now.

Shay lifted me into his arms and carried me with long strides through the restaurant. I nestled my face under his chin not wanting to look at the many faces staring our way. He approached another door and kicked it open with his foot.

He carried me through the doorway into a vast and glamorous foyer with marble flooring. Above us an enormous chandelier rained light upon us, the glass droplets looking familiar.

As did the grand staircase.

"Chrysalis?" I whispered, as he carried me towards the stairs.

But how?

I realized the drive in the limousine had been a ploy to make me believe we were going out. Instead, the limo had merely turned around and come back here.

Bringing us back to his sacred place.

Shay pressed his lips to my forehead, his kiss soothing me as we ascended into the heart of Chrysalis, his hauntingly beautiful words finding me again.

"Setting you up to fly."

CHAPTER TWENTY-FIVE

Shay

I CARRIED RUE UP THE CENTRAL STAIRCASE AND ALONG THE hallway, holding her close, inhaling her sweet perfume. Her arousal was just as alluring as the scent she'd dabbed on her chest earlier.

My brilliant dark angel with her unique and exquisite needs.

My dick had gotten so hard at witnessing how well she'd been enjoyed and worshipped. I remembered the arousing thrill of having her writhe against me while she was being watched by the elite members of Chrysalis.

I'd even felt a twinge of jealousy—an emotion I rarely felt.

I'd had to remind myself this was not about me.

Nor would it ever be.

She'd shown herself to be brave and beautiful and profoundly true to herself. Owning her sexuality.

She had trusted me enough to play out her desires, obeying me in every conceivable way and bravely performing my erotic orders. Her dark fantasies had been explored and brought to life.

She was with her own people now. The kind who reveled

in passion. The kind who'd long ago discovered the ecstasy of Enthrall.

And the profoundness of Chrysalis.

She'd be safe here.

Now, she needed nurturing. I'd been the one to take her to the heights of pleasure and it was me who would also remain with her as she came down.

Once inside the luxurious private suite, I carried her through to the marble-tiled bathroom. She sat on the edge of the tub while I ran water to fill it, pouring in copious amounts of bubbles. They frothed and their spicy scent wafted around us.

I lit a candle for her.

Running my hand through the heated water I asked, "How are you feeling?"

"Good." She stretched languidly. "It was everything I wanted it to be."

"I'm glad."

"Thank you."

"Pleasure's all mine." I quirked a smile.

I eased off her shoes, gently taking one and then the other and placing her heels in the corner.

Watching her come alive in each of those scenarios had been exhilarating. I'd felt a respectful envy seeing our senior Dominants, Grantchester and Sinclair, getting to experience her intimately. And that jealous twinge.

Ridiculous.

I'd always taken a sordid pleasure from sharing my submissives. But now, I felt my protective side rearing up.

It made no sense.

Shaking it off, I ran my fingers over her painted toenails, admiring her feet.

"We were at Chrysalis all along," she said sleepily.

"This place is a small village."

Since Richard had taken over as the director, he'd added a five-star restaurant. Guests didn't have far to go for a fine-dining experience. It also provided another setting for the kind of session we'd just enjoyed.

It was a good place to test obedient submissives.

When the tub was full, I gestured for Rue to stand. She turned around so I could ease her out of her dress. I tugged it down and helped her step out of it. From now on, whenever I saw her wearing this I'd remember our experience today.

Once the dress was off, I hung it on a hanger.

Then I knelt behind her and ran my hand up her legs, placing my palm on her ass, her cheeks round and plump. She was the kind of woman I was drawn to. Someone confident in her own skin.

Owning her femininity.

She looked over her shoulder at me.

I grinned. "Just admiring you."

She pressed her palm to her chest. "You make me feel…"

She made me feel the same way.

Even though these feelings surged, I pushed them down. They had no place here. No future. It was merely her coming down from that scene.

"I'm taking out your Ben Wa balls," I told her, tugging on the string just below her vagina. I eased them out and set them near the sink.

Naked, she took my hand for balance and stepped into the tub, then lowered herself into the warm water, the bubbles frothing over her, her locks falling over the back of the tub and her shoulders.

She was like a sea goddess having no idea of her beauty in this moment.

My thoughts drifted to how Grantchester and Sinclair had handled her so well, and with compassion.

They'd coaxed her gently and had performed brilliantly.

Maybe De Sade was right. Maybe Grantchester was a better fit than me.

Then again, the way Rue responded to me was worth more introspection.

Kneeling beside the bath, I reached for the sponge and caressed its softness over Rue's breasts, dragging it down over her stomach and around her ruby pierced bellybutton. She arched her back as I stroked it up and down between her thighs.

I recalled Rue mentioning the possibility of having another piercing, that she wanted my initials on a piece of jewelry she wore.

I applied more pressure to the sponge and she rocked her hips against it, suspended in a state of craving. A need so intense it might be seen as a challenge by a junior Dom.

Her constant craving made her a rare and sacred creature.

I knew how to honor her nymphomania.

I continued to massage the sponge along her clit, circling until she hummed her pleasure, her eyelids fluttering. She bit her lip, hips rocking to ride the sensuous design of this perfect pressure, thighs shaking as she came.

I made sure she continued to come down from the extraordinary event at Imperial. The memory made me smile. She'd fallen for the ruse, and it had been intriguing to watch her limits being pushed.

It was up to me to reassure Rue that what she needed was normal. So, I again brought her to the height of bliss where she could remain in this reverie. Suspended at the height of her arousal, flicking her clit this time with my finger to ensure she remained on the precipice and then slowing to guide and control her release.

She trembled through another orgasm. "Again," she whispered.

"I know," I said. "Part your thighs a little more."

It was the way she looked at me with gratitude, with longing, as though she felt just as connected to me as I did to her.

As the world slipped away, I allowed myself this quiet time, these moments away from my hectic schedule.

Taking care of her felt cathartic.

I could almost believe Rue was meant for me, that the gods

had delivered this exquisite creature into my world to keep all the chaos and drama at bay.

Giving me time to worship her.

Rue's eyelids fluttered and her rosy lips pouted, which I'd come to read as her tell of needing to come.

Her silent request for more.

This time, I caressed her breasts with the sponge and worked it roughly over her nipples—they were erect, her breasts swollen with desire.

Again, she climaxed with a shudder, her painted toenails curling, her sighs and gasps and moans echoing around us.

Finally, she settled down as though only now sated.

"Thank you for understanding," she whispered, breathless.

"That's what I do," I told her. "Ensure your fulfillment."

"You don't mind me…?"

I gave her a crooked smile. "How can I? Making a beautiful woman come again and again…"

"It's just that…I crave this…all the time."

"I can see that."

"It's not a problem?"

"Not here, no. It's a benefit. Soon you'll undergo submissive training and—"

"I'm already trained."

"You're not Chrysalis-trained."

Her frown deepened. "Will it be you?"

"I believe we've found you a master who is a suitable match."

Water whooshed around her as she sprang up. "What do you mean?"

"We've found a Dom who will honor your predilections."

"Not you?"

"I'm willing to facilitate your time here—"

"What was that in Imperial?"

My back stiffened. "How do you mean?"

"Why was it you with me in the restaurant if you had no intention of keeping me?"

"We were ascertaining who might be the best fit, which Dom you connected to best. You responded well to Grantchester."

She looked confused.

"The gentleman who sat at the booth opposite ours."

"The one with the girlfriend!"

I brushed a wet strand of hair out of her face. "She's his submissive."

"Won't she mind?"

"She does what she's told."

"He already has a sub."

"She's completed her training. She'll now meet the demands of Chrysalis."

"He loses her. Like I'm losing you?"

"Silence," I demanded.

She'd been drawn to Grantchester. He'd responded well to her, too. His nod of acknowledgment after she'd withdrawn from beneath his table indicated his interest.

Again, I was hit with that sense of injustice of having to hand her over to him.

Rue shook her head. "It's either you or I'm not staying."

"It doesn't work like that. You gave consent. You are here for the duration."

"Duration?"

"You gave yourself over for one week—total immersion. There is no leaving."

She grabbed my arm. "It has to be you."

"Our Doms are of the highest caliber." I cupped her face with my hands. "You have to trust me."

Her face fell and she looked a little lost.

"I'll keep track of your progress."

Water swirled as she settled back against the tub.

"What are your concerns?" I asked.

"I'm not good with too much pain. Just enough to please my Dom, that's it."

"We know."

She gave me a weak smile.

"I'll visit."

"I want to please you."

"Then please Grantchester, Rue. That is how you please me." I brushed a strand of hair out of her face. "Perhaps Sinclair is more your type?"

She pursed her lips, frustrated with how the conversation was going.

Rue wanted me.

And my cock wanted her.

And my heart was warning me that I was close to demanding I be the one to possess her.

Back in Imperial, I'd ruminated on how it would feel to lose her. I'd reassured myself that I could keep my emotions separate from my actions.

"You must be hungry?" I said. "We skipped dinner."

Her smile widened, letting me know it had been worth it to skip a meal at Imperial—exchanging it for something else entirely.

She was no different than the others.

This lie sat like a rock in my chest.

I'd grown fond of her.

Not fond, no. Something more intense, something tangible, something…

There was a knock at the door.

"I'll get that," I said, pushing up.

"I'm not ready," said Rue.

"You're ready when I say you are."

I left her there and closed the door behind me.

CHAPTER TWENTY-SIX

Shay

R UE WANTS YOU TO BE THE ONE.

I knew it. Of course, I did. I'd been in denial while running that bath for her.

Leaving the discussion unfinished felt wrong.

She deserved my time.

Letting her soak in the tub would give her time to think about how much she'd enjoyed her brief time with Grantchester.

Could I bring myself to hand her over to him?

At the other end of the bedroom, Scarlet Winters beckoned. Our former senior Dominatrix never seemed to age.

She visited the dungeons here with her husband Ethan. They kept their visits private because he was a D.A. and dabbling in BDSM wouldn't go over well with the public.

Scarlet looked stunning in a Prada suit. She looked stunning in anything, really. All that long, dark hair and post-baby softness.

"Hey," I said.

"Surprise!"

"It's good to see you," I told her.

She pulled me into a tight embrace, her familiar perfume of white lilies reminding me of a time when we'd all been together, not scattered like we were now. It made me wonder if I was the only nostalgic one.

"How are you?" I said.

"Good, really good."

I looked her up and down. "Motherhood agrees with you."

"I've left the baby with Ethan. He's already texted me twice."

I chuckled.

"He's an adorable dad. I shouldn't complain." Scarlet led me to the other side of the room. "How's Rue?"

"Excellent."

"I heard she excelled at Imperial."

"She did. We're just deciding who the best fit is for her."

Her expression turned thoughtful.

I tried to read her. "Is there an issue?"

She gestured towards a side door and we walked over and stepped out into the hallway.

I looked around to make sure we could still talk privately.

She gazed up at me, concerned. "Faulkner's here. We needed a reference for her," she explained. "That's how he found out."

"That's fine," I reasoned.

"Richard conducted a background search on Rue. It included hearing how well she'd behaved under her last tutor."

"Of course."

Scarlet rested a hand on my arm. "It appears Rue belongs to him."

"She belongs to herself."

"She's his sub."

"*Was* his sub."

"You warned Faulkner to cease her training?" She folded her arms.

I loved this about Scarlet, always looking out for everyone. I needed her on my side.

"He took her to Pendulum," I said.

"Which is not ideal. I get that."

I'd done the right thing by keeping Rue out of Pendulum. Bringing her here and ensuring her safety within the confines of Chrysalis. There was no guilt there.

"Shay," Scarlet said. "He's here to take her back."

Fuck.

"There's a code," continued Scarlet. "We don't trespass into clubs or steal subs."

"Her Domina asked me to remove her from Pendulum."

Scarlet nodded as she put the pieces together.

"Yeah, so before you accuse me of stealing submissives—"

"I had no idea." She frowned. "Won't her Domina feel the same about her?"

"Rue is no longer at Majestic."

"Carrie Quinn?"

"Yes, that's her."

"Do you want me to escort Rue to Faulkner?"

"She's not going back to him."

She let out a frustrated sigh. "He's in Richard's office. Talk to him at least."

"Why are *you* here?"

"I know him," she said softly.

"In what capacity?"

"I was his mistress when he started out."

Because that was how it was done. Every Dom started out as a sub. It was the way of things—although Cameron was an exception to that rule. And I was, too, because I bowed to fucking no one.

I shook my head. "I refuse to let him have her."

Richard came strolling down the hallway towards us. He patted Scarlet's arm with affection.

I braced for his demands, ready to take the hit.

He turned to face me. "Trying to make my life interesting?"

I folded my arms, ready to argue. "I've never asked for anything until now."

"I'm the one who signed off on Rue being here, remember?" he said.

I shoved my hands into my pockets. "I'm listening."

"What are you to her?" he said.

"I'm navigating her through the process."

Richard studied me. "You wouldn't be averse to Faulkner training her here at Chrysalis, then?"

"Win, win," said Scarlet. "Rue stays."

"You could watch over them," added Richard.

I drew in a calming breath. "There's a chance he'll take her back to Pendulum."

Richard gave a nod. "Or we do it another way."

"Which is?" I glanced from him to Scarlet.

Scarlet and Richard both answered my question with glares.

I shook my head even as my chest constricted with their suggestion.

"I don't see the problem," said Richard. "You're an hour away from giving her to Grantchester."

I tried to hide the truth. I'd grown fond of Rue. Her passion aligned with mine. Her predilections mirrored my own. If I was looking for a partner she'd be my first choice.

Only I wasn't going anywhere near a relationship.

"Grantchester's not right for her," I said.

"Sinclair?" asked Richard. "He's in."

"That's a good choice, right?" said Scarlet.

"No, not right either." I threw in a nod of conviction.

Richard looked amused. "So neither one is right for her?"

"I'm the right person to decide who would be the best Dom for her."

"And yet the Dom can't be you?" asked Richard, quirking an eyebrow.

"I have commitments," I reasoned.

Richard raised a finger to stop me there. "As you're staying, you might as well watch over your sub."

"*My* sub?"

"We listened to you. Now you need to do the same and listen to us." Richard folded his arms defensively. "Do this for Rue."

"Not a good time for me."

He opened his palms in a gesture of surrender. "This is your place as much as ours."

I appreciated what he was saying but I'd always been *their* guardian. I was the one who put the fires out—and I didn't need to complicate matters.

"I have to leave from time to time, business and such," I said with a note of finality.

"I'm fine with that," said Richard. "Lotte will watch over her when you're not here."

"That would work, right?" Scarlet affectionately rested her hand on my arm.

Was I really being forced to take on one of the most beautiful women I'd ever seen and own her?

Protect her.

My gut clenched with the possibilities.

I wanted her.

Wanted to play and push and possess that beautiful woman. All I had to do was keep my heart closed and my mind focused on giving her the best experience.

"I'll continue for now," I said quietly.

Scarlet went to say something and then seemed to think better of it.

Richard turned to Scarlet. "Prepare the Harrington Suite."

I looked from one to the other. "You expect Faulkner to carry out the ritual where he hands her over willingly?"

"Yes," said Richard.

"You offered him membership?" I said, only now putting the pieces together.

Scarlet looked at Richard with surprise. "Did he really say that? Faulkner's agreed to give up Rue for membership at Chrysalis?"

"He did." Richard's gaze met my own. "It's settled then?"

"How could anyone in their right mind give her up?" I felt a pang of truth in that statement.

Scarlet gave me a kind smile, as though saying *exactly.*

CHAPTER TWENTY-SEVEN

S HAY REAPPEARED IN THE DOORWAY.

Resting my head against the back of the tub, I admired how ruggedly handsome he looked. I was consistently struck by his powerful presence.

I was suddenly hit with the realization that he knew how to give me everything I'd ever needed.

He knew how to satisfy my desires.

Shay pushed off the doorjamb and came closer.

The tension between us felt dangerously alluring.

"Dinner will be served in your room," he said. "I will also allow a glass of wine."

"I'm just going to stay in here until I wrinkle up."

Shay towered over me. "Out."

"No."

No matter how attractive those men were at Imperial, I'd always be thinking of Shay.

"Don't question me," he snapped.

Aroused by his sternness, I pushed up until I was standing

before him naked and dripping wet…soapsuds kissing my body, bubbles sliding over my left breast—which he seemed to notice.

He grabbed a towel. "We've decided."

Uneasiness slithered up my spine. "I refuse."

"Your punishment will be severe if you continue to defy me, Rue."

His harsh words made me giddy with want.

"Obey," he said gruffly.

With a nod, I stepped out and turned, letting him wrap the towel around me. He dried me off and my body shuddered beneath the smoothness of the towel and the firmness of his touch.

"Who, then?" I said softly. "Is it the man you mentioned?"

"The one you want."

I spun around and peered up at him, my heart hammering in my chest because what he was insinuating was too good to be true.

"You?" I was breathless.

"Kneel."

Exhaling in a rush, I gave a soft moan of relief, my cheeks flushed with happiness. I sank onto my knees, returning my focus to him.

I wanted to read the truth in his gaze.

"We must have no secrets between us," he said.

"I'm yours," I whispered.

"Bedroom," he said. "Go."

Scurrying that way, my heart swelling with emotion, I made it through the door and all the way to the foot of the bed. Turning, I knelt and held a submissive pose.

Footsteps followed me.

I was his. He was the only one who had ever seen me for what I was.

Shay knelt before me. "I'm a harsh master. Much will be expected." He reached for my hands and turned my palms up. They tingled with the warmth of his touch.

"How long were you with Faulkner?" he asked.

"A week."

He tipped up my chin. "Palms always up. You know that."

"I'm a little…" *Thrown by you.*

"After your show of confidence in the restaurant, that surprises me."

"It was because of you."

Just sharing the same oxygen with him made me lightheaded; indulging in such stunning arousal at his bidding. I'd lost count of how many times I'd come today. This terrible thirst only he could quench.

With him I reached that pinnacle.

"Slow your breathing."

"Will you sleep with me?" I shook my head to clear my mind. "I mean tonight."

He pushed up and looked down at me. "If you believe you can tolerate me fucking you over the course of an entire evening—"

"Yes, sir."

He could fuck me for an entire year straight and I'd be happy.

Shay pointed to the bed. "Present yourself appropriately."

"I want it all," I said, pushing up. "Everything you think I'm worthy of."

Ignoring the chill on my naked skin, I hurried onto the bed and lay back, spreading my thighs wide, offering myself to him.

Silence filled the room as he surveyed what was his.

Shay glared down at me. "It's not happening in here."

Raising my head, I tried to read his meaning.

"Have you heard what we do in the Harrington Suite?" When I started to move, he gestured for me to stop. "No, keep that position. It pleases me."

I spread my thighs even wider, showing off my pussy. The arousal I felt was making me giddy, my body trembling with need.

He was to be mine and I his.

"Faulkner is here to claim you." Shay gestured for my obedience. "We've come to an agreement. However, when a submissive belongs to a Dom, even temporarily, there's a rule for how the transition takes place. A ceremony."

"I don't care what happens," I said, "as long as I become yours."

"It's a tradition. A way to make it known that you are under my command."

His words resonated like a chant. The promise of salvation.

I didn't mind an erotic ceremony. I just hoped it was highly sexual and didn't involve any pain.

My flesh ignited like I was already there—even with these unanswered questions.

"Sir, what happens in the Harrington Suite?"

CHAPTER TWENTY-EIGHT

Shay

I'D ALWAYS ADMIRED MY WILLPOWER, BUT HAVING TO LEAVE Rue with her body inviting me to take her hard and fast meant reaching a whole new level of self-control.

I'd left her to prepare for tonight.

Our senior Dominatrices would make sure she was ready.

By leaving Chrysalis for several hours, I would be able to think this through—away from temptation.

This place wasn't bad. It was just so fucking loud.

I'd have one drink. By the time I returned to Chrysalis the liquor would have worn off.

Anyway, cancelling tonight's opportunity to spend time with this special someone wasn't an option.

It's easy to tell who your closest friends are. They're the ones who—no matter how much time you've had to spend apart—make you feel like no time has passed at all.

When it came to this Navy buddy and my ex-commanding officer, I felt nothing but respect for Henry Cole. Cameron's older brother had shown the kind of bravery that most men weren't capable of achieving in a lifetime.

We were two retired frogmen in a sea of civilians.

The Edison was not my kind of bar. I was surprised it was his, with its swanky décor, dark-themed rooms and loud music that screamed decadent youth.

Everyone was looking down at their phones—even the bartender. It annoyed the hell out of me, but then I had to admit I'd glanced at mine several times, too.

Just in case any update came out of Chrysalis.

Not Henry though, he was too much of a gentleman and too old-fashioned to fall into that tech trap. With his impressive height, broad shoulders and confident swagger, he drew attention from everyone we walked past.

Both of us had donned a different kind of uniform now—jeans and T-shirts with tailored jackets, because we weren't that slovenly yet.

This post-industrial venue was set in the sub-basement of a renovated power plant, located on the corner of Second and Main off Harlem Place Alley in L.A.'s historic core.

A strange thought popped in my head—perhaps Rue would like it here. Maybe I'd bring her, like we were a couple.

"This way," shouted Henry, leading me down a long corridor, cognac in hand.

We moved away from the noisy action toward a quieter corner, finding leather-covered chairs in a seating area that was more private.

"Makes me feel old," I said, taking the seat beside his.

"My assistant booked this." He shook his head. "I told her I was meeting you. For some reason, she thought this was what we were going for."

"She probably doesn't know L.A.," I said.

"She lives here." With a smile, he added, "And so do I."

"Since when?"

"A week ago."

"Cameron didn't say anything."

"He thought it best to wait and see how I liked living here before we announced it."

"Cole Tea headquarters is now in L.A?"

He gave a nod and that confident smile still looked good on him. No arrogance, merely the assured look of someone who had a different kind of benchmark…a man of his word, someone who could be trusted.

Someone who'd almost died for his country.

Every day we lived was a gift.

I knew they'd completed construction on Cole Tower. Cameron had given me a tour, but not mentioned having his brother here.

"You've got to come visit," said Henry.

"Of course." I leaned back, grateful at the thought of having him around. "You look good," I said. "How have you been?"

"Can't complain. How about you?" he said. "Going old school with the beard, I see."

Because we'd all worn beards back in Afghanistan.

Caressing it, I gave a nod. "It's a change."

"Have you heard from anyone?"

"Only a few. You?"

He looked away. "I didn't exactly leave Afghanistan on a high note."

"Jesus, you left there a fucking hero."

That old familiar guilt found me again, that he'd been the one captured. Henry had gone back in to rescue one of our own. Mortar fire had cut him off. That mission had left one dead and Henry in the hands of the enemy.

The terrorists had inflicted the kind of cruelty that was hard to stomach. I didn't want to think of their name, let alone say it. They didn't deserve one more brain cell wasted on them.

Henry Montgomery Cole had sacrificed it all for his men.

For me.

I owed him my life.

I was courteous enough not to bring up his PTSD. We all had it to a degree—it was an old enemy waiting to rise up and ruin our fucking day.

I'd seen first-hand how it had ravaged his life, his psyche and his heart. He was doing better now; though with him in New York and me here I'd not been around to witness any further flare-ups.

He seemed to read my thoughts. "I'm doing EMDR therapy. Seems to help."

"I've heard of it," I said. "Eye movement desensitization."

He waved that off. "How are you doing, really?

"Great."

He gave a slow nod. "Look, Cole thinks it best I don't bring it up, so I won't."

"Bring what up?"

"Have you ever considered seeing him in a professional manner?" He raised his hand. "Not the crazy shit he does but the more traditional therapy."

"I don't need it," I said calmly. *Because I didn't.*

"Okay, well, you know it's available if you ever decide you do."

"I appreciate it, Henry." I raised my glass. "But I'm fine."

Sometimes, when I woke in the middle of the night and thought back to our time in Kabul, I knew it was this guy here who'd gotten me through it all.

We had an unbreakable bond.

"How's the wild side?" he said, snapping me out of my musing.

"Still wild."

He gave me a devilish grin. "Bunch of reprobates."

"It's cathartic. It's my version of EMDR, only with my dick."

Our laughter filled the room.

God, I've missed this. Missed him.

"Funny how you wish you were back there," he said. "But when you were there all you could think about was home."

"Even after everything, you wish you were back?"

He looked thoughtful. "Before Charlie Foxtrot."

"I don't remember much."

"Maybe we're still running from ourselves." Henry watched my reaction.

"Maybe."

He leaned forward and stared at me. "You saved my life that day, Gardner…made a hard decision."

I tasted grit—trying to see through goggles in a sandstorm, my vision blurred.

Deafening blades cut through the thick air as the Black Hawk helicopter turned around—dust being the enemy of flight, making it impossible to extract us.

Movement from over the ridge…a mountain lion appearing.

The sound of a bullet.

Mine.

The look on Henry's face…horror.

Then relief.

Saving one life but taking another. I killed that stalking lion.

"We survived it," I whispered.

"Shay?"

A part of us would always be left in that country…a part of our soul.

My soul.

"What do you remember?" he said softly.

I gave him a look that told him I'd been prepared to die for him.

Henry shook his head. Words weren't needed between us.

We sat quietly for a while, people watching, taking in the crowds that came and went around the bar.

"Cameron still feels bad about how I left Afghanistan," Henry said. "He's just in need of therapy."

"I think he sees someone."

"No harm in it, right?" Henry studied me.

"Cameron did what he had to do for you, debriefed you. He was the right man to be brought in, although his bedside manor leaves a lot to be desired."

And it had been Mia who'd persuaded Henry to leave that cabin in Big Bear and rejoin society.

It had all seemed to come full circle.

The way the ice melted was fascinating. No two pieces disappearing at the same rate.

"Let's change the subject," Henry said gently.

"Sure."

"Does Cameron still…?" Henry waited for my response.

"No comment."

"You always were a loyal bastard."

"He deserves it."

"He's my younger brother and it's hard to see him any other way."

I decided to change the subject again. "How's the business world?"

"I have a few ideas about where I want to take Cole Tea."

"I look forward to hearing more."

He leaned forward. "Want another?"

I glanced at my near-empty glass. "I have a thing tonight."

"Thing?" He arched a brow. "Oh, a thing, thing."

Henry was open-minded but me sharing the "deets" would probably push him over the edge.

"New guy?" he asked.

"A woman."

His brows shot up. "Oh, well she's lucky. Want to tell me about her?"

The ice had melted in my glass. I sipped the diluted liquor and mulled over what was safe to share. "It's early."

"Bring her over for dinner. I'm staying at Hotel Bel Air."

"Bel Air?"

He pressed his tongue into his cheek. "Yeah, you can expect a visit from me at Chrysalis. Stone's throw away."

"I'll give you a tour if you want one."

He smirked. "I have a lifetime ban."

"Cole's not there anymore." I smiled. "I mean Cameron."

"I'm sure he'd love that…me in his old stomping ground. Sneaking around and seeing what you all do."

"Don't knock it until you've tried it."

"What happened to old-fashioned gentleness with a woman?"

"We have that."

He didn't look convinced. "Each to his own."

"Trust me, the women run the show."

"Really?" He gave a nod. "Now that I'd like to see."

"When was the last time you dated?" I asked.

"Not sure I'm cut out for…domesticity."

"Then you've not found the right person."

He downed his drink. "Come work for me."

"I have a job."

"I'll double your salary."

"I'm flattered." I finished off my drink. "Don't share this with Cam, but I'm thinking of leaving Enthrall. I'm ready to take CloudSource to a new level."

"Your app? I use it every day, you know that, right? I love it."

"I'm glad."

"It's great software. All my texts disappear into a secure cloud! Inaccessible to anyone, the kind of reassurance social media doesn't provide."

"It's gaining traction."

"I'll buy shares when it's time."

"I appreciate that."

"If you ever need financial backing…"

"That's good to know, thanks."

"I never saw you leaving Enthrall."

"I'll always be available to consult."

He raised his glass. "To CloudSource."

I raised mine. "Here's to risking it all."

I needed more time, though. Taking that kind of leap was risky.

Henry gestured for the barman to bring us more drinks. "Remy Martin's XO."

"I'm only having one."

Henry gave a nod and corrected the order.

Then he turned back to me. "When was the last time you saw Mia?"

"A few days ago."

His brow furrowed. "They seem happy."

"They are."

"That rug rat is as cute as hell."

"I hear you spoil him, Uncle Henry." That made me chuckle.

Henry accepted his drink from the barman and then leaned back in the leather seat. "You got a photo of her?"

"Who?"

"The woman you're seeing tonight."

I fished out my phone and swiped toward the only photo I had of Rue. I'd taken a screenshot from her Instagram. She was posing at the beach beside a surfboard—though it wasn't the time I'd caught her riding the waves at my place. It had been taken on another day. She looked tanned and windswept and so fucking pretty.

I showed her to Henry.

His expression went from being surprised to looking impressed.

"She's just a passing…" I struggled to finish the sentence. "You know."

Henry blinked at me like I was insane. "She's…wow."

Yeah, I once thought that before reason kicked in. I was just going to let her use me and when she was done, she'd be nothing but a memory.

"Is she into…?" asked Henry.

I hesitated to answer, not wanting to betray a trust.

His smiled widened. "Goddamn, if you aren't perfect for each other."

"We're not even close to that level of relationship—"

He raised a finger to silence me. "Let me live vicariously through my Lieutenant, okay?"

Glancing at the photo again, I felt a rush of emotion. Soon I'd be seeing her back at Chrysalis.

Even if it was just for a filthy, erotic game.

"Tell me more about CloudSource," said Henry. "Let's talk about your strategy moving forward."

I leaned back in my seat, comforted in the knowledge that I had the best friends in world.

CHAPTER TWENTY-NINE

Shay

H ENRY AND I PARTED WAYS AT THE EDISON.

Seeing him had been cathartic. It always was, and I promised to make a concerted effort to spend more time with the oldest Cole brother—especially since he was now living in L.A.

The Coles really were an extraordinary family.

What Cam had done at Chrysalis was equally compelling. He'd helped so many people here, but trying to tell Henry that was challenging. It was a concept even I had trouble understanding.

I stopped off at home to shower and then change into a black tuxedo for tonight's soirée.

The drive back to Bel Air was pleasant. Probably because I knew I was heading back to Rue.

As usual, I made my way around the back of the manor and entered Chrysalis via the private door.

I preferred jeans and a T-shirt to a tux, but I had to follow the dress code. This starched shirt and bowtie weren't exactly me.

*When in Rome…*or more specifically, Chrysalis, I honored the rules.

Loosening my tie, I headed down the long hallway toward the Harrington Suite. The cognac I'd shared with Henry back at The Edison had eased my tension.

I'd be showcasing my predilection for exhibitionism in the most decadent display. This tradition of handing over a sub to another master had gone on for years.

The only time it had been broken was for Mia, because Cameron had not deemed her ready. And no one was going to argue with him.

Rue, however, would revel in the display of power exchange.

None of us were shy about sex. We'd all gotten over the hesitation of watching others fuck during our first days here. Now, we were all relaxed with each other and as close as friends could be.

Trying to get in the right headspace, I focused on what Rue would need.

The ritual was imminent.

Just the thought of taking her again made me hard.

Back in the military, with all its rules, we had to let go of our individuality. Here, it was celebrated.

Something continued to simmer inside me; a stark jealousy for anyone who touched Rue.

These rapid-fire thoughts were disrupted when I saw Jake heading my way, all black-tie swagger and untamed confidence. Breaking my fucking heart still seemed to agree with him. De Sade walked with the kind of arrogance that turned heads.

"Hey," he greeted me.

"Is Rylee here?" I asked.

"No."

I gave a nod. "See you later."

"Don't be like this."

"Like what?"

All the work I'd done on regaining some semblance of peace was on shaky ground because he was literally the storm I'd craved. The edge of this hurricane felt addictively alluring.

My thoughts returned to the room down the hallway where a beautiful woman waited, which helped my resolve, if I was going to be honest.

Thinking of Rue steadied me.

"Rue's in the Harrington," said De Sade as though reading my mind.

I imagined how she'd be feeling and what she'd be wearing. How she'd respond to my return. She thought she wanted this, but when it came to reality it was an entirely different experience. I'd be reading every micro-expression, checking in with her to make sure she wanted to continue with everything we offered.

I wondered if Faulkner was in there yet.

I tried to walk around De Sade. "I'm late. Excuse me."

"You're still angry with me."

"I just…"

I didn't want to say I was concerned, that I thought Rylee was probably going to hurt him again. It would come across as sounding bitter and lacking compassion.

My dignity was still intact, at least.

His mouth twitched. "Go on, say it."

"You deserve to be happy." I looked over his shoulder.

"It's me, Shay."

Why did he have to say my name like that? Like he used to? Like on those Sunday mornings when he'd bring me coffee and the *Times* because he knew I loved working on the crossword.

I often finished the puzzle before he'd even gotten the first word. He liked that about me. What I liked about him was fucking everything.

"What do you want me to say?" I snapped.

"We can still be friends."

"I don't want you in there," I bit out.

Didn't want to take a chance on any fallout.

Because *I* was the fallout.

The collateral damage.

I didn't want anyone else close to this.

It's just a fuck in a room with a submissive. At least that's what my brain was trying to convince me to believe.

No, it was a trap within a trap.

Maybe Rue and I could be more if I ever had the time to mess up my life again.

Only I don't.

My heart contracted with that thought, and then hardened into granite.

De Sade turned to look back toward the suite. "I think she's good for you."

"Rue?"

"It's good to see you happy."

"I'm just facilitating her time here."

"Right."

"You want to watch me fucking someone else? Is that it?" I snapped.

He really did find this amusing.

He moved closer and met my gaze. "Make this permanent with her. Don't just carry out the ceremony only to give her away."

The rumor had reached him. Or maybe he just knew me.

"You need her, Shay."

"Fuck off." I walked away.

I hated the fact he still affected me like this, like all I had to do was see him and I again felt him breaching my defenses.

But Rue was the ultimate palate cleanser.

I'd be able to shake these thoughts in her presence.

Inside the Harrington Suite, I took in the fancy ballroom, its chandeliers sending shards of light over the occupants.

All attention was on Rue.

My submissive was on her knees in the center of the room with her palms up, her pose flawless.

She wore a satin masquerade mask, her piercing blue gaze meeting mine. She returned a nod of serene readiness.

Her bright lipstick made her mouth look even more enticing.

I felt eager to wrap my arms around the waist of that tight fitting bodice and rip off her thong. I'd have to be wary of her spiked heels.

Maybe one of them would accidently find its way into Faulkner's heart. That would be a fucking tragedy.

For a second, I questioned whether letting him touch her was going to be something I could handle.

And there was the bastard himself, heading my way looking suave in a black tuxedo.

"You okay?" I asked.

"Yeah, why?"

"No doubts about this?" I checked his reaction.

Faulkner made eye contact. "I'm doing what's best for her."

His reputation for training subs and taking them to Pendulum preceded him like the iceberg hit by the Titanic. The fact he'd gotten a membership was a miracle.

Richard had arranged this for me.

"I'll take care of her," I told Kaison.

"I'll hold you to that."

"We're safer than Pendulum."

"You were right. She wasn't ready."

His words felt a lot like an apology. At least here Rue was in command of what she wanted; she got to choose her fantasies.

"How can you give her up?" I said.

"She's insatiable."

"I know."

"You're more patient."

Rue was worth all the time I had to give.

"I always wondered what this room looked like," he mused.

"Now you know."

He gave a nod. "Beautiful, isn't she?"

Even Rue's wildness was alluring. This was what it looked like when a woman lived out her dreams in a safe space.

"Let's make this session about her," I reminded him.

"You're the one with the reputation."

I gave a shrug. "Good or bad, it's probably true."

"And why shouldn't I be concerned for her again?"

"It's my bad side they crave."

I walked away from him and approached Rue.

CHAPTER THIRTY

T HERE HAD TO BE AT LEAST ONE HUNDRED DOMS AND
their submissives at this black-tie event.

This was the kind of ceremony I'd never believed I
could be part of—not here at Chrysalis, anyway. This event was
reserved for exclusive clients.

Shay had made it happen.

The guests here could have stepped out of Vogue with their
impressive masquerade masks. Some submissives sat by their masters' sides, all dressed like they were attending a fashionable ball.

A vast mahogany table with ornately carved legs loomed not
that far away. Light rained down from a chandelier that was almost as striking as the one in the foyer. It sent shards of light
twinkling over my body.

A thousand shockwaves shuddered through me—or that's
how it felt. Like I was drunk on erotica.

I'd been primped and beautified by the staff, my hair styled
so that it flowed over my shoulders. A makeup artist had been
brought in to pamper me.

No expense was spared in preparing me.

When Shay strolled in, I kept my focus trained on the hardwood floor. I wasn't going to fail before he'd touched me.

I burned for Shay's touch, his strength. I trusted him to make this more about pleasure than pain, too.

Saying goodbye to Faulkner brought mixed emotions. For a while, he had been my universe. I'd not minded him loving other submissives. That had always been part of our agreement.

There were so many of them to love and to make love to—he trained them all and we were made aware of this from the start.

I'd never looked at another man until Pendulum.

Never wanted another master.

Until now.

Weeks ago, Faulkner had decided I was a perfect fit for Pendulum, promising all my fantasies could be realized. Only that night had come to a crashing halt.

Tonight I felt like Shay would put things right.

Lotte approached me, looking elegant. "Ready?"

"Yes, mistress," I said.

How could I not be?

I'd demanded this from Shay by the pool.

As he and Faulkner walked towards me, I leaned low and forward, assuming the correct pose with my face down and butt in the air, arms outstretched before me.

"Up." Shay's voice sounded gruff.

I rose up, still kneeling.

When they both stood before me, I understood. I peered up at Faulkner and then Shay, waiting for that nod of permission to begin.

Shay tore at his necktie and dragged it off, which was so damn sexy. He looked so gorgeous in that tux.

"Do you submit entirely?" he asked, gesturing that he gave me permission to speak.

"I submit."

"You understand the purpose of this evening?" he asked, more for the crowd than me. All that was to transpire had been explained in the finest detail to me.

Shay paused, looking toward the door.

It was De Sade.

No!

Shay wouldn't do that to me. Set that man loose on his submissive? Panic shuddered through me.

Shay read my terror.

"Excuse me." He walked toward De Sade.

My adrenaline spiked as I observed their strained interaction.

I could run—though I'd not get far.

They were exchanging heated words.

De Sade pivoted and walked out of the ballroom.

Shay headed back towards us, his right hand tucked into his trouser pocket with an elegant confidence.

Unfazed.

"He's not coming back." Shay glanced at Faulkner. "I'm here to take ownership."

Relief washed over me.

"Begin," coaxed Shay.

Rising up, still on my knees, I unzipped his pants and eased out his cock, his length and girth still intimidating. My mouth stretched wide over his tip. I did my best to bring him to the back of my throat.

As I continued to blow Shay with a perfect rhythm, I reached left for Faulkner, my hand trailing up his thigh as my fingers found their way to his zipper. I pulled it down and eased him out, feeling his familiar erection grow in my grasp as I stroked him.

"A good start," encouraged Shay.

I moved from one to the other, honoring each dick with licks and laps until they'd drawn their bodies closer, their tips almost touching, making it easier for me to bounce back and forth.

They tasted of control and power.

This was the ultimate rush. I was the one they'd chosen, and

I had them shuddering at the end of my fingertips, my mouth claiming one and then the other.

"Up," ordered Shay.

Responding quickly, I pushed to my feet.

He knelt before me and eased off my thong, his firm fingers trailing down my thighs, his touch like an electric pulse.

Faulkner appeared to be deferring to him. Letting him take the lead.

Stepping out of my thong, I reached out and leaned on Shay's shoulders for balance as he removed that strip of silly material.

Then I assumed the pose with my hands behind my back.

His fingers explored my pussy, exposing my folds and running along my wetness, causing me to shudder in delight.

"Show your clit," he demanded as he rose to his full height.

Bringing my hands down, I eased apart my labia. He gripped the back of my neck, forcing me forward to show me off to the hundreds of faces. Forcing me to watch those who watched us from the shadows.

He turned me around in a circle for all to see. See what I willingly shared in this erotic pose.

His fierce grip twisted me around and then he dragged me towards him, his mouth looming close to mine.

"Want more?" he said.

I leaned in to whisper in his ear. "I'm yours."

"Soon." Shay walked me toward the table.

Faulkner sat on the edge of it with his cock in his hand as he worked his length, as though teasing me with it.

Following Shay's direction, I leaned toward Faulkner and rested my hands on his knees for balance, dipping low to deep throat him.

With my butt out and spine curved, I continued to present an excellent form in my posture. Shay's hands trailed down my spine and he untied the straps of my bodice, pulling at the silk strands. Even as I continued to pleasure Faulkner, Shay stripped off the bodice, leaving me completely naked.

Except for my spiked heels.

Shay's fingers were gently probing my sex. His cock tapped against the delicate tissue.

He shoved all the way in, stretching me and then stilling for a beat to let me acclimate to his size.

I lifted my head to breathe through the discomfort of him growing within me, the increasing pressure and tautness of an impossible size.

As though sensing what I needed, Shay reached around and pressed a fingertip to my clit, circling and eliciting pleasure. My body relaxed and I was able to accommodate him, able to move in time with his thrusts.

"You will not come yet," he said, his voice deep and firm. "Not until I grant you this honor."

"Yes, sir," I managed.

Faulkner's hand on the back of my head redirected me back to him, forcing me to bob my head and take him all the way to the back of my throat until it closed around him.

Lifting my head, I glanced over at the many masked faces staring back. Perhaps they coveted our experience as we shared our exquisite performance.

"All these people are watching you, baby," said Faulkner.

Shay withdrew from me.

Faulkner slid off the table.

Strong hands spun me round and then lifted me upon the table. Leaning back, using my hands for balance, I opened my thighs wider as they ordered.

I sat facing them now. My legs spread.

They both knelt in front of the table.

They took their time; one leaning in and dipping between my thighs, then the other devouring my pussy, causing my thighs to tremble. My breaths stuttered as I tolerated this blinding pleasure of savage tonguing.

If I came, I'd be failing to follow a command to hold back, to hold on, and not find release before having permission.

"Master," I pleaded as they remained unrelenting in their savage passion.

Impossible to obey.

Shuddering, coming hard as each one continued to take turns nestling between my trembling thighs, each mouth searching, flicking, and demanding more of my clit.

Arching my back, I marveled how any submissive could not find release. How any soul could have the finest men possessing her with this level of intensity and not bow to an orgasm.

My moans echoed around the great hall as they offered their adulation at the shrine of my womanhood, worshipping me with feverish mouths.

They knew I'd climax. They were unrelenting.

My obedience was theirs to break.

I reveled in their fascination. Their ability to own me without reservation.

"I'm going to…" I was on the verge, and nothing was going to stop me from coming.

Shay rose and grabbed my throat and the shock of it made me gasp. With Faulkner not breaking away from between my thighs, I was held still by Shay's grip, his hand tight around my throat so that each breath was a struggle.

His hold heightened my climax, my moan breaking through and my body violently shaking as I reached a pinnacle, coming hard and harder still.

The world fell away.

All I knew was him. The man holding my throat with the grip of a king.

In a flurry of movement, Shay had me off the table, flinging me around so that I was leaning over it with my butt pushed out again. The only sound in the room was my heavy breathing as I tried to come down from the euphoria.

"What do subs get when they come without permission?" snapped Shay.

"Punished!" I managed between breaths.

Shay slapped my ass.

His palm continually slammed heat into my flesh with a fierce spanking that sent wave after wave of delight through me. Gripping the edge of the table tighter, I felt Faulkner's fingers rim my puckered hole at the same time.

They were trying to drive me toward madness.

How was I to keep standing through this erotic attack? My thighs weakened as waves of lightheadedness shook me.

"Please," I begged.

"Remain still," Shay demanded.

"Yes, sir," I tried not to squirm.

Shay continued to shower me with delicious spanks and Faulkner had stepped to the side and was caressing my pussy.

They were demanding the impossible.

We were a fast-flowing river together—falling downstream into an abyss of nothingness.

Like a harmonious poem, never ceasing.

Moving against the rhythm of the slaps, I rocked in sync, feeling almost hypnotized.

Shay's hands gripped my hips and his cock sank all the way in, sending shockwaves of pleasure into my taut muscles as he stretched me wide, spiking my arousal again.

Dazed and dizzy, I glanced at the crowd, exhilarated to be watched by all these voyeurs.

Digging my fingernails into the table's wood, I forced myself to remain upright, grateful for Shay holding me up with his strong hands at my waist.

Emotions swirled as I surrendered and came again, mind drifting with the rush.

Like a well-choreographed dance, I was pulled and pushed and twisted this way and that until I lost count of how many times I climaxed.

I reveled in the beauty of the moments that followed, silently worshipping these brilliant men.

Faulkner rounded the table and came to Shay's side, each

man standing before me and taking turns thrusting their cocks into me—one sliding all the way in and then stepping back so the other could fuck me, bringing a constant wave of bliss.

My moans of pleasure echoed around us, intermingling with their gruff groans and heaves and thrusts.

Like a ragdoll I was moved again.

This time, Shay sat on the edge of the desk and lifted me up so that I sat on his lap with my back to his chest.

I felt the cold drops of lube being circled around my ass by Faulkner.

He lifted me slightly with ease and slid his cock all the way into my ass. Leaning forward a little, my breathing was stilted by a discomfort so shocking all I could do was wait out the pressure until the burning sensation lessened. In its place I felt a riveting pang.

Shay pulled me back and hugged me. "You okay?" he asked.

"You're too big," I gasped out.

"Relax," he soothed. "This is what you asked for, remember?"

Yes, I had.

Soon, I would be filled with both men.

But for now, I needed to settle into the intensity, the searing of body and mind.

Shay continued to hold me with a reassuring strength.

I widened my thighs and Faulkner stepped between them.

"Ready?" he asked, glancing at Shay as though checking in with him, too.

"Answer him," demanded Shay.

"Yes," I managed, "Please, sir."

Faulkner kept his gaze on me as he slid all the way into my pussy.

Slowly, he set about a mesmerizing pace, gliding in and out until all I could do was rest my head against Shay and let them have their way. Let them take me all the way to nirvana.

These dazzling sensations became my only reality. I was

tranced out by being taken by both men at the same time, pleasure coiling in my pelvis and then rising and rising as I flew skyward.

Becoming more.

Becoming *his.*

Rejoicing in this erotic show, like I was a prima ballerina and this was my dance.

Only now feeling free.

Obeying them.

"Together," Shay demanded of us.

I was the first to fall again, coming so hard my mind blanked out. I was only vaguely aware of the heat spilled within me as both men came.

They'd conquered me.

Stillness.

Whispers in the shadows.

Shay's voice near my ear. "You were exquisite."

"I pleased you?" I wished I could see Shay's face.

"No one has performed this ceremony better," he replied, caressing my hair, adoring me.

I felt like a precious flower in the wildest of gardens. Finally sated.

After catching my breath, I watched as Faulkner stepped back a few feet. He bowed low as though he'd just conducted an orchestra—bowing to me.

Then he walked away, tucking himself into his pants as he headed for the exit.

My former master had turned me over to my new one.

It was done.

Shay owned me.

He now possessed me entirely.

Finally, I was *his.*

CHAPTER THIRTY-ONE

Shay

RUE WAS ASLEEP.

I was naked and spooning behind her, nestled within the warm bed and breathing in her delicate fragrance.

Usually, I'd be scrolling through my phone, hoping to fall asleep. Or reading late into the night, alone, and okay with that. With her beside me, it felt like I'd been missing something and just hadn't realized it.

None of that mattered, not really.

I'd carried her out of the Harrington and brought her up here. The luxury suite would be ours for the duration of her stay.

We'd taken a hot shower together. I'd scrubbed her like I was removing all traces of Faulkner from her body—wanting nothing but my own scent on her.

My possessiveness was getting out of hand.

For now, Rue was mine.

She needed to know she was under my command. No other man could touch her unless I gave them permission.

And something told me I wouldn't.

Just thinking of how she'd thrived and flourished in the Harrington Suite made me want her again.

Either way, we could never be together after this.

That thought felt like a knife to my throat.

"I can't believe I'm here," she whispered.

Running my fingers through her hair, I tried to soothe her back to sleep.

"Can I ask you something?" she said quietly.

"Sure."

"Will you be staying tonight?"

"Have I not respected your needs?" I reached around and cupped her pussy.

"Yes." She exhaled in a rush.

I kept my hand there. "How do you feel?"

"A little sore."

"I meant emotionally?"

She looked over her shoulder at me. "I really...like you." She let out a big sigh and turned away.

"Falling for your master is expected."

She gave a frustrated sigh.

"Are you able to let go of him?" I asked.

"Faulkner?"

Yes, Faulkner. Only I'd not wanted his name mentioned in our private space.

"I only want you," she said softly.

Kissing her head, I let that serve as my response.

How he'd given her over to me was something I'd never understand. Although, when the dark hour came for me to nudge her away, perhaps I would.

It was easy to be fascinated with Rue.

Enjoy her company.

I caressed her clit and felt it throb and swell beneath my finger, teasing her until she fell asleep again.

She was just a submissive and I was merely the man who was going to protect her from herself.

Like I protected everyone.

Easing out of bed, I sat on the edge and reached for my shirt, pulling it on. I needed to walk this mood off, this sense of guilt that attacked from all sides.

I put my pants on and slipped on my shoes, unable to disregard this uneasiness, this sense of losing her like it had already happened.

Not falling for her was the kindest decision I could make for myself.

I peered back at her and it made my heart ache, seeing the sleeping beauty with her serene face, red locks spilling around her like a mystical nymph captivating in every conceivable way.

Drawn to her, I leaned in and planted a kiss on her nose, gentle pecks trailing over her freckles, as though kissing each one was humanly possible.

She opened her eyes, gazing up at me.

"Hi," I whispered.

"Hi."

"Tell me what you want?"

"I want you to be happy."

The promise of a different life.

My mouth crashed against hers, tongue forcing her mouth wider. I needed to taste her like this, needed to be closer.

Our first kiss felt frenzied and demanding.

How could so much intimacy have passed between us and only now were my lips sealed to hers—as though claiming her like this would fix everything?

When I moved away, she raised her head and pressed her mouth to mine again as though needing more.

I broke away and glared at her. "This doesn't make you special."

"What?"

"I need you to remember that."

"Yes, sir," she said, her tone shaky.

I pressed my lips to hers again, punishing her for how she

made me feel, forcing a fierce control on her in an attempt to prove she meant nothing to me.

Yet at the same time I hungered for more. I heard her soft sigh as she yielded beneath me.

I cupped her face as my kiss became more frenzied, as though it was easy to possess her.

Own her.

Punish her.

My thoughts disappeared into stillness.

We could have been anywhere, but we were here in this private bedroom, beneath this delicate chandelier. Together.

Within Chrysalis.

I could feel myself yielding to her. Her body trembled as it bent to mine.

Breaking me apart.

Breaking me open.

She might as well have been forcing her way through this wall I'd built, crashing onto the other side.

Finding me.

I was unable to pull away, despite wanting to fight against the inevitable hurt and destruction. I refused to listen to the voice that warned this was the wrong way, because it felt like the only way.

I jerked away and turned from her so she couldn't see what she'd done to me.

"Shay," she said softly as I left our bed.

I opened the door and walked out, leaving her alone.

CHAPTER THIRTY-TWO

TWISTING MY WRISTS, I TRIED TO PULL OUT OF THE CUFFS. It was useless.

Naked, with my back against tile, I tried to catch my breath as Master Shay strolled in.

He was bare-chested and shoeless, wearing only tailored slacks.

I'd been prepared for him.

Stripped and secured and now on show.

Last night, he'd walked out of the bedroom after kissing me like I meant something to him—even though before that he had told me otherwise. I clung to hope.

Just as De Sade had advised me to do.

It was closing in on lunch time.

Shay had been gone for hours. Seeing him made my flesh heat.

I'd waited in this intimidating room for thirty minutes, hoping he would show up.

He moved around as though this had always been inevitable. Us together again.

It was easy to guess what this room was for. The checked floor giving it a classy appearance, but it was a water room, nonetheless. The floor dipped onto another level to collect water that would gather around my feet.

I'd heard of these sessions where the pressure of a hose was used instead of a whip.

In that usual domineering way I'd grown addicted to, Shay closed in on me, his expression unreadable. He checked to make sure my wrists were contained within the cuffs.

Yesterday, I'd been showcased in the Harrington Suite and I'd exceeded their expectations, according to Lotte. I'd responded well to my old master as he'd given me over to my new Dom.

How could this not be permanent?

I trusted my master not to be too harsh or bring too much pain in this session. And it was water, right? How bad could this be?

"Let's begin," said Shay, strolling over to the other side of the room. He grabbed one of the fire hoses and dragged it off the clip on the wall.

He turned the handle on the faucet and water shot out the end of the hose. He carried it over to me.

I jolted with shock as the water pressure hit my abdomen. After initially being startled, I realized it felt good.

The stream of water was waved over my pelvis.

This felt like someone had turned on a shower and directed the showerhead at me—the kind that would feel delicious when pointed between my thighs.

Shay used a crisscross technique over my body, forcing water over my waist and gliding it down my stomach and thighs, before finally dragging it across my breasts.

When the water stream was directed between my thighs, my body jolted from the extreme sensations. I felt the rise of an orgasm.

I kept moaning.

Until Shay redirected the stream of water down to my toes,

starving me of what my clit desperately needed—that pressure returned.

"Again," I pleaded.

It was the way he bit his lip, that twist of a devilish smile. He rested the tip of his tongue in the corner of his mouth.

"Please, sir," he said gruffly.

"Oh, God, please, sir."

He jerked the water stream back up to my sex, teasing me, bringing me close.

My body shuddered from the intense pleasure caused by the delicious pressure.

I let out a deep-throated sensual groan.

He dragged the water stream away again and teased my nipples with the hose.

"Sir!"

"I didn't give you permission to speak."

He lifted my chin and pressed his lips to mine. Our mouths clashed as our tongues warred with a devastating passion. He forced my lips wider so he could savagely kiss me.

"Master, permission to speak," I whispered against his lips.

"Speak."

"Don't edge me, please," I stuttered. "Carrie edged me for two days when you returned me from Pendulum. That was my punishment."

He seemed to reconsider. "Let's make up for it."

"Choke me," I demanded.

He grabbed my throat and tightened his hold, observing my reaction.

I mouthed, "Tighter."

"Stay with me," he coaxed.

My lungs felt strained by the lack of air.

"Come," he soothed.

The shock of pleasure bursting against my clit from where he'd pointed the spurting water sent me reeling.

Yes, and yes, to all things yes, my mind chanted as I slipped away.

I needed him. Yearned to have him show me he felt the same way.

I'd only known this man for a few weeks and already I'd fallen hard for him.

I was fading fast into a beautiful darkness, disappearing into a blinding climax.

My thoughts dissipated as the pleasure surged.

Out of the blissful dark, I heard Shay speak my name.

"Rue."

I felt the sensation of a strong arm around my waist.

"Rue?"

My hands were freed from the cuffs. I was lifted and then lowered onto the tile floor, being held in his arms.

I awakened to see his beautiful face.

"You okay?" he asked.

Raising my head, I looked around, recalling where we were.

"How do you feel?"

"I don't think I've ever come that hard," I said, breathless.

He chuckled and then his expression turned serious. "You should have told me you're not into edging."

"I'm into coming."

He grinned, bowing closer and planting a kiss on my nose.

Shay's stomach grumbled.

He shook his head. "I forget about food when I'm around you."

"Oh."

"I mean, when I'm in here I…" He pushed to his feet and helped me to mine. "Let's continue."

I stood beside him and folded my arms. "It's hard to focus with your stomach making noises."

Shay looked affronted. "Don't break protocol."

"I'm not going to continue one more second until I've seen you eat something."

"I'm fine.

"You're neglecting yourself. Let me look out for you, too."

"Don't."

"Don't what?"

"Be this…" He swept his hand through the air.

"Cadence," I said my safe word with panache.

Strolling over to a rack in the corner, I threw a towel to him and grabbed one for myself.

We dried off and then both of us slipped into the luxury robes provided.

"I'm thirsty," I said, knowing that would work on him. "Your submissive needs water."

"That wasn't enough water for you?"

I dragged him toward the door.

"This is totally out of order, Rue."

"Oh, shut up, sir." I guided this big hulk of a guy along the hallway.

We found the kitchen stocked up with enough food to feed a small army. I brought out of a plate of lasagna and proceeded to microwave the dish. Shay sat at the kitchen counter watching me. After it was heated, I served up two china plates of food, grabbed some cutlery and poured us both a glass of water.

We settled in, sitting opposite each other at the kitchen counter feasting on Italian. The food tasted deliciously home-cooked.

I smirked. "Was this cooked in the Imperial kitchen?"

"It was."

"Amazing things happen in there," I joked.

Shay dabbed his mouth with a napkin. "I didn't realize how hungry I was."

"See?"

"You've settled in well."

"I'm versatile."

"I can see that."

I watched his reaction. "I savor our times together."

"I enjoy spending time with you, too."

"Other than surfing," I said, "what do you do in your time off?"

"I don't have much time for anything other than work."

"I hike around Laurel Canyon." I took my last bite of food. "We can hike together, if you like?"

His expression changed to concern.

"Or you can never see me ever again after this," I said. "If that makes things easier."

"Why would it make things easier?"

I'd just be one of the other submissives when the time came. I'd see him pass by from afar. That was my destiny. Our future set out before us.

"You grew up in Beverly Hills?" he asked.

I knew where this was going. He would see me as privileged and find another reason to point out our differences.

"I was spoiled with love," I began. "My mom came from Georgia. She taught me the meaning of gratitude. It was a very southern upbringing."

"Sounds idyllic."

I felt a stab of fear that if I didn't connect with him now, I never would. "What do you like to do?"

"I really am a workaholic." He nudged his plate away.

"Do they not give you time off?"

He shook his head. "I micromanage."

"You must have something you look forward to."

His mouth twisted as though he was mulling it over. "I've been saving up to buy some property. I've managed to place a bid on a great piece of land. I'm going to build a house on it."

"Where?"

"Malibu."

"That's incredible."

"Maybe I'll take you to see it once the deal goes through."

"I'm free next week," I said softly.

Shay seemed contemplative. "Rue…"

I shrugged. "It was a silly thought."

He sat up straight on the stool. "No, I like the sound of it."

"But?"

"It's just a matter of finding the time."

"Tell me about it…the place."

"The plot is on the ocean." He lit up. "Once the house is built, I'll be able to walk from the patio and put my feet in the sand."

I smiled. "That sounds like a dream come true."

"I'm going to need advice on decorating. I wouldn't know where to start."

"I can help."

"I'll be doing a lot myself. It'll keep the cost down."

"Right, good idea."

He looked away, his expression crinkling into warmth.

"I'll do the dishes," I said, grabbing my plate and then his and heading over to the sink.

Shay joined me. As I rinsed them off, he took the plates out of my hand one by one and placed the china in the dishwasher.

It was kind of cute, us doing the dishes together, like a glimpse of another life—the kind I'd always craved but was too scared to believe in.

"Come here," said Shay, arms out.

I rested against his warm body, my cheek on his firm chest.

I was giddy with the thought that he was finally letting his guard down.

His lips pressed the top of my head as though marking the moment with a kiss.

Standing within his strong, warm embrace, I wished with all my heart that I knew what this man was thinking.

CHAPTER THIRTY-THREE

Shay

T HE SEAMSTRESS CONTINUED TO FUSS OVER THE TRIM OF Rue's deep green bodice, which was sprinkled with faux diamonds.

Even the light worshipped this submissive—sunrays bursting through the window shimmered over her.

Yesterday, we'd found time to get to know each other when we'd had a casual lunch in the kitchen. It felt good to get to a place where we felt comfortable. That way, we'd be able to push our limits and be honest about our expectations.

"I've never been to a ball before." Rue raised her arms as pins were placed down her left side. "I'm so excited."

"I'm glad."

The thought of her wandering off into the halls of Chrysalis made my stomach clench. I'd be keeping a close watch over her.

A Chrysalis event meant no expense was spared. Luxurious elements took center stage as new submissives were showcased.

Rue would stand out like a rare gem. Her charisma would keep the attention on her all night.

"When do I get the wings attached?" asked Rue.

"After your fitting," said the seamstress. "You're going to look like a Victoria Secret model."

"They're all skinny," Rue retorted.

"Rue, you're perfect," I said. "You're all woman. If I was into worshipping women, I'd have built an altar to you by now."

Both women stared at me.

"I mean it's not that I don't worship you…" I shook my head. "I just do it in my own way."

"That is the most romantic thing anyone has ever said to me," she whispered.

Where the hell had that come from?

This wasn't like me.

I wasn't the romantic type.

Rue's costume was stunning. Her wings would slow her down with any luck.

Everyone was going to be drawn to her. She was a magnet. At some point in the evening, other guests would flirt and maybe she'd flirt back. She'd probably want to stretch those silver wings and fly off with someone.

I shouldn't care.

This was the agreement between us.

Locking her up in a castle would be a stellar idea. Not letting anyone see her.

Because that made total fucking sense.

There was a fault line in my heart.

I suddenly realized the awful truth. I'd fallen for her. It was hard to tell when or how or even why.

These feelings were devastatingly different.

Maybe it had been those minutes that had passed between us in the kitchen when she'd made me lunch, nurturing me. I'd forgotten what that felt like.

Or maybe it was the first time I'd found her in Pendulum.

It was like a shattering of all that had gone before and a future that threatened to self-destruct if I didn't get a handle on this.

"You like it, right?" Rue's voice brought me out of my musings.

I shook off the melancholy and nodded. "It'll do."

She looked relieved, showing no vanity as she glanced at her reflection in the mirror. She offered the seamstress a kind smile and then looked at me all wide-eyed and eager.

Dashing billionaires would be hiding in the shadows to sweep her off her feet.

It was inevitable.

As reality sunk in, my desire for her intensified because seeing her like this, like an erotic fairytale nymph, made me want to keep her.

She's not yours to keep.

The cruel truth of my dark musing.

"Out," I ordered the seamstress. "I need to talk with Rue."

She scurried out of the room.

"Am I in trouble?" asked Rue.

I stalked toward her and knelt, dragging her thong down her legs. "Get out of this," I growled.

She lifted her legs as I helped her step out of her thong. This was the outfit she'd be wearing when I sent her away.

And I hated her for it.

Leaning in, I kissed her pubic bone as though that alone would soothe my heartache. As though the process of letting her go had already begun.

My mouth glided lower.

She tasted of peace and safety and all the things I'd never known, her clit soft against my tongue at first, and then the small bud began to harden.

I lavished her with a harsh punishment as though she'd already left me—her sighs and moans and the rocking of her hips proving she was close to coming.

Relentless, refusing to let up, refusing to let go and forgive her, I owned her pussy like I had a right to it. Like this woman was mine.

She dragged her delicate fingers through my hair, her hands

settling on the back of my head, holding me to her, holding me as though she was just as addicted to me as I was to her.

Her climax snatched her breath away and caused her to tremble against me. Feeling her ride through her pleasure with me as the catalyst made me harder.

I fought to ignore my own needs and just give her more.

She shuddered through another orgasm.

Softening my claim on her, I lapped tenderly, because that's what she deserved. That's what she had to be given to sustain her serenity.

And I knew that. Knew what she needed and just how to deliver her over to the other side of peace.

"I feel seen," she whispered.

No one would treat her with more reverence.

No other man could adore her like I was now, like I would have done in the future if we'd had more time.

She suddenly drew in a sharp breath, her expression full of concern as she stared toward the doorway.

I turned to follow her gaze.

De Sade was standing there.

Pushing up, I walked toward him, anger a snake curling in my belly, throat constricting with a firestorm of words.

He backed off. "I need to talk with you."

"You should knock."

"I knocked."

"You should have knocked louder."

"I can see why you didn't hear." He looked over at Rue with an awed expression.

The same expression I'd seen on the faces of so many others when they laid eyes on her.

I studied his reaction, as though seeing him bewitched would explain my reaction when I was in the room with her. I needed to understand this obsession.

"I'll wait outside." De Sade stepped back into the hallway.

We were alone again.

I faced Rue. "Get dressed."

"I don't think she's finished, sir," Rue said, her voice timid. "The seamstress, I mean."

"She can come back later."

Which was ridiculous—I was literally telling her to dress so that no part of her was exposed.

I ran my fingers through my hair. "You'll eat lunch in your room."

"Without you?"

"Yes, Rue, think you can handle that?"

She seemed hurt, but I was already closing in on the door. I paused and looked back at her. "You look…"

She gave a bright smile of understanding. Because she saw through me, too.

"Thank you for the bodice."

"Try on the shoes."

She grabbed the box off the bed, her mouth curling at the edges. "I like it when you choose what you want to see me in."

"You like them?"

She peered under the lid. "They're perfect."

"That's what I thought." I dug deep into my kindness.

No, that wasn't strictly true. Rue brought it out in me.

Looking back at her, I tried to say something to undo the harshness I felt when around her. I'd lost the ability to reason when she was in close proximity. She was like a goddess with the ability to break through my fake demeanor.

Heading into the hallway, I went after De Sade.

He gestured to have me follow him down the hallway. Other than Cameron, De Sade was the only other person who was never intimidated by me. Even at my worst.

"What do you want?" I said.

"You closed down Enthrall? What's going on?"

"I'm on it, Jake."

"It would be great to get a heads-up if something is going down."

"We've attracted a photojournalist," I said. "I'm dealing with him."

"Does he know about Chrysalis?"

"Not as far as I can tell."

"Okay, good." His eyes narrowed. "Is he after someone specific?"

"This is why you interrupted me?" I snapped

"No, actually."

"What. Do. You. Want?"

"Sometimes you surprise me, Gardner."

I folded my arms across my chest, showing my impatience.

"You never signed it?" he said.

I stared at him, trying to unscramble his words.

Jake's expression was stoic. "The submissive contract. You just wrote *to be determined*."

Those seeds of doubt I'd had in the breakfast room.

The gut feeling that rarely let me down.

"Names were put forward," he said.

"What?"

"Dominic—"

"Dominic considered you?" I felt a stab of concern.

"My seniority does give me that honor, yes."

We both knew how much Dominic hated me, too.

"What are you saying?" I snapped. "Dominic considered you for Rue's master? What about your wife?"

"She likes to watch."

I gritted my teeth together, trying to suppress my annoyance at Dominic.

The air grew heavy.

Here we were again. De Sade thrusting me into a sea of chaos.

He was the master of pain, only I'd never considered his specialty being wielded outside a dungeon.

My concerned gaze held his. "Tell me you didn't sign the contract?"

Uneasiness slithered up my spine when I saw pure arrogance in his eyes.

"All *you* had to do was sign it," he said.

"So you did?" I seethed.

"Rue would have gone to Grantchester. I knew you didn't—"

"Why didn't you call me?"

"You were out with Henry."

"How did you know that?"

"Lotte told me. Didn't want to interrupt your dinner."

"It was just drinks." I could have taken a call or answered a text.

Even now, I hated the distance between myself and Rue and it was merely a wall between us. The thought of losing her completely caused a wave of dread to surge over me like a tsunami.

I'd kept putting it off.

Because seeing her with another man was unbearable.

De Sade gave me a smug little smile. "Now if you'll excuse me, I'm going in to talk with my new submissive."

CHAPTER THIRTY-FOUR

Shay

I BLOCKED JAKE FROM MOVING PAST ME. "No."

He looked amused. "No?"

"You're not going in there."

"You know there are rules, right?" he said.

"It was agreed. Richard and Scarlet—"

"Scarlet doesn't work here."

"Richard is still the Director."

De Sade reached into his pocket and whipped out a piece of paper. He unfolded it. "Notice my signature is *not* on the contract."

What the fuck.

He shoved the form at me.

I felt equal parts anger and relief as I scanned the last page.

"You're welcome." The asshole probably found this funny.

I inhaled a deep, cleansing breath. The thought of losing Rue had filled me with too much dread.

My adrenaline was still spiking.

De Sade reached into his pocket and took out a fountain pen. It looked familiar.

"So Dominic put you up to this."

I should never have put Rue at risk. My feelings for her were so intense I'd tried to deny them.

I grabbed the pen and pressed the contract against the wall. Scanning it quickly to make sure what I was signing was the submissive contract, I signed my name along the last line of the page.

It felt so damn good.

I handed the pen back to Jake.

We swapped a look and he gave me a compassionate smile. The kind that told me he got me.

I watched him wander off toward the stairs.

Standing at the top of the steps, I thought about how I'd felt while placing my signature on that form.

Rue was mine.

This way, I could still be her hero—make sure she remained safe.

I could go back into the room with Rue, but I wanted to tell her later. Make it special…give us something to look back on.

Following Jake, I descended the stairs, two steps at a time. When I got to the bottom I headed for Richard's office.

It was empty.

Making myself comfortable at his desk, I got ready to do some work at his computer. His screen was the size of a fucking house, for God's sake.

He'd taken over Cole's space after he'd been handed the reins. Richard made it his by adding touches of his personality to the décor, but he'd left a few items that reminded us of Cameron.

Cole leaving as the director of Chrysalis was one of the harder transitions for us. We admired Richard, but Cole had been the once beating heart of this place.

My team had sent over a report detailing Enthrall's security footage. Deciding to check it out for myself, I scanned it over carefully. Darryn hadn't returned to Enthrall, which was good, but the reason for him being there initially still wasn't clear.

Working methodically, frame by frame, I scanned the footage

from Enthrall's perimeter recorded weeks ago, logging who came and went—names, license plate numbers, deliveries, and the coming and going of staff.

I reversed the footage all the way back to the hour that Darryn had tried to infiltrate Enthrall. Later that morning, he'd gotten stuck in the elevator—a quick-thinking Lotte had sealed him in there.

When the elevator doors finally opened, he'd tripped out. More evidence I'd not touched him, and his wrist sprain had nothing to do with me—though I might have strong-armed him to get him to hand over his camera.

And then escorted him out of the building.

A minute later, there I was on the footage seen with Darryn climbing into my Rover parked out front.

There was me driving off with him to go get his wrist X-rayed at Cedars. We'd had his car towed to his address in Santa Monica— the one that turned out not to be his place.

I jolted forward when minutes later, right at the bend in the road, I saw my car pass a Mercedes-Benz.

It was Cameron's car heading toward Enthrall.

Continuing to watch that morning's footage, I followed Cole to the front door.

The near miss was heart-stopping. Zooming in on Darryn's face through the windshield, I could see he'd not even clocked the car or driver heading in the opposite direction.

Something told me Darryn was interested in only one client. And that mark was Cameron Cole.

I read that Darryn's background check indicated he had once worked for TMZ. Now, he was a contractor for hire.

According to a copy of his tax records that we'd obtained— illegal, I know—Darryn actually lived in an apartment in North Hollywood. That Santa Monica house was his way of trying to shake us off.

Richard was leaning on the doorjamb of *his* office.

"Hey." I sat back.

He knocked on the door, even after seeing me. "Can I come in?"

I liked "considerate Richard," the guy who'd slowed down since meeting Andrea.

"I've located Darryn," I told him.

He approached the desk. "Really, where?"

"North Hollywood."

"Are you going to pay him a visit?"

"I will, yes."

"Any idea who his target is?" Richard waited for my response. "Not me, is it?"

I shook my head. "Still looking into it."

I'd not told a lie—it was more of a delay tactic. They'd hired me to deal with threats so they didn't have to.

Richard studied me. "He's not after Andrea, is he?"

"Not as far as I can tell."

"You'll keep me updated?"

"Absolutely," I said, smiling. "Can you arrange for Rue to visit the spa?"

Richard grinned back at me. "You're spoiling her? Has she done anything that warrants a massage?"

"She has to put up with me."

Richard gave a nod as he headed out. I trusted him to make it happen.

I worked for another hour, up until hunger got the better of me. I stood and stretched, then made my way toward the kitchen.

I was glad to find the place empty.

It meant I could take the time to think everything over during a quick lunch. Rue was right—I needed to pay more attention to my diet. To everything, really. In that respect she was a great influence.

Opening the fridge door, I tried to figure out what I was craving.

The chefs at Chrysalis always made sure our kitchen's fridge was well-stocked. It meant staff and guests could enjoy flavorful meals and snacks in between the dining room's hours of operation.

Reaching in, I went for the chicken pasta. I could almost taste the pesto sauce. I brought the bowl over to the kitchen counter and scooped some onto a plate, popping it into the microwave.

"Thank goodness I found you," a female voice said from behind me.

I pivoted and looked over at Lotte who was standing just inside the kitchen door.

I took the plate out of the microwave and set it down. "Hey, Lotte."

"Carrie Quinn's here"

I smirked. "She wants to join us. Get her membership ready."

"I'm serious. We have a pissed off Dominatrix demanding to see you."

"Rue was at Majestic for a while."

"I read that in her file."

I glanced over at my plate of food, yet to be eaten. "Invite her in."

"Carrie says she prefers to wait in her car."

"Can this wait a while?"

"I'm guessing no."

"Okay, I'll deal with her." I headed for the door.

"Is that chicken pasta?" Lotte nudged by me and walked over to the kitchen counter. "Can I have the rest?"

I gave her a warm smile. "Sure."

My stomach was polite enough not to grumble.

Lotte dipped her finger into the sauce and licked it off. "We'll keep Rue safe."

She may be a pasta thief, but Lotte was also one of the kindest souls around.

I left the kitchen and took long strides down the hallway toward Chrysalis' front door.

Making my way out, I walked toward the town car parked close to the entrance. The driver's door opened and a chauffeur got out. He walked some distance away, after probably being ordered to give us privacy.

I rapped on the dusky back window.

The car door sprung open.

"Mr. Gardner," Carrie's terseness sounded familiar. "Get in."

I climbed inside and sat opposite her. "This could have been a call."

"It could have been, yes." She sneered. "However, I doubt you'd have put Rue on the phone."

"She's allowed to make her own decisions."

She mulled that over as though sucking on a bee, her mouth twisting with distaste. The bitterness of failure. "I sent you to rescue my submissive from Pendulum. And somehow, she has found her way here."

"It is curious, isn't it?" I leaned back and crossed one leg over the other.

"Rue left our House without honoring her contract."

She'd not told me that part.

"We don't keep them prisoner, Carrie."

"Unless your name is Cameron Cole."

I gave her a thin smile. "If you'll excuse me."

"You and I have some business to discuss." She sat back.

And here it was—the predictable first strike.

I'd expected it, but it stung nevertheless.

Ambitious women like Carrie always had a wild card up their sleeve—an ulterior motive.

"Let's hear it," I said.

She looked toward the manor. "The cost for Rue breaching her contract is substantial."

"Let her out of it, Carrie."

"We must set an example. Once a hundred K arrives at Majestic, she will be released from her commitment."

I uncrossed my legs and rested my elbows on my knees. "That's how much she's worth to you?"

She bristled. "Rue has unusual needs."

I could have added that Rue had informed me she'd been starved of pleasure while there. It was better not to feed this two-headed monster.

"Just so we're clear," I said, "you're saying Rue may stay here as long as we send funds?"

"This is a confidential request, for Rue's sake."

"For Rue's sake?"

"As her Domina I know what is best for her."

"Not anymore you're not."

"Ask Faulkner what I did to him."

He'd not mentioned anything about it, which would have been helpful now.

"Don't make me find it necessary to dig around Majestic," I said. "I've brought down more superior houses than yours."

"I can see you're captivated by her."

I reached for the door handle. "We're done."

She leaned forward. "I want to speak with Rue alone. That way you can't influence anything she might want to tell me."

That idea made the hairs on my nape prickle. "I'll see if she wants to speak with you."

"I'm sure the council at Chrysalis will want to make this scandal go away." She narrowed her gaze on me. "It's certainly interesting that a security issue is caused by the head of security."

I opened the car door. "Blackmail doesn't work on us."

"Time will tell."

There was a strict policy of not paying out. That policy wouldn't change even for someone like me. The optics weren't good, either. I had to make this go away and fast. For everyone's sake.

A sinking feeling hit me as I thought about what I'd have to do to appease Carrie and keep Rue from having to return to Majestic.

"Rue is capable of making her own decisions," I threw in.

"How far do you think my power goes?"

"I imagine all the way up your ass."

She gave me an unpleasant smile. "Unlike my contemporaries, I don't willingly give up my submissives."

Any retort I made would be wasted. She'd made up her mind.

She added, "There will be consequences if you don't comply."

My brow arched playfully in response to her threat.

"Keeping our reputations intact," she said. "We all want that, right?"

"If we decline?"

"I wouldn't advise it."

"You're crossing dangerous ground," I said sternly.

"You've set a bad precedent," she said. "Moving submissives like chess pieces to fulfill your needs."

"You asked me to remove her from Pendulum."

Carrie looked off toward Chrysalis. "The directive was to bring her back to me."

"Thank you for forwarding her contract with Majestic." I forced a smile. "We'll take a look at it."

I exited the car and headed back to Chrysalis.

Once inside, I went to check up on Rue. Though telling her about Carrie's visit was not going to happen.

I didn't want her worrying that she'd ever have to go back to that place. I wanted to keep her in the right headspace.

We had a ball to attend and seeing her reach her full potential and fulfill her fantasies was everything.

CHAPTER THIRTY-FIVE

Shay

I HAD ONCE HEARD RICHARD SAY THAT HE BELIEVED OUR SOULS were made from the stars. He could be surprisingly poetic when he wanted to be.

My own philosophies were more pedantic. More earthbound. Human nature had always fascinated me. That's why I was drawn to Cameron. His understanding for the human condition was compelling.

What I did know was this: people are generally creatures of habit. Most people love routines, choosing the same time to wake up, to eat. Same time to carry out all those other privileged practices we get to do in the western world.

Darryn Amara was no different.

From his online presence to his existence in the real world, he was an asshole. My contempt for him only briefly lifted when I realized what a mess he'd made of his life.

Darryn was a gambler. He owed enough money to get him into trouble. Pushing aside both ethics and morality, he was trying to reap those losses.

Entering Mel's Diner, I saw him sitting at his favorite booth eating his favorite lunch, looking disheveled and unshaven—and seemingly lonely after his recent divorce. I almost felt sorry for the bastard.

When he saw me he pushed to his feet.

"Sit down," I said.

Darryn slumped back into the seat.

I wouldn't be eating, not with him. Breaking bread with this kind of man just wasn't going to happen.

I waved away the menu being offered to me by the waiter, also turning down coffee.

"Had a feeling I'd see you again," he said.

Between us sat an empty plate stained with grease. I dragged my focus back to him. "You know why I'm here," I began.

"To give me more money?" he chided.

Right, because this idiot deserved another check from us after cashing the last one we'd written to try and get rid of him.

Only, he had no intention of going away.

The stakes were too high.

I'd been watching him use his damaged wrist with ease since I'd arrived. Before I could ask about it, he spoke up.

"How did you find me?"

"Library card." It was sort of true—his memberships had come up in a search. More specifically, I'd found Darryn via his phone, thanks to the towers pinging his location.

"What's this about?" he asked.

"Who sent you to spy on us?"

"I'm just a freelancer for hire."

"No matter how many photos you take or how many jobs you work, you will never catch up financially. Your wife took the house. Your children don't know you. Your life is going down the drain."

"What's your point?"

"Gambling debt gone." I leaned back. "How does that scenario sound?"

"Like a lie."

"Because you're not used to dealing with decent people." I removed the contract from my inner pocket and slid it over the table to him. "You have five minutes."

He leaned forward and glanced at it. "No comment."

"They are paying you just enough to keep the lights on. Not nearly enough to turn things around. Now that's what's called—"

"Keeping me on the hook."

"I'm your way out, Mr. Amara." I reached into my jacket pocket and pulled out a pen.

"If you know this much then you know about the rest. You don't need anything from me."

"Tell me their name." I set the pen by the contract.

"It's nothing personal," he said.

"Sign the contract. I'll order you more coffee."

"Don't want any."

"You have three mugs of dark brew at breakfast. That one was your first."

"That's not sinister at all."

Because when it came to me and my team, we were the best.

"As you can see, finding you was easy—despite the false Santa Monica address."

He picked up the pen and scanned the contract. "I should have a lawyer look at this."

"A lawyer would advise you against blackmailing us—a crime punishable by prison time. We could sue you to the full extent of the law."

"Shit."

"Take this as your chance to wipe the slate clean. Avoid prison."

"They're the kind of people you don't piss off."

"Neither are we."

"I'll never feel clean." He nudged the coffee mug away and then changed his mind and brought it closer. "Tell me I won't regret this."

"Doing the right thing can feel like the wrong thing sometimes. That's your conscience."

"I don't know…"

"This is enough money to wipe out your debt. You'll be able to move back to London. Be near your kids."

He let out a sigh. "God knows what they'll do if they find out it came from me."

"We're good at what we do."

"Clearly, but…"

I reached for the contract as though I'd changed my mind.

"Come on, man."

"Who were you sent to photograph at Enthrall?"

He sat back.

"Talk," I said. "Tell me who you're working for."

CHAPTER THIRTY-SIX

Shay

OUR SWORDS CLASHED.

We went at each other hard backwards and forwards like we meant it. My épée bent against Cameron's chest guard. I leaped into the air and pumped my fist.

I'd won the match.

I wore a grin behind my mesh mask.

I'd finished Cole off with a swooping flèche.

We lowered our swords, bowing to each other. With that gesture, it was safe to rip off my mask.

Cameron pulled off his, perspiration spotting his brow, his hair disheveled.

The fight to the death of egos was over.

Though I'd wanted to dive right into business, Cole had insisted we fence first—as though life could wait for the drama.

Being at Cameron's Beverly Hills home was a good way to get rid of the bad taste left in my mouth after seeing Darryn Amara this afternoon at that L.A. diner.

Money. A great influencer. It made people like him be willing to break the law.

"Being pissed off suits you." Cole gave me a wry smile.

He swaggered over to a corner table and laid his sword across it.

Finding the time to fence had been challenging with our conflicting schedules.

Maybe he needed this, too—a respite from life, burning out the tension with some elegant violence.

Cameron's razor-sharp focus zeroed in on my distracted look. "Want to talk about it?"

I didn't need Cole digging around my psyche. "How are things with you?"

He thought on it and then said, "Really good."

"You're both content to have given up the scene?"

"Hello to you, too."

"Just saying."

Cameron picked up a bottle of water from the table and unscrewed the lid. I watched him take a few gulps.

"How's the new submissive?" he said.

"Rue?"

"The one you have no emotional connection to?" He arched a brow.

"There's affection for her."

"Right."

"She's sweet-natured."

"That's how I found her."

"Just come out and fucking say it, Cole."

"Say what?"

"You know me better than I know myself. Tell me what's going on inside my head."

"How would I know what's happening inside your head?"

"Because that's how you work. You get inside a mind and gnaw away until you get to the problem."

"Gnaw?"

"You know what I mean."

"I hear you've signed the submissive contract."

"Is nothing private?"

"Richard told me."

That made me smile because Cole usually began with a shocking accusation to rile me up.

"Having feelings for her makes you uncomfortable." He rested his palm over his heart. "When this awakens, watch out world."

"I'll take some antacid."

Cameron looked amused. "Why do I sense it's serious?"

"You have a problem at Cole Tea," I said, attempting to change the subject.

He waved a hand in the air. "Let's focus on you. You're standing before me right now. You're important. Let's seek out a solution."

"I don't have a problem." I looked away, trying to find the words. My stomach clenched with dread.

"You have to be the one to say it," he reasoned.

Turning my épée in a circle, I thought about how to express my feelings. "I don't want anyone to touch my submissive tonight."

He gave me a kind smile. "That's a problem because…"

"That's her kink."

"You gave her time at Imperial. Maybe she got it out of her system."

"She's fascinated with the scene."

"That was before she fell for you, Shay."

I shook my head. "I have no right to dictate what she does."

"Do you want to?"

"I don't think we're heading in that direction."

"Rue is drawn to someone she has chemistry with," he said. "I saw the way she looked at you at Enthrall."

I blinked at him. "What am I meant to do with that information?"

He laughed. "You tell me."

"Look, this is trivial compared to why I'm here."

"Okay, let's change the subject, if that feels safer."

"It's not that."

"I'm here. I will make time for you, Shay. You know that."

"You have a corporate spy at Cole Tea."

He'd been about to take another drink of water, but he paused.

"Darryn Amara was part of that corporate attack," I said. "He was hired to photograph you at Enthrall by a major competitor."

His expression remained surprisingly calm.

"I observed no photos of you on his phone when I examined it."

"He let you?"

"Didn't give him a choice. Anyway, he's contained. For now."

"I'll call Henry."

"I'll forward you the info I have so far."

"I would appreciate that."

"We'll increase your personal security. No more letting guards off for the evening."

He gave a salute.

"Sorry to deliver the bad news," I said.

"Still impressing me after all this time, Gardner." He finished the bottle of water and set it back on the table.

"It's what I do."

"Let's talk about what's happening tonight at Chrysalis."

"With Rue? I just warned you there's corporate espionage going on at Cole Tea and you want to chat about my relationship?"

He gave an approving nod. "I like how that sounds. A relationship."

"It's not official."

Cole closed the gap between us. "You're on the precipice of something incredible."

His opinion meant everything to me. "Rue is special…"

He threw a towel my way. "My chef made a salad for lunch. Mia's at a play date with Raif. We'll have privacy to talk more. We'll call Henry from the kitchen."

"Sounds like a plan."

"I know you don't want me in your head, Shay, but at least let me say you're ready for love."

I knew he'd take it there. "There's too many…"

"Shadows?" Cameron patted my back and guided me out of the room. "My specialty."

CHAPTER THIRTY-SEVEN

S HAY STROLLED IN LOOKING TALL AND DASHING IN HIS BLACK tuxedo.

He drank me in, seemingly devouring my body.

My fingers caressed the ruby collar that fit snuggly against my throat.

Tell him.

Tell him you don't want to be with anyone but him.

"You look—"

I spun around, showing off my curvaceous deep green bodice, turning to show off my wings.

His satisfied smirk looked sexy as hell.

My costume was a butterfly midflight.

"They're a little restrictive."

"You'll find a way, I'm sure."

Considering this was Chrysalis and the play was daring and wild and all kinds of kinky fun.

"Want to share your thoughts about tonight?" he asked.

"I need to go slow."

Sensing my reticence, he closed the space between us and looked down at me. "Consent is yours to give, Rue."

Which was why I'd fallen in love with this place.

He was wearing a different cologne—a combination of sex god and something earthy, like leather and ash; an intoxicating aroma.

This man was all I'd ever wanted and ever dared to dream of having.

I was going to have to watch him with another woman tonight. See him play hard.

Shay strolled over to the mirror. He reached into his pocket and pulled out a black masquerade mask, securing it to his face.

I watched his reflection. This strikingly domineering man would be my guide tonight.

He turned to face me.

I followed his lead and moved over to the mirror, putting on my masquerade mask. With my titian hair, I'd probably stand out.

Maybe I'd cross paths with the other dominants from Imperial. Maybe we would see Kaison Faulkner.

"We'll get a drink first," he said.

"Before?"

"Before we explore."

He meant before we see what goes on within the rooms. Within the dungeons. And all the corners where lovers like to meet.

"Your safe word?"

"Cadence."

He twisted his mouth. "If you forget it, say stop." He shrugged. "In case you're in a high stress situation."

"What kind would that be?"

"What we did at Imperial was nothing compared to what will unfold tonight."

"Oh?"

"It's what you want, right?"

"Is it what you want?"

His fingers reached for my mask and adjusted it. "This will be everything you want it to be."

"Whatever pleases you, sir."

"Right—remember to address me as Dom or Master or sir. Never use my name."

"I'll remember, sir."

He reached into his pocket again and drew out a long, thin chain. He clipped it to my collar. "Ready?"

"Yes, sir."

I'd never be ready to see him with another member.

Before our time at Imperial, we hadn't bonded like we were now.

He opened the door and gestured for me to go ahead of him.

The music grew louder, an operatic splendor welcoming guests.

We descended the stairs.

Gripping the banister, I tried to be careful walking in heels, and felt grateful when Shay reached out and took my arm.

The place was humming with partygoers. The men looked sharp in their tuxedos and the women were wearing elegant long gowns. Submissives were mingling with the ebullient crowd; all of them in erotic leather and lace outfits.

Holding hands, we strolled into a vast room.

A server offered us bubbly from a silver tray. I was handed a glass and Shay took the other flute of champagne for himself.

We tapped our drinks together and sipped our bubbly.

Something between us had changed.

Instead of looking at the guests, we were staring at each other. Our connection felt even deeper.

My body felt heated despite my skimpy bodice.

"You look…" he began.

"You, too," I whispered.

Shay's brows furrowed and he looked annoyed.

"What?"

Shay led me away, hurrying me through a wide doorway. We brought our drinks with us.

I glanced back and saw Kaison. Even in a masquerade mask I knew it was him. He'd stopped short of following us.

Shay turned back to look at him. "Not yet."

I tried to read what he'd meant by that.

A man dressed like a butler closed the door behind us.

This felt like an exclusive and very private conclave of Chrysalis. The light had a deep blue hue and the music was louder with a rhythmic base.

I was as curious as I was nervous, my eyes trying to adjust to the dimness. Blinking, I saw leggy women dressed as submissives escorting men into the darkest corners.

Marble columns lined the venue.

At the outer edges of the glamorous room, guests were fucking—the scene dreamlike beneath the sensual lighting. On a burgundy couch, four lovers were entwined and writhing together in perfect unison.

An erotic vision unfolded as I was led on through.

We found our way into the center of the room.

"On your knees," demanded my master.

Obeying quickly, I knelt and peered up at him, waiting for my next command.

"Take it in your mouth," he ordered.

Reaching up, I unbuckled his belt and unzipped his pants.

Unfolding around us where sexual encounters of every description, a beautiful vision of passion and lust.

Of affection and love.

"Look at me," he demanded.

Leaning forward, I took him in my hand and then waited for permission. He gave it with a nod.

I kissed his cock reverently.

"I approve," he said, his tone edgy.

"Please," I begged.

"Suck it."

I lavished affection onto Shay's enormous shaft, lapping and sucking and leaning low to draw his balls into my mouth, suckling them and then returning to the width of his cock.

"Good girl," he said huskily.

Knowing he was looking down at me with admiration gave me the rush I yearned for, my arousal spiking.

Gripping him with my right hand, I cupped his balls with my left. When his hand came down on my head as though anointing me, I began a faster pace, wanting to please him more.

"Take it deeper," he demanded.

And I did, swallowing his tip each time it was thrust to the back of my throat. I enjoyed the silky feel of his iron-hard length in my palm.

His fingers clenched my hair, controlling my pace.

Then, still gripping locks of my hair, he dragged me to a standing position.

I was spun round and nudged against a post, my thong ripped from me.

He'd tucked himself away, but I knew, just knew, he was straining against his sleek black pants.

With my hands on the post and my butt out, I leaned forward and bit down on my lower lip. At some point there would be pain. I'd always known it would come at last but had been scared to think of it.

When Faulkner had insisted on my punishments, they had been cruel and agonizing but I'd endured what had been expected.

Now, I would have to face my new master's demands.

I was on display.

The one to be watched.

I felt alarmed when I saw my master standing beside me, holding nothing. He merely stood close to me with his left hand on the post.

"Have you ever been paddled?" he asked.

I shook my head no.

"Then it's time you were," he said.

He made me push my butt out farther while leaning against the pillar, making sure my pussy could be viewed easily.

My Dom gave a nod to someone behind me.

Sir wasn't going to be delivering my punishment.

"Don't turn around," he ordered.

The first strike on my butt was gentle, more of tap with the flat of a wooden paddle, as though testing my endurance. A hit to my sex sent a shock of pleasure through me, my arousal increasing.

"Look straight ahead," Sir demanded.

He didn't want me to see who was wielding the paddle. My imagination was running wild.

Feeling the tension of holding this position and wanting to please him—please them—I tried to remain quite still.

I'd been deemed worthy enough for Chrysalis—deemed ready for this private party where the elite roamed. I wanted others to have no doubts that I could perform to their standards.

The paddle increased in tempo against my flesh, as though whoever was spanking me had been briefed to go easy.

This certainly wasn't how it had been at Majestic, where punishment came in severe forms. Afterward, I'd been showcased for the welts on my flesh.

These strikes fell into a delicious rhythm; now and again striking my pussy with a moderate thrash, causing me to swoon with the pleasure of it.

Heat spread across my cheeks.

My face flamed behind my masquerade mask.

Falling into the rhythm of the paddle, I let go, trusting my master to know how much I could take. Relaxing, allowing myself to enjoy the combination of light and dark, of heat and cold where the strikes did not find me.

A command was called out—an order to cease.

For the first time I could remember, I moaned because my punishment had stopped. The chain around my neck tugged me sideways and I continued to walk beside my Dom. I wanted to turn around but the way I was led dissuaded me from looking back.

Glancing left, I saw a blonde submissive sitting in a high-backed chair, her legs wide and leaning over the armrests, exposing her. Her thighs were strapped in so she couldn't move.

An elegant dominatrix was spanking the sub's pussy with her hand, tapping away at her fast. The sub squirmed in her seat, jaw slack, her moans rising over the music.

When she appeared to be close to release, the spanking slowed as though to draw out her climax. Her arousal soaked her sex, leaving her thighs wet, looking deliciously erotic.

"You like that?" asked Sir.

I suddenly felt self-conscious.

Because of him…

I wanted to please him.

We continued to stroll down hallways with Sir leading me on by that silver chain.

Until we reached a certain door.

He stepped forward and planted a kiss on my forehead.

"I want to give you everything," he said. "And for that I can't continue with you. I must let you go on alone."

"I don't understand."

"I'm…fond of you," he admitted. "Totally my fault. It means I am compromised with what I can offer you. What you need. What you are asking for."

I'd asked for so very much.

"They know you don't tolerate pain well. What they can give you is everything you asked of us. There will be no ending of pleasure. You'll be cycled through orgasms. Only when you are sated will you leave the room."

Confusion flooded through me. "What's behind the door?"

"Not what, Rue…who."

"Don't leave," I said, feeling breathless.

"My last order is this: Don't disappoint them." He leaned by me to turn the handle and open the door. "In you go."

Last order?

Was this him letting me go? Sending me away?

Stepping inside the dimly lit room, I saw a four-poster bed.

The door closed behind me.

When I turned back, Sir was gone.

I faced the four men who were waiting for me.

I knew what this was.

The four men in tuxedos looked suave and relaxed.

Kaison Faulkner was talking with Master Sinclair and Master Grantchester, all three of them sharing a glass of what looked like bourbon.

A little ways back from them, De Sade sat in a high-backed leather chair. He patted his knee, indicating I should sit on his lap.

CHAPTER THIRTY-EIGHT

ALL I COULD THINK OF WAS BELONGING TO SIR.
I didn't want anyone else to touch me. Not De Sade. Or Kaison Faulkner. Or Doms Sinclair or Grantchester. Not even with my Dom present.

This felt like I was betraying him.

I gripped the doorknob, trying to find the courage to leave.

Kaison strolled toward me.

All I'd wanted was this—I'd even defined this as the ultimate fantasy in my file. Yet now, as the reality sunk in, I felt different.

Because of Shay.

Faulkner curled his fingers against my cheek. "Take off your clothes."

My throat tightened, panic surging.

"You've been very naughty," he said.

Adrenaline surged in my veins.

"It's okay," said a reassuring voice from across the way.

It was De Sade.

Kaison flicked one of my wings. "You would never have survived Pendulum."

Nodding furiously, agreeing, I refused to look at him.

He stroked my hair. "You were my favorite."

"I belong to Master Gardner," I said.

I tried to remember my safe word, and couldn't.

De Sade pushed up from the chair and strolled over. He was so damn tall, his athletic physique intimidating. His fingers trailed over my collar. A tug and my chain slinked to the ground near my feet.

Peering up at him, I remembered how he'd earned his name.

He leaned around me to grip the doorknob. "Come on," he said, opening the door and taking my hand.

He led me out and away from that small chamber, down the long hallway.

"Shay asked me to watch over you in there," he said. "He would never have left you without a guardian."

We entered the breakfast room, crossing the short space to the glass door.

De Sade opened the door and gestured for me to go outside. "Tell him how you feel," he said, and walked away.

Shay stood by the swimming pool, his hands tucked into his pockets, deep in thought.

"Sir!"

He pivoted to look at me. A kaleidoscope of emotions crossed his handsome face—his mask was off now.

Approaching him, I tried to read how he felt about me disobeying his order. He looked off toward the house as though contemplating it.

"Want some company?" I said, trying to sound casual.

"I can't stay, Rue."

I replayed his words in my head. "Why?"

His expression was now void of emotion.

"Is there someone else?" I asked.

"No."

"Are you leaving to see someone?"

"Rue, there is no one else." He stepped back. "Be safe, okay."

"Wait."

He closed the space between us, towering over me. I craved this connection between us that went so deep I couldn't imagine where it ended.

His thumb brushed my lower lip. "One last kiss."

"One last kiss?"

Shay's strong hands cupped my face.

His mouth came down on mine with forceful passion. His tongue tangling, fighting for the control I gave him.

I sighed deeply into his mouth because this is what he did to me. He helped me find my center.

He drew my sighs into him, taking on my sins. Taking on all that was wrong with me. Yet again proving he was the best kind of man.

I was nudged away.

I felt a surge of pain at this sudden loss. This rejection.

"Run along. Go be slutty," he said dryly.

I hated him for saying it. "Is this why you warned me not to get close to you?"

He looked down at the sparkling water. "There is only one way I'll know the game is over."

"It should never have begun."

His gaze met mine. "It was on this spot that you once demanded I give you what you wanted."

"I know...but..."

He exhaled slowly. "The thing about Chrysalis is you get to change your mind. You're in control of *your* body."

"Which was why you saved me from Pendulum."

"Yes."

"De Sade told me you asked him to watch over me just now."

Shay looked off. "The Great Red Dragon and the Woman Clothed with the Sun."

"What does that mean?"

"It's from a William Blake painting…the balance of good and evil." He shook his head as though rising from a nightmare. "No one questions De Sade."

"Only you," I bit out. "I don't want anyone else."

"I'm fulfilling my end of the bargain."

"I'm…in love with you."

"Don't be ridiculous."

"Cadence!"

"*Now* you use your safe word?" he said.

"I didn't know how to tell you I'd changed my mind."

"How about, 'I've changed my mind,'" he said dryly.

"Cadence!" I repeated.

"Yes, I heard you the first time."

"Are you disappointed in me?"

"What are you talking about?"

"You're pushing me away."

"For your own good."

"Whatever happened to you in Afghanistan still haunts you. You pretend nothing affects you, but it does. The wall around you is too high for anyone to breach."

"You breached it," he said softly.

"I'm sorry. I shouldn't have said those things."

"I am rather fond of you."

"Fuck you!"

"Excuse me?"

"I mean, fuck off, *sir*."

Shay's stony expression remained unchanged. "Wanna come with me?"

"What?" I froze, too shocked to move.

"We could leave."

"Am I allowed?"

"Technically, no."

"Will you get in trouble?"

"I've never cared what others think."

He'd literally stolen me out of Pendulum and was stealing me out of here, too. This was outrageous and scandalous and totally against the rules.

And yet, we both wanted to escape.

Shay helped me peel off my butterfly wings.

If anyone came looking for me, they'd find them discarded in a corner. It was as though I'd not only outgrown my personal chrysalis, I'd also discarded my wings.

What I'd been searching for had been right in front of me all along.

Wearing Shay's jacket over my shoulders to keep me warm, I walked alongside him with my hand in his.

We slipped out unseen.

Shay collected his car keys from the valet.

We were on the road and heading toward the Pacific Coast Highway within minutes, my head resting on his shoulder, desperate for closeness.

Shay had one hand on the steering wheel and his other held mine, as though he needed to touch me just as much.

Both of us were leaving that world behind because something else, something remarkable, loomed on the horizon.

From the moment I had met him, during those dazzling first minutes in the confines of Pendulum, I'd sensed he'd become an important part of my life.

I wanted this man so much.

It was his commanding presence, his honesty and integrity. The fact he'd tried to protect me.

He did all of that without thinking of himself.

Although I didn't know how long I would have him all to myself, I would hold on to every second like it was our last.

Reaching out of the car, I let my hand feel the breeze rushing through my fingers. I wanted to hold back time itself. Slow everything down.

Glancing over, I took a mental photograph of him.

A lifetime would never be enough.

We arrived at his beachside home an hour later, the L.A. traffic having slowed us down.

Once out of the car, Shay picked me up and carried me toward the house. He made me laugh with his hero swagger as he entered the house.

It was swift and sure, his hands on me like a man on fire. He shoved me against the wall in a passionate frenzy.

Shay undid his belt, unzipped his pants, and lifted me up. I wrapped my legs around his waist and felt the pressure of him against me.

I cried out at his first thrust, desperate for more.

He banged me against the wall, both of us gasping and clawing at each other's bodies, like we were drowning and coming up for air. Like fucking was the only act that might save us.

His hips fiercely pounded me, my body responding by opening for him—my heart welcoming his brand of darkness. His control caused my body to become slack as he flew us into the stratosphere.

It was hot and heavy and frantic—both of us stealing orgasms in a frenzy.

He lifted me suddenly, moving us over to the kitchen table and fucking me there, too, before carrying me effortlessly over to the couch. We rolled onto the plush rug in the center of the room, moving together more slowly this time, gliding against each other.

Until we were finally sated and breathless and content.

Shay rolled off me, dragging me into a hug. We lay still, catching our breath. I rested my head on his chest, hearing his heartbeat, feeling safe in his arms.

"Warm enough?" he asked.

"Your body is like a furnace," I said. "So yes."

He kissed the top of my head, and his lips remained pressed against me as though this was his way of saying he was glad I was with him.

I took a deep breath, feeling peaceful. "This is paradise."

"Because you're here."

I heard the rhythmic woosh of waves on the sand.

"Let's surf tomorrow?" he said.

"I'd like that."

"We'll order in everything you need," he said. "That way you can stay here for the rest of the week if you want."

"I'd like that, too."

"If you change your mind and want to go back to Chrysalis," he said, "I can take you. You know that."

I moved my head to look up at him. "You are my Chrysalis."

That made him smile.

He dragged his fingers through his beard, his expression thoughtful.

Finally, he said, "It wasn't what you wanted in the end?"

"I'm evolving. Finding myself."

"It's possible to lose yourself all over again. Life is like that."

"Were you going to leave without saying goodbye?"

"Honest answer?"

"Yes."

"My jealousy got the better of me."

"Seriously?"

He stared down at me. "I've become obsessed with you."

"I like you being obsessed."

A lingering silence fell between us, broken only by the sound of cresting waves.

"I'm a complicated man."

"Why is that?"

"Stuff happened and I can't get over it."

"What happened?"

He swallowed hard and stared up at the ceiling. "You don't want that in your head. It's bad enough that it's in mine."

I studied his face, wondering if he could ever go there with me. "I shouldn't have brought it up."

Not after how perfect everything had felt.

If I could somehow learn his secrets, I'd be able to reach him.

He shook his head as though coming out of a trance.

Seeing him hurting and unable to work through his pain made my heart ache.

"Hey." I brought his focus back on me. "We're here, in this wonderful place. Together."

He smiled.

"You're a good man," I said softly. "Never forget that."

The smile vanished. "I'm the worst kind of man."

"You really think that about yourself?"

"No one comes back the same." He gave a shrug. "It's just how it is."

"Can nothing be done?" Could no one help this man?

"Let's take a walk on the beach," he said. "Clear our heads."

"I like that idea."

He pushed himself up and offered me his hand. "We should get dressed first, of course. We don't want to scare the neighbors."

I fell against him, giggling, and hugged him tight.

CHAPTER THIRTY-NINE

Shay

RUE SWAPPED A BRIGHT SMILE WITH ME AND THEN LEAPED onto her board, both of us riding the wave in toward the shore.

This…*this* was living. I'd forgotten what it felt like to have fun.

I inhaled sharply through the rush of adrenaline, feeling truly alive inside, using every muscle in my body to stay on my board.

Glancing to my right, I saw Rue shredding the wave with ease, taking a snapshot in my mind.

She was a dangerous force. A charismatic goddess I couldn't get enough of—coaxing me and pulling me until no resistance was left.

It felt like this wave was also carrying me into my future.

That's how we spent our morning—catching waves and stealing kisses and hugs and just being together. Forgetting the world and selfishly enjoying each other.

One more wave.

And then another.

Back on shore, I made my way over to where we'd laid our stuff. I grabbed a towel for me and another for Rue.

She hurried over and took it. "That was amazing!"

"Nothing like it."

"I'm so hungry," she blurted out.

"Hungry for…?" I waggled my eyebrows.

"I'm going to need to stock up on calories just to keep up with you. I thought I was fit but I'm not compared to you."

I reached for her, pulling her towards me and kissing her, tasting salt and smiles and the happiness I'd forgotten was possible.

My life had finally slowed down.

Rue grinned against my mouth. "You taste like the ocean."

"You taste of…"

She pulled away a little. "What?"

"Bliss."

She threw her head back and laughed.

I carried our surfboards up the beach towards the house.

God, she's going to kill me with that smile.

Nothing felt more natural than taking a shower together, facing each other and lathering each other's bodies with soap, stealing more kisses.

I cupped her face and planted kisses on her freckles.

Being with her was everything.

After showering, we dried off and dressed in jeans and T-shirts. I'd ordered in everything Rue might need, including extra clothes, along with flip-flops and a swimsuit for her.

I'd also placed a food delivery.

After a light lunch, we spent the rest of the day snuggled up on the couch watching movies on Netflix—after we finally agreed on what we both wanted to see. Fighting over the remote, we had a laugh at how natural it felt to act like a couple.

This felt like a vacation to me. I'd have to return to work tomorrow, but Rue could stay here for as long as she wanted.

Later that night, I cooked us steaks and prepared a Greek salad. We carried our plates of food out to the balcony where we watched the unending waves, munching on pita bread and sipping white wine.

"I made a mistake," I said absentmindedly.

Rue set her glass down and turned to look at me. "How?"

"I regret making you leave this place, taking you back to Majestic that day. I'm not sure what I was thinking."

"It was the right thing to do."

"Was it though?"

"I signed up to be there." She went to say something and then held back. "It's fine."

"Have you heard from Carrie?" I watched her reaction.

"She's left me a message to call her. I will."

"Want me to handle that call for you?"

"No, I've got it."

"You don't have to go back after this, Rue. You know that, right?"

She gave me a wistful smile. "Thank you for this. It's helping me regroup from the burnout I didn't know I had."

"You've not been a nurse that long."

"I bond with every patient. My colleagues tell me I must toughen up. That it gets easier. But I went into nursing because I care about people. I think about them after a shift. Wonder how they're doing."

"That's admirable."

"It's also why I'm frazzled."

"You've got to learn how to manage your emotions," I said.

"I don't want to end up hardened."

"I think that's hard to avoid if you don't want to end up depressed." I gave a shrug. "Well, you can stay here for as long as you want."

"Thank you."

"I won't let you out of my sight again." I flashed a smile.

"I won't let you out of mine."

She tucked her feet beneath her. "This morning was fun."

"Your dad must have been a great surfer. He was the one who taught you, right?"

"Yes. I thought I'd never feel like that again."

"Like what?"

"Happy."

"I'm glad."

"Where did you grow up, Shay?"

"San Diego."

"Are your parents there?"

"Just Mom. She still lives in the house I grew up in."

"And your dad?"

"He left when I was twelve." I shrugged. "We did okay."

Cole had helped me work through my gnarly childhood where my father's discipline was a fine edge between strictness and cruelty. It had nothing to do with me and everything to do with Dad's own demons. That's what I'd come to understand from the brief therapy sessions I'd had.

But wallowing in self-pity just wasn't me.

"It was a happy time for the most part," I added.

"Are you close to your mom?"

"Yes. I need to go see her. I owe her a visit. Work gets in the way."

"Maybe we could take a drive down there?"

"She'd love that—she'd enjoy meeting you."

"I love the San Diego Zoo."

"I can take you there."

Making plans with Rue felt natural.

"We had this framed print in the living room," I began. "I couldn't remember it not being there. With my first bonus check, I went out and actually bought the original painting for Mom one Christmas."

"Really?"

"I went through Cameron's art dealer." I smiled. "It was my first time purchasing a piece."

"Your mom must have been thrilled."

"It didn't exactly go as planned."

"Why? What happened?"

"When she unwrapped it, she looked bewildered. I couldn't understand why. She explained that my aunt had given the old print to her, and it was more about the memory of the day she'd been out with her sister than the painting itself."

"Oh."

I shook my head. "She ended up hanging the one I got her in the bedroom. She wanted to look at it before going to sleep."

"Because it reminds her of you."

"I've never been into owning things, you know. Don't care for having a lot of stuff. I think it's because when I served abroad, we had so little. I got used to being without. I like the freedom of being able to move around."

"You'll miss this place."

"It's going to be hard to leave it."

"But it's great you're building your own home," she said.

I stood and picked up our plates. "I'll grab dessert."

She didn't need to know what was on my mind. That not everything worked out the way we want it to.

That piece of land had been a fun dream for a while.

But Rue...she was more important.

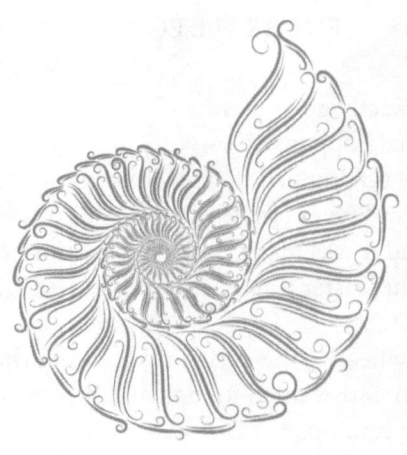

CHAPTER FORTY

I'D SPENT THREE DAYS IN THE BEACH HOUSE.

It felt like hardly any time had passed.

Time moved easily here.

Shay was at work. I missed him when he wasn't here, but knew he couldn't take a vacation on such short notice.

I had no regrets for leaving the ball. Not one. Because I felt like I'd found more than that place could ever give me.

This was everything I'd ever wanted.

Going back was still an exciting prospect but I imagined it would be different with Shay by my side.

With him, the man of my dreams.

Now that I was alone, I was able to explore the place and check out each room. The house must have cost a fortune. Everything was elegantly decorated with tastefully detailed ceilings and a beach lover's theme that made it feel homey.

I ended up in the office, checking my emails.

Shay had given me permission to use his computer. The fact this place belonged to Cameron Cole was intriguing. It really was nice of him to let Shay stay here. Though I assumed owning different properties was just another smart investment for a businessman.

Maybe Shay and I would be able to double-date with him and his wife, Mia.

There were a few emails waiting in my inbox, but not too many and nothing urgent. A couple of them were from Carrie Quinn, which I didn't want to open.

A devilish sense of nosiness came over me.

I reached for the left drawer and pulled it open. Peeking in, I saw a bunch of fancy fountain pens and a notepad from the Dorchester Hotel in London. There was a doodle on it—a drawing of a Dachshund. It was super cute, and it made me wonder if Cole had drawn it for his wife. Nudging that aside, I pulled out a photo-magnet of the London Eye.

Putting the magnet back, I closed the drawer and opened the one on the right.

Finding a folded piece of paper, I opened it, even though I knew it was wrong to snoop.

My heart stuttered at what I was looking at—a receipt from Majestic. Reading it further, I saw my name and then realized what I was looking at.

Shay had paid off my contract with Majestic. It was right there in ink. The amount was so high I'd believed it would be impossible to pay off. I'd used up all my funds to buy a membership at Chrysalis—just to be closer to Shay.

At some point I'd planned to return to Majestic and finish out my time there.

The amount Shay had paid was impossible to fathom.

I suddenly understood what he had done.

What he had given up.

With a shaky hand, I reached for my phone.

I hated myself but there was no other way. I scrolled through my contacts and punched Carrie Quinn's number.

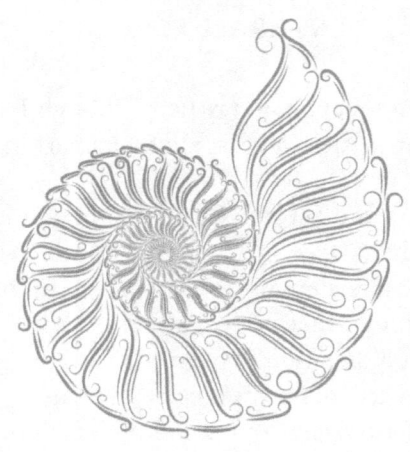

CHAPTER FORTY-ONE

Rue

TRYING TO KEEP IT TOGETHER, I STARED OUT THE WINDOW waiting for the silver BMW to appear in the driveway, hoping Carrie would get here before Shay returned.

Nausea welled in my stomach at the thought of having to leave this place.

I wanted to stay more than anything.

But I couldn't.

Even though every moment we'd shared had felt perfect.

Too perfect.

Something this wonderful can't last.

I'd always been good at reading people. Now, as I replayed every interaction we'd shared, the truth hit me like a thousand jagged shards of reality.

Shay had done what he believed was best for me—even though it would be a financial disaster for him. I could never live with myself knowing he'd lost that land. He was stubborn like me. He'd never let me refuse his gift of paying off my contract.

I made my way back to the kitchen and found a piece of paper and a pen. Then I set about writing the letter that would sever our ties, my hand shaking as I explained the reason I was leaving.

We are just too different.
Forgive me.

                    —Rue.

It was over.

I felt like all the air had left the house as I walked toward the front door.

I headed outside to the waiting BMW.

When I opened the car door, Carrie's rich perfume hit my nostrils. It triggered me, taking me back to the hellish days and nights I'd spent at Majestic.

"How did he take it?" she asked.

"I left a note." I pulled on my seatbelt.

"Do you think he'll come for you?"

"No," I said. "I don't think so."

Because that note would leave no doubt in his mind that we were done.

My chest tightened with grief.

It hurts to breathe.

"You deserve to be treated like a queen, Rue."

"That's how he treated me."

I felt dazed and bewildered that something so perfect could be shattered so easily.

We drove away.

The growing distance felt like a lifetime of pain opening between us.

I could tell him all that was in my heart. But after this it would be too late.

Carrie navigated us onto the Pacific Coast Highway.

He was the first man I'd ever fallen in love with. We hardly knew each other, but you know…you just do.

Shay Gardner was all that was good in this world. What hurt the most was I'd failed to tell him that no man would ever come close to him.

"You okay?" said Carrie.

"You promise to return his money?" I asked sternly.

"Of course."

I gave a nod, reassured that the return of Shay's funds would mean he'd be able to buy that piece of land he'd had his heart set on.

I refused to be the one to steal his future.

He would never have let me return to Majestic.

And after I'd been back there at that Glendale House, and done all those things they get us to do, he wouldn't want me.

Because another man touching me was something he couldn't stand.

Caressing my chest, I knew this ache would be permanent.

Within an hour, we'd made it back to The Grove Apartments. I turned to face Carrie. "Promise me you'll return his money today."

"We will."

"I'm not coming back," I said. "I'll send you the money."

"Glad to hear."

She didn't need to know it was my membership payment for Chrysalis which Richard had sent back.

I went to open the car door.

"He doesn't deserve you, Rue."

"You're wrong," I said. "It's the other way around."

I exited the car and headed up to my apartment building.

CHAPTER FORTY-TWO

Shay

One Week Later

T HE DECEMBER RAIN HAD FINALLY CEASED, LEAVING THE
air cool and fresh.

Richard turned the engine off. He was quiet and
thoughtful, respectful even—everything a good friend could be
at a time like this.

"You okay?" he asked.

"Never better," I lied.

He'd been checking in on me frequently over the last week.
Since finding that note from Rue, I'd gone back to being my usual
grumpy self.

The check I'd written to Carrie Quinn to get Rue out of her
contract at Majestic had been sent back to me—a week too late.
I'd lost the bid on the land I'd wanted to buy. It had gone to someone else.

But I cared more about what I'd done to Rue.

I assumed that the returned check meant she had returned to Majestic.

I could have called her.

I was still struggling with the role of jealous asshole.

Maybe next week I'd reach out to her, see how she was doing. Maybe I'd get Lotte to check on her. That way Rue wouldn't have to deal with me.

Maybe she wouldn't even take our call.

I climbed out of the Audi and walked away, needing a few minutes to regroup.

From this vantage point, the ocean view looked spectacular. Malibu's coastline was endless and vast and the sight of the vivid blue seascape was a welcome change from desert browns.

If I had binoculars, I'd be able to see the land I'd once dreamed of owning. It made me wonder if Booth had any idea how hard this was for me.

Richard had avoided revealing the reason we were here, but I knew...

We needed somewhere private to talk—just not his place, apparently, which was a fifteen-minute drive away.

I'd broken the cardinal rule of Chrysalis.

There was no coming back from that.

I stepped closer to the cliff's edge, seeing a sandy pathway to my right that led down to a golden beach.

If I was alone, I'd kick off my shoes and head down to the cold water to soak my feet.

A car door slammed behind me.

The talk was coming.

When Richard joined me, I could instantly feel the tension between us.

I turned to face him and read his expression, trying to figure out how to make this easier on both of us.

On the way here, we'd discussed everything from how well the New York Giants were doing this season to how he was looking forward to flying off to Italy to reunite with Andrea. The one subject we had avoided was me removing a submissive from Chrysalis.

It was a bad look all around—their head of security being the one to break the rules.

For God's sake, I'd fire me.

Richard stood next to me looking out at the blue ocean. "Nice."

"You want to do it here?" I asked, hoping that nudge would get him to start so we could get this over with.

"Do it here?" he said, sarcasm in his tone. "In the middle of nowhere?"

"We could have done this at your place."

"And be seen with you?" He shook his head. "Fuck, no."

Really? What an asshole.

I looked east. "You're up there, right?"

"That's right."

"I fucked up," I finally admitted. "I know that."

"Do you, though?" he said sourly.

"Are you going to tell me what the consequences are?"

"We're waiting on someone."

My shoulders slumped; the last thing I needed to see was disappointment in Cole.

"Have you ever read *Story of O?*" asked Richard.

"What?"

"The book."

"No, but I saw the movie."

"Cole has been giving that book to subs as reading material."

"How is this relevant?"

"At the end of the novel, Odette is so broken-hearted that her master has left her, she asks for permission to kill herself."

"Not in the movie, though, right?"

"Can't remember."

"That's fucking dark."

"It really is."

"Why would Cole give anyone that book to read?"

"He wants to see how they will react to that part of the story. He wants to know how stable they are."

"If they relate to O, they can't stay at Enthrall?"

He shrugged. "Have no idea what goes on in his mind. Nor do I want to."

"Are you saying I might be…?"

"Unstable."

"Are you fucking kidding me?" I snapped. "I was having…"

"Fun?"

"Yes, Richard, I needed to let my hair down."

"Shay, it's a joke. Why are you so serious all the time?"

Maybe I was in a bad mood because I'd lost Rue—and quite possibly my job.

"We returned Rue Asher's membership fee," he said. "Admin error. She didn't need to pay."

"Oh, okay."

"Thought you should know."

I could hear the familiar slicing of blades cutting through the air. Off in the distance a helicopter was approaching fast.

Maybe that was my punishment. I was going to become fodder for a billionaire looking for an idiot to land on. Or maybe Cole would accidently set down on Richard's Audi which would provide no end of entertainment.

My past had caught up with me.

My talent, which was my willingness to sacrifice everything for Chrysalis, was also my weakness, apparently.

Richard shielded his face from the blast of air. "Always a dramatic entrance."

Cole's expertise was impressive. He navigated the helicopter toward a smooth landing, setting the chopper down.

Here came the one man confident enough to eviscerate me.

I squeezed my mouth shut so I didn't eat a flying leaf or a stick, silently swearing at the bastard for blowing us both into tomorrow with those blades.

Cameron turned off the engine and opened the door. He climbed out, ever mindful of the still-whirling chopper blades.

He walked over to us, his swagger confident.

Gone was his tailored suit and in its place he wore jeans and a white T-shirt—his choice of battle garb for this war with me on a Malibu hill.

His hair was ruffled and he had a five o'clock shadow that I wasn't used to seeing on him. To be honest, he looked sleep deprived. Oh, the joys of parenting.

I imagined that the unknown corporate spy within Cole Tea was also weighing on him.

Having to hear his reaction to my behavior over the last week made my chest tighten.

He joined us on the precipice. "Some view."

"Thinking of buying it?" I asked, preferring small talk.

"This shit hole?" Richard scoffed. "No."

"It's not bad if you can tolerate the sound of crashing waves," said Cole. "How does anyone focus?"

Seriously, this place was a goddamned slice of heaven and if they couldn't see it, they were insane. More than this, both were wealthy and probably couldn't imagine the rest of us still holding on to reality—no matter how terrifying.

"How's Rue?" said Cameron.

"Haven't spoken with her." I'd tried not to think about her.

Because her note had made it clear we were simply a blip in time.

Maybe I couldn't resist thinking of how it felt to run my fingers through her hair…or brush my lips over her delicate freckles. I couldn't forget how it felt to press my lips to hers and feel the softness of her kiss, the tenderness of her embrace. The sound of her laughter was imprinted on my brain.

And the stillness she brought—the feeling I was no longer chasing time.

No longer running from myself.

Cameron patted my back as though reading my thoughts. "Well, this is not easy on anyone," he began.

Turning to face him again, I tried to read what my punishment would be—but it was clear.

Their secret glances revealed this was hard on them, too.

I deserved it.

Cameron stepped away and put some distance between us, seemingly thoughtful, like he was trying to find the right words.

"If it helps," I offered, "I've already fired myself."

I'd also lost the girl.

And forced my boss to cut me loose.

This San Diego boy once had nothing, and because of it, had remained terrified of losing anything good that came his way.

Bravo, my self-fulfilling prophecy had come true.

"You have a great future, Shay," said Cameron.

That was something you told an intern, not someone like me—a man who'd once had the privilege of being Cole's right-hand man.

I swallowed the lump in my throat. "Am I banned?"

"What do you think?" said Richard.

I looked toward the sprawling ocean. The distance to the horizon was not as far as I felt from my friends right now. The friends who had always been there for me. I'd been there for them, too.

We'd been more like a family. Like the one I'd never had.

"This will free you up to put more energy into CloudSource," said Cameron.

"Henry?" He'd betrayed my trust.

"Henry didn't say anything to me," said Cameron. "But I'm glad to hear you guys talked about it."

They had more faith in me than I did.

My leaving was always going to be on my terms…when I was ready.

Never like this.

Hadn't I earned a pass? I'd given years to Chrysalis…dedicated my life to it. I'd given up so much.

"It's time, Shay." Cameron shared a look with Richard.

"This is it, then?" I said. "I'm just to walk away?"

Cameron drew in a breath. "There's a compensation package."

"You don't need to ask me to keep quiet," I said. "You'll always have my loyalty. I'll always love you fucking bastards."

"Well, if you put it like that," said Richard. "We'll throw in your pension."

Cameron raised his hand to silence him. "You were the best thing about Chrysalis."

He'd used the past tense.

And it stung.

"What do you think?" said Cameron.

"About what? You firing me? Feels like shit."

"You told us you've fired yourself," said Richard.

"Right." Because details were important with these two.

Cameron grinned. "What do you think about your severance package?"

Was this funny to him? God, he was infuriating.

After seeing my annoyed expression, Cameron opened his arms wide in a sweeping gesture. "You're standing on it."

"Standing on what?"

What they were suggesting was my severance package was the equivalent to acreage, and this land was worth millions with that priceless view.

I looked down at my feet. "What are you saying?"

"This lot. It's yours," said Richard.

I was hit with doubt. "I can't accept this."

"You can and you will," Cameron said firmly. "This is non-negotiable."

I was trying to keep air in my lungs as I processed this stunning revelation.

Cameron rested his hand on my shoulder. "You've earned this."

"I don't know what to say."

"Words aren't needed, my friend." Cameron gave a warm grin.

I took a deep breath of the fresh ocean air.

"Enthrall. Will I be allowed back?" I asked.

"Of course," said Cameron.

"Just not as your security advisor?" I clarified.

"You're always welcome," said Richard.

"Soon, it will be time to take CloudSource to the next level," said Cameron. "Richard and I insist on being early investors."

This was a lot to take in.

A town car with blacked out windows drove stealthily toward us, parking nearby.

I wondered if they'd brought Rue here.

Crazy wishful thinking.

CHAPTER FORTY-THREE

Shay

A PPROACHING THE TOWN CAR, I RAN THROUGH ALL THE things I might say to Rue.

I reached for the door handle, my heart racing surprisingly fast.

It opened before I could touch it.

I stepped back, surprised.

"Not who you were expecting?" Henry offered a warm smile.

I accepted his offer to climb in and sit opposite him, the brief hope of seeing Rue ripped from me.

I suppressed my disappointment.

At least I was still welcome at Chrysalis.

That plot of land was six times as large as the one I'd set my heart on. It was going to take time to get used to the idea of it being mine. They really were the most generous men I'd ever known.

Today had been mind-blowing.

The town car's divider rose and cut us off from Henry's driver.

"How are you, buddy?" said Henry.

"Do you know what they just gave me?" I leaned back, trying to comprehend it.

"Yeah, not bad. Not bad at all."

It was the most incredible gift I'd ever been given. Cole knew I wouldn't have accepted it any other way.

"I'm out of a job, though. Did they tell you?"

"You didn't get the offer?"

"Offer?"

"Cole Tea wants to hire you as a consultant. We want to be CloudSource's first company. That alone will give you what you need to take your business global, with us on your resume as a major client, right?"

"Can I think about it?"

He looked surprised. "Do you really need to?"

"I don't want to take advantage of friends."

He rubbed his jaw, looking thoughtful. "Shay, you're not even working for Cole Tea and you discovered a breach in our company. That's how good you are."

A million thoughts raced through my mind.

He beamed at me. "We want to welcome you to the family. *Again.* Only this time on my side of things."

I'd always been made welcome. The entire family had made me feel like one of them.

Henry's expression turned solemn. "We need you to find him."

"Your spy?" I said. "Could be a woman."

"True."

"I can do that."

"The photojournalist, Darryn Amara, won't he let our enemy know they are exposed?"

"We paid him well. If he breaches the non-disclosure he's screwed. We can send him to prison."

"You trust him?"

I sat back, thinking. "Time will tell."

I recalled what Darryn had told me at the diner—that a rival company was tracking all members of the Cole family. He'd also revealed a Trojan horse had been sent into Cole Tea's L.A. office.

A week ago, I'd written up the report and handed it over to Cole.

"Cameron's been selfishly holding on to you for too long." Henry's gaze met mine. "Untangle this mess for us."

"I will certainly try."

"We appreciate it." He looked out the window toward where Cameron and Richard were talking. "You can begin building here whenever you like."

"It's beyond generous."

"You've saved our asses so many times, Gardner. I was beginning to doubt you had any faults. Though apparently, you do."

"Rue?"

"Stupid fucking rules." He smirked.

"They told you, then? What happened at Chrysalis' ball? That I whisked her out of there?"

"I'd have done the same thing."

"Still, rules are rules."

"When something doesn't go our way there's usually something better waiting on the other side."

I recalled Lotte saying something like that. Maybe, just maybe, I'd introduce them one day.

"Thank you for coming all the way out here."

He looked shocked. "You literally saved my life, Shay!"

I shook my head. "You had it."

"Had what?"

"The situation."

"Which I understand is hard to talk about."

"It's forgotten, Henry."

"Before you come work for me…"

"Sign a contract? Of course."

"Well, yes, but something else."

"What do you need from me?"

"One therapy session with my brother. Just one. It's worth considering."

"Is the job contingent on it?"

"Humor me."

I glanced over at Cameron. "Sure."

He reached out and offered his hand. "Welcome aboard."

We shook on the future.

My world didn't feel so upside-down anymore.

"Do me one more favor," said Henry.

"Another?"

"Don't use Cameron's interior decorator. He literally installed a chandelier that looks like a cock in his Beverly Hills home."

I laughed. "Good advice."

"You have one more stop, I hear?"

"Really? They didn't tell me that."

"Good luck."

After saying goodbye to Henry, I exited the car and strolled back toward Cameron and Richard. They'd migrated toward the edge of the hill and were admiring the view.

My view.

I was still reeling over that revelation, now seeing it differently from when we'd first arrived. I took in the surrounding scenery—the place that would become my home. This sacred earth.

Henry's town car glided back down the hill.

Cameron gestured to the helicopter. "Next stop Cedars-Sinai?"

Was I that transparent?

They'd always seen through me. Always would.

"Your brother just offered me a job," I said.

"Hope you accepted it," said Cameron. "You're working for me and Cole Tea, too. How does that sound?"

"Great."

Like a dream job with the kind of responsibility I'd craved.

Cameron added, "You have our support to launch CloudSource to the next level."

Pride filled me, knowing I had this chance at something special.

"Go celebrate with a friend," said Richard. "You know...*her.*"

Maybe seeing Rue again to offer an apology for that misstep over Majestic was as good as it got under the circumstances.

"Come on," said Cameron. "It won't be the first time I've landed on the helipad at Cedars-Sinai. I'll alert traffic control and the ER."

"Isn't that reserved for trauma patients?" I asked.

"You're a trauma patient," said Richard. "Trauma of the heart."

"Yes, thank you, Richard, for that insight." Cameron rolled his eyes.

"How do you know she's working today?" I asked.

Then I remembered this was Cameron Cole. He'd have thought of everything.

Even flying in a helicopter, it would still feel like it was taking a lifetime to reach her.

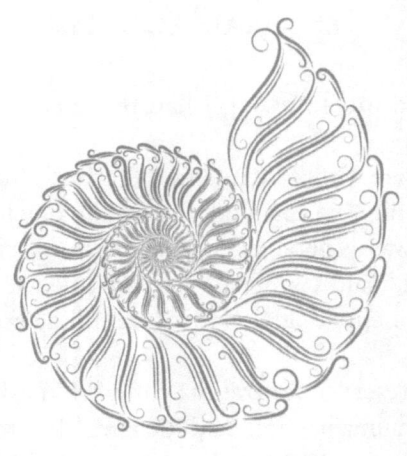

CHAPTER FORTY-FOUR

THE ONLY WAY TO COPE WITH THIS CHAOS WAS TO surrender to it.

Get into the zone.

Adrenaline has you moving fast. Going from room to room and circling the central nursing station like a pro.

Admitting and discharging patients constantly, carrying out doctor's orders—thinking on your feet. And in the middle of all this you're giving everything you've got to save the lives of those who come to Cedars-Sinai ER for help.

It's easy to forget to eat or drink anything. Taking a pee is the last thing you get to do sometimes. When the place is at maximum capacity everyone sacrifices their own comfort.

Until a supervisor insists you take a break.

The end of the shift comes up so damn fast it's mindboggling. Only then am I aware my hair's a mess and my feet are killing me.

One of the best things about my job is not having time to dwell on what's going on in my personal life.

No time to think of *him*.

There's just a dull ache that won't be soothed.

The new normal.

"Can you stay for a few minutes?" asked Sharon, my super-visor and one kickass RN.

"Sure," I said.

"I need you to go up to the helipad. Can you greet the guest who's flying in?"

"A patient? Need me to help admit them?"

"No, just make sure they know how to get down here."

I headed to the elevator and waited patiently for the doors to open, my legs aching from all the walking I'd done.

A hot shower was in my future, and a hot meal.

And later, that warm bed.

I stepped inside the large elevator and rode it all the way to the roof. It was big enough to house a team of life saving specialists when a patient was flown in and we needed the space to work on them.

The doors slid open.

I saw the whirling blades of a helicopter.

Stepping out onto the roof, I watched it lift off the helipad and fly west.

A lone man was left standing on the roof.

I tried to process why Shay Gardner might be up here while scanning the area for someone else.

God, he looked sophisticated even wearing a casual jacket, jeans and boots. His hair was ruffled and his beard looked a little unruly.

"Hey," he called over. "Have a second?"

"I'm expecting someone."

"I think that's me."

"Why are you here?" I smirked. "To offer up a kidney?"

"I'd give you my whole damn body if you asked for it."

"That doesn't sound like the Shay I know."

"Let me get this off my chest, okay?"

"Sure. Why not? This is totally normal being up here and—"

"A little enthusiasm would be nice."

Like rising out of a daydream I said, "You flew in for me?"

"Yes. Do you have time to talk?"

"Yes, of course." I stepped closer to him.

"I remember that day...the way the lights fell on you in that dungeon. The way your hair looked. The collar around your throat. I wanted you, and it scared me how obsessed I felt. I've tried to hide it and deny it. Those days at the beach house with you were the happiest I've had in ages. I felt like myself again."

"I'm sorry I left like that," I said. "Forgive me."

"Was it me?"

"Never. You would have lost the land."

"I'd have lost a fucking planet for you." He smiled. "You're okay?"

"No. Because I miss you."

He rested his palm over his heart. "Me, too."

"Shay, I didn't want to be the person who ruined your future."

"You are my future."

His words resonated like a dream I'd been too scared to hope for.

"I couldn't get there," he said. "Couldn't let you in. I couldn't be the man you wanted."

"I've wanted you from the first second I saw you."

"I'm...broken, Rue."

"You're like the rest of us, then? Aren't we all a little beaten up? I will always look up to you. So many people do. I hope you see it. See how important you are to so many people."

"You deserve happiness."

"You're really here because of me?" I held my breath.

"You inspire me to be a better man," he said. "To face my demons."

"We can face them together."

"If you still want me..."

I ran and leaped on him.

He caught me and my arms went around his neck, my legs wrapping around his waist.

I kissed him so damn hard, showing him how much I'd missed him.

Our kiss deepened; nurturing and fierce and tender and as our tongues caressed. We were sharing what we needed to tell each other: That we had found our person. The one we'd been destined to meet.

We were saving each other in our own crazy way.

Finally, I pulled away. "I need to get home and get out of these scrubs and take a shower."

He gave me a provocative smile. "Want some company?"

"I would love that."

"My ride's gone." He looked skyward and then turned back to me. "Looks like you might be stuck with me."

I beamed back at him.

"Rue, I have so much to tell you."

"I can't wait to hear it all." I offered my hand to him, feeling the strength of his grip. "I want to show you my place."

We headed into the elevator and rode it down to the ground level.

We walked out of Cedars hand-in-hand and for the first time in forever I felt like his equal, this beautiful and complicated man who'd protected me right from the start.

Now, it was time for me to nurture him.

CHAPTER FORTY-FIVE

Shay

A Few Days Later

CAMERON COLE STOOD NEARBY, HIS HANDS IN HIS pockets, already in doc mode.

This had once been his permanent office back when he'd run his psychiatric clinic out of this impressive Beverly Hills space.

"Not sure this is necessary," I said, walking around the room. "But Henry thinks this will be good for me, and Rue agrees."

"I'm glad," said Cameron.

"She's forgiven me for interfering in her life."

"You did what you believed was right. It was generous of you to pay off her contract."

"Things are really good between us now."

"You're great together, Shay."

His armchair sat in the center of the room and there was another high-backed chair opposite his.

Was I ready for this session?

"You really think this will help?" I asked.

"It's getting harder for you to remain emotionally unconscious."

"I suppose."

"Waking up...breaking down and breaking out. It fucking hurts."

"A doctor who swears...I like it," I said. "That's where you got the name for Chrysalis?"

"Positive disintegration—like the metamorphosis of a caterpillar. The breakdown is growth."

"Wow."

"Let's go meet your true self." He gestured to *the* chair.

I hesitated to sit.

"Do you miss it?" I asked. "All of this?"

"Yes."

I offered a sympathetic smile. "What made you choose psychiatry in the first place?"

"The brain is the most complex puzzle to solve."

And he loved puzzles. "Right."

"The office is closed. No one will bother us."

"Are you still consulting here?"

He gave a nod. "Perk of the job."

"How do you fit it all in?"

"I could say the same about you." He gestured to the seat opposite his. "Let's start with how you're feeling today."

Finally, I took the seat opposite him, feeling vulnerable. And a little silly, really, because this was probably eating into his valuable time. "I'm good. Rue and I are going slow."

He nodded.

"We're getting to know each other."

I was used to this part—where Cole mirrored my body language.

So damn obvious.

I didn't mind humoring him. Maybe I'd get something out of

this? Finally appease them all by showing I was a well-adjusted man with nothing to hide.

Those shadows Cameron had hinted at were merely ghosts from my past that were easily chased away.

"I'm assuming we're going to talk about how abandoned I felt after my dad walked out on us?"

"We can."

I gave a shrug. "I've never known anything else."

"Henry's been doing well with Rapid Eye Movement Therapy."

"He mentioned it. Not sure I need that. I'm glad it's helping him, though."

"What's your favorite time of year?"

"Are you going to ask me my favorite color next?"

"What is it?"

"Seriously?"

"Why not?"

"Blue."

"Blue. Mine, too." He smiled.

I stared at him. "Don't ask me anything freaky."

He nodded. "Do you want to talk about Rue?"

"Well, okay…Rue and I have been surfing together. We have that in common. We both love it."

"What else do you have in common? What do you like to do?"

"Eat Italian food." Just thinking of Rue made me relax. "We like watching movies and taking long walks on the beach. Is this really meant to help?"

"Worst time of year, Lieutenant?"

He'd used my rank and it made me nervous.

"I fucking hate November."

"Is that so?"

"I glanced at my watch. "How long is this going to take?"

"You have to be somewhere?"

"I'm taking up your time."

"My time belongs to you today."

My foot bounced with the sudden tension I was feeling in Cole's presence. "I'm a crap patient. Sorry."

"Let's try some hypnosis."

I gave him an amused look. "Bit hokey for you."

"Close your eyes."

I settled back, doing what he asked, squeezing my eyelids closed, just going along with it.

Outside the window I heard the sounds of traffic.

Cole spoke up. "I know a little about what you went through. I was there for a brief time."

"I know."

"I never got as close to the mountains of Afghanistan."

My throat tightened with the mention of the place. "They dominate the landscape."

"I hear the wildlife is something?"

"It is."

"What kind of animals roam there?"

"So many. Like the wildcats. They look like the most pissed off animal on the planet. Birds you've never seen anywhere." I shook my head. "When you're camouflaged, they can get really close."

Cole began counting me down and down and down.

Three. Two. One.

His voice trailed off in the background as he guided me under.

Deeper.

And deeper.

Taking me all the way back.

My breathing slowed and I felt strangely sleepy.

"Tell me more." Cole's voice sounded distant.

"So much to see."

"Tell me about that day," he said. "Visibility was low."

Henry would have told Cameron that. "We were caught in a sandstorm."

"What do you see?"

"We're on reconnaissance. Henry's here. Sergeant Matt Dias."

"What do you hear?"

I turned my head in the direction of the blades. "The helicopter is turning around."

"Turning back?"

"It's too dangerous for it to continue. We're in a sandstorm."

The chopper was flying south.

I squinted as though trying to look through the storm. "Hard to see…"

"Go on."

"My goggles are blurry. Sand in my face. Mouth." I wiped my face trying to remove the grit. "You know how it gets."

I was there again.

I tasted dirt despite the scarf that covered my mouth.

"What's Henry saying to you?" said a distant voice.

Looking that way. Looking right.

Trying to hear over the blades.

I blinked as though that might make it easier to see through my goggles, and then wiped grit from the lenses.

Henry was pointing his gun toward the ridge.

The signal to move.

I leaned into the storm, sweat snaking down my spine in the heat, my rucksack heavy. My M4A1 carbine was pointed at the ridge.

"What do you see, Shay?"

"I see…"

Squinting…I could see something staring back through the whirling sand.

A lion.

God, he was beautiful.

"Can I open my eyes?" This wasn't working.

"Not yet."

This was insanity.

It made no sense.

"What do you see, Shay?"

What do I see?

"Sand. Mountains. Henry. Dias."

"And…"

"That…mountain lion."

"Close?"

"Fifty feet away, maybe?" I squeezed my left eye tighter as I peered through my site with my right. "What the hell is it doing?"

"What is *it* doing?"

Doesn't make any sense. "What's on its face?"

"Tell me."

I glance at Henry, trying to read his expression. Does he see it?
I shook my head. "It's gonna hurt him."

"Seconds to decide," said a distant voice.

"His eyes." I swallowed hard. "Intelligent. Shit. It's down. It's down."

"You got it?"

"I shot it." I sat upright. "I shot it dead."

No, no…that doesn't make any sense.

Nausea welled up in my tight throat.

I tried to make out what I was looking at.

It had been a clear shot.

A sob broke from me. "I couldn't let him kill Henry." I leaned forward and rested my face in my hands.

"What happened?" asked Cole.

"I shot a…boy. Fifteen, maybe younger." I glared at Cole. "I shot a boy!"

"Say it again," he coaxed.

"It wasn't a lion. It was a boy." Tears stung my eyes.

I let out a wail, filled with self-loathing.

Why did Cameron make me remember such a thing?

"We had to release this," he said. "It had to come out."

I let out another howl of pain. "That boy had no idea of the consequences of carrying a gun, wearing that uniform. They trained him to kill and he was only a kid!"

"*They* trained him."

"Why should I have a life? Why should I know what it is to fall in love or have a family? He can't…because I stole that from him. I stole his life." I sat back, stunned.

"What else do you remember?"

"He came out of nowhere. He pointed his weapon at Henry."

It had been a split-second decision.

"You saved Henry's life," said Cole softly.

"I know, but…"

I'd killed someone so young.

"How are we just meant to go on?" My words flowed in a torrent. "How are we meant to see all that? Do those things and have any sense of peace ever again?"

"I'm sorry," he said softly.

"You take a life. You save a life? What does it all mean? I trained for it. I know that. But nothing prepares you for…"

"The men who set that boy on that path," he said calmly. "Do you think they hold responsibility?"

"Yes. No. I don't know."

"Of course, they do."

"They were murdering indiscriminately. We did the best we could to bring some semblance of peace."

"How many lives did you save?"

"Too many to count."

"You're a hero, Shay. You have to see yourself as we do."

"Will I ever learn to live with this truth?"

"This is a good start, Lieutenant." Cameron leaned forward. "You left something of yourself back in Afghanistan. Let's keep going with more sessions. Let's get that man home."

I gave a slow, steady nod. He was right. I'd come this far, faced this much—and I was deserving of the help being offered.

My shoulders dropped and I mulled over what all this meant.

I had so much work to do if I wanted to recover from this trauma.

Doing this alone was impossible.

Maybe this was what De Sade had tried to tell me. I would need help to deal with these demons.

"Thank God for friends," I said.

"You risked your life for yours, Shay." Cameron pushed to his feet and offered me his hand. "Now it's our turn to put you first."

I stood before him. "Thank you for not giving up on me."

"Never."

"Henry will be pleased. He knew I couldn't face this alone."

"And you never will have to," said Cole.

Something dark inside me had lifted.

A part of me had cracked, and for the first time I felt light flooding in.

I'd carried this burden for so long. Clearing these dark corners of my mind meant I had room to let others in.

And maybe, just maybe, enough space for love to enter, too.

EPILOGUE

Shay

THERE WILL BE PAIN BEFORE THERE IS REST.

Truth can sometimes hide in the shadows, but mostly it finds its way out into the light. My cruel truth had finally risen into view. My mind had once hidden agonizing memories to protect itself.

This was the only reason I had been keeping everyone at arm's length.

My personal crucible of combat had been fought and won.

Facing what had held me back in all areas of my life felt cathartic. I felt ready for what lay ahead.

Standing barefoot in the sand, I drew in a deep refreshing breath while taking in the view. This place was fucking amazing.

The sun was taking a bow, getting ready to sink below the horizon.

The air felt cool and cleansing on my face. Finally, I felt like I was home.

Enduring hours of therapy with Cameron had resulted in

the equivalent of acid draining from my heart. I was no longer afraid to seek help.

Cameron had fulfilled his promise to wait until I was ready to talk—just as all my friends had. They had endured my closed-off nature, my stubbornness.

I'd entered the shadows and faced my biggest fear—that when my friends discovered what I'd done while serving abroad in the name of war, they would hate me for it. Or at least look at me differently.

My fears had never been realized. If anything, revealing what I saw as weakness made them love me more deeply because they'd seen my authentic side. My real side didn't scare them. What worried them was me trying to hide my trauma.

I'd made mistakes, but never with malice.

Refusing love was a punishment that was testimony of my humanity. I had carried the weight of my actions and that alone proved I was aware of the value of life.

Learning to forgive myself was all that was left. Stepping out of the darkness.

Letting it fall away.

My friends had refused to give up on me.

I choose happiness.

And I chose to be the best person I can be for *them.*

I'd never been one to pinch myself—until now.

It felt like I had always been destined to consult for Cole Tea. I looked forward to working with Henry again. I suppose we'd always been destined for this. Two brothers-in-arms bonded for life.

I turned and looked toward where *they'd* gathered on the ridge overlooking the ocean—Cameron, Henry, Richard, Mia, Penny, Lotte, Scarlet and Jake.

And my sweet Rue.

They all gestured for me to join them.

They'd brought champagne for us to celebrate. Tomorrow I would start building my new home. Cole had told me I could stay at his beach house for now.

My friends always made me feel like I was family.

I marveled at how that sacred earth would soon become the foundation for my future. I was no longer shielding my eyes at what was to come.

Rue descended the bank and then pulled off her shoes, heading my way.

They'd probably sent her down to get me. I'd just needed a few minutes to catch my breath. Soak everything in.

Her hair blew across her freckled face. Her warm smile greeted me like it always did with kindness and warmth, her figure looking deliciously curvy in a summer dress.

I took a mental picture of her, wanting to remember her like this forever. She looked carefree.

When she reached me, I pulled her into a hug, burying my face in her hair and inhaling her scent of flowers and freedom.

"You okay?" she asked.

"Just taking it all in."

"Of course. Take as much time as you need."

I wanted to talk with her alone first and she seemed to sense it.

She looked at me with a quiet understanding. "It's peaceful, isn't it?"

"It really is."

"You earned this, Shay." She squeezed my hand. "Don't forget that."

"I can't wait to show you the architectural design." I swept my hand through the air. "We're going to have huge windows all the way across the house so we get a full view of the ocean."

She leaned against me. "I'm so happy for you."

"This is the kind of house that deserves a family."

She blinked up at me, processing what I was saying.

"Just a thought." I broke into a smile. "One day."

"Sure you're up for that level of happiness?" She nudged me with her elbow.

I pivoted to face her. "I wanted to ask you something."

"Okay."

"Do you think you'd ever consider going steady with me?"

"You mean exclusive?"

"I've learned that, with you, I'm possessive."

"I'd be enough?"

"Would I?"

"I think I've found my match." She grinned at me.

"It doesn't mean we can't play from time to time—just with each other. We'll make our own rules."

"I want that. More than anything."

"And I want you to know how I really feel about you." I pulled her to me and she tipped her face up to me inviting a kiss. My lips fell upon hers, our kiss soft and slow and then frenzied as our tongues lashed together. We were letting each other know that even though we could be wild and dabble in fantasies, our center together would always hold.

Instead of telling her I loved her on the beach that very second, I merely reflected my feelings in a kiss. During the weeks and months and years that followed, I would tell her how I felt about her every single day.

We got each other.

And, finally, I knew myself, too.

We were the space between dust and dark matter—a brilliant stardust. An enduring light.

The secret, it seems, is to never forget that love is how we stay there

ALSO BY
VANESSA FEWINGS

THE ENTHRALL SESSIONS
ENTHRALL, ENTHRALL HER, ENTHRALL HIM,
CAMERON'S CONTROL, CAMERON'S CONTRACT,
RICHARD'S REIGN,
ENTHRALL SECRETS, ENTHRALL CLIMAX,
ENTHRALL ECSTASY AND ENTHRALL SHADOWS

The **ENTHRALL** Spin-off series
THE CHANDELIER SESSIONS
CHANDELIER DREAM
CHANDELIER SIN
CHANDELIER ENTHRALLED

THE ICON TRILOGY from Harlequin:
THE CHASE, THE GAME, and THE PRIZE

PANDORA'S PLEASURE
MAXIMUM DARE
PERVADE LONDON and PERVADE MONTEGO BAY
PERFUME GIRL
THE STONE MASTERS VAMPIRE SERIES
THE RAVISHING—With Ava Harrison

ABOUT THE AUTHOR

Vanessa Fewings is the *USA Today* and international bestselling author of the ENTHRALL SESSIONS and THE ICON TRILOGY from HarperCollins along with many additional novels. ENTHRALL has been optioned for film. Her books have been translated into other languages around the world. She now lives on the West Coast with her rescue Foxhound, Sherlock.

vanessafewings.com